完

文

Kanbun

~an historical novel~

by Jon D. Mills

ISBN: 978-1089194408

Book design: Y42K Publishing Services
http://www.y42k.com/bookproduction.html

Dedication

This work is dedicated to the fond memory of
Robert E. Cady, Jr. and Steven J. Ostro

Contents

Foreword

Some who read this work will recognize parts of the story, while for others it will be unfamiliar. The life and times of Uechi Kanbun are unaltered, but I have created a story to match the little that is known about his life, especially in China. The skeleton of the tale is factual; the body is historical fiction. For those who wish to learn more about Kanbun, there are other sources available, though mostly in Japanese. Chief among them is an exhaustive work entitled, *Okinawa Karatedo: Its History and Methodology*, whose authorship is ascribed to Kanbun's eldest son, Kan'ei, but is in fact a work compiled by Takamiyagi Shigeru. Though that referential work contains inaccuracies and shortcomings, it was enormously helpful in sorting through materials to form the basis for this novel. I owe debts of gratitude to many others as well, some living and others not, for whom I have heartfelt words and thoughts of appreciation.

Confusion can arise when transliterating people and place names into English because there are multiple systems for this, both formal and informal. There are the local pronunciation of a proper noun, the standard dialect, foreign usage, and more options that vary with accented syllables. An individual may have a familiar name used by family members and close friends, another that is related to one's formal or official title, and then there are nicknames, adopted names, and posthumous names. For purposes of practical consistency in a complicated maze of linguistics, I identify people by the word order customary in their country, i.e. family name followed by given name.

7

To pronounce the names of the most significant people in this book, it is helpful to use the Oxford English Dictionary pronunciation standard as follows:

Uechi Kanbun (上地 完文), oo-ay-chee kahn-buhn or in Chinese, shan-di wan-wen;
Jou Tsuhe (周 子和), *joh ze-he* or in Japanese, *shoo shee-wa.*

The sons of Uechi Kanbun, Uechi Kan'ei and Uechi Kansei, told me that their father studied under Shusabu in Nansoe of Fujian Province, China. It was learned that the "sabu" of Shusabu is the Fuzhou dialect of standard Chinese *shifu* (師傅), or teacher in English. It is an open question of why Kanbun would use the Japanese pronunciation of 周 (shoo) coupled with the Fuzhou dialect of 師傅 (sabu), unless his teacher was surnamed Shoo and someone other than Jou Tsuhe. Compounding the mystery is Kanbun's statement that he studied in Nansoe, even though there is no such city or village in Fujian Province. There is the village of Nanyu, which when rendered in the local dialect sounds like Nanyoi and was the home of Jou Tsuhe, which only adds to the puzzle. To this day, there is no concrete evidence that Kanbun knew or even met Jou Tsuhe, and the Uechi family and their students in Okinawa believe the identity of Kanbun's teacher is unknown.

Jon D. Mills, 2019
Jdmills4452@outlook.com

Izumi

It was in the Northern District of Ryukyu in the Kunigami County on the Motobu Peninsula in the Village of Izumi that Uechi Kanbun, and his younger brother Kanso, were born. Their grandfather, Uechi Kansho, had built a family home in the hillside community when his eldest son, Kantoku was still a youth. It was a traditional farmhouse that stood upon a platform raised about the length of a child's arm above the ground and with a simple thatched roof overhead. All of the houses in the villages, counties, and districts of the country were raised slightly on posts, which themselves sat upon heavy stones that were half submerged and firmly grounded in the thick soil compacted with volcanic ash, red brown clay, and moist tropical air. This short space between the ground and the under flooring of the house provided space for the breezes that lifted off the ocean and rose up the densely green hillsides to circulate and cool the rice reed tatami mats that absorbed moisture and provided cushion and comfort for the inhabitants of the homes. The thick, moist air prevented the soil in the surrounding rice and vegetable fields from rising into dust and settling in the houses. The mud that did collect on the straw sandals worn by the villagers in upland agricultural communities stayed outdoors as they removed their hand woven straw footwear before entering their homes. As a result, the interior was dry, neat, clean, and welcoming. Only tropical insects, multicolored snakes, green lizards, or nocturnal rodents occupied the space between earth and floor. Indeed, it was this style of raised living space above the earth that separated man from nature. Man made his home on a slightly elevated plane, above the soil, in an exceedingly modest but significant ascent toward the heavens.

Since ancient times, the Royal Family in Ryukyu had enjoyed favored relations with the powerful and cultured Imperial Court across the sea to the west in China. Indeed, the name of the island kingdom "Ryukyu" was a Chinese reading of the abstract characters for "Jeweled Orbs" and so it was that the small archipelago appeared from the larger continental land mass to west. In a case of magnanimous disposition by the nearby and mighty continental power, the Chinese Court extracted modest tribute from its vassal the Ryukyu Kingdom. This consisted more of ceremony and courtesy than substantive value, in return for which China provided bounty and protection. This covenant provided the people of Ryukyu the opportunity to trade with the Chinese mainland and to enjoy relative prosperity and stability in the region. The trade, diplomatic, and cultural exchanges between the Ryukyu Kingdom and the Imperial Court in China were conducted chiefly between the port of Naha, which was overseen by the Royal Castle of Shuri above the approach to the harbor, and the city of Fukushu in the Chinese maritime province of Fukken. However, in a repetitive cycle often lasting centuries, the Chinese imperial dynasties would sag under the weight of an overextended military, bureaucratic inflexibility, and official corruption. It was during one of these periods in China that the powerful Shimazu Clan of the military government on the Japanese mainland to the north had begun probing the Ryukyu Kingdom for opportunities to expand its reach of power. During the middle part of the seventeenth century in the dying throes of China's Ming Dynasty and its eventual overthrow at the hands of Manchus who swept in from the north and proclaimed the new imperial era of the Ching Dynasty, the Shimazu laid its strongest claim to Ryukyu. In the early seventeenth century, they were emboldened by Japan's own new era of centralized and forceful administration by the Tokugawa Shogun in Edo, the capital city that more than 250 years later would become known as Tokyo. Shimazu maintained a tangible influence over the island chain to the south, though the Ryukyu Kingdom was able to retain some degree of domestic political freedom for an extended period of time.

While continuing during this new era to pay symbolic deference to the Ching emperor in Beijing, the people of Ryukyu found that the Shimazu overlords from the Japanese mainland would exercise restrictions on their native traditions and civil life. In time, the Ryukyu Court in Shuri Castle, which gradually became disengaged from its Chinese moorings to the west while falling subject to Japanese pressure from the north, was no longer able to support its own extensive domestic commitments. As military commanders who were in turn sanctioned by the Tokugawa Shogun of Japan, the Shimazu overlords forbade the people of Ryukyu to carry weapons such as swords, the traditional symbol and substance of power of the samurai class. Rather than confront what was undoubtedly a better armed, trained, supported, and more powerful force from the mainland that generally refrained from interfering with non-military local affairs, increasingly the people of Ryukyu turned their attention from distant overseas powers to local livelihoods. However, in a practical and sincere response, they continued to practice unarmed and defensive military training, mostly in secret. At first, they developed a systemized set of movements from informal dances that suggested parrying and counter thrusts, avoiding and re-engaging, which was borrowed from the Chinese envoys that stayed at Shuri Castle and was known in Ryukyu as *toodi* or "Chinese Hand." Central to the values of the Ryukyu Kingdom, which included the practice of *toodi*, was the concept of courtesy. Indeed, it was enshrined over the main gate leading to Shuri Castle in the carved characters for 'The Land Where Courtesy Reigns' for all to acknowledge as they passed through. For the people of Ryukyu, courtesy, respect, and gratitude were nearly synonymous; one without the other rendered it meaningless. Over time, because of the official ban on swords and other military weapons, *toodi* became combined with indigenous forms of weaponry using implements from the farm or fishing boats and household tools. It came to be known first as *toode*, which implied the same origins as Chinese Hand, and then later as *karate*, an ambiguous term that satisfied the interests and culture of the Japanese overlords. The ostensible submission by the people of Ryukyu to the prohibitions of the Shimazu Clan veiled their stout-hearted maintenance of native traditions and way of life. As a consequence, the Uechi family ancestors, who in earlier times had been granted land, an income, and an official position as samurai, like many others originally employed by the Shuri Court and the central government of the island kingdom, began to cast about for a sustainable means of livelihood. The Uechi family members retreated to relative obscurity in the northern end of the main island of Ryukyu and sustained themselves modestly with agriculture and fishing. For the next two centuries, the Uechi family, one generation after another, lived quietly and peacefully, benefiting modestly from the natural gifts of land and sea, observing their customs, maintaining their traditions,

12

practicing *toode*, and sustaining their attachment to the Ryukyu island chain.

In the latter half of the nineteenth century, Uechi Kantoku, Kanbun's father, had grown to take responsibility for the family livelihood. He and his family decorated the inside of their home with simple and seasonal crafts made from straw, banana leaves, and other plants that grew on the hillsides or from pieces of driftwood, shells, and seaweed they brought in with their fishnets. Kansho and Kantoku also wove the reed sandals they all wore outdoors. At different times during the year, they would sit together on the veranda in front of their modest home, and Kanbun watched as his grandfather and father took several handfuls of dry rice straw and tore them into thinner strips. Next, they trimmed the ends with a short sharp knife to make them equal in length. Then, they gathered several handfuls of the rice stalks and rolled and braided the light brown plant tightly and powerfully in their hands that had been roughened by digging in the fields and hauling lines and fish in their boat. After working the thin straws together for a while, it became thicker like rope. They repeated this process until they had several of the cords ready for weaving. They held one cord firmly between their toes while they pulled on it tightly and shaped it into a flat oblong. From there, they wove pieces of rice straw between the cords until the sole of the rice straw sandal was complete. Finally, they took a single piece of straw rope, threaded it through the soul near the toes, stretched both ends soundly around their ankles, and tied a knot. In this way, they could easily slide their feet into the sandal and hold the front end firmly with the threaded strap. Kansho and Kantoku repeated this craft a few times until they had made different sizes and pairs for each member of the family.

At New Year, their mother, Tsuru, made special tasty dishes using out-of-the-ordinary ingredients that visually and traditionally symbolized health, wisdom, long life, and good fortune, while Kansho and Kantoku would pound sweet rice into sticky cakes that they ate wrapped in seaweed and flavored with soy sauce. Kansho wove a toy horse from rice straw, decorated it with a bit of bright red cotton material, and set it beside the candles and incense laid out in front of the family altar. Here, the Uechi family prayed for the repose of their ancestors. In spring, Kansho tore, bent, and knotted banana leaves into hats to protect them from the heat of the tropical sun bearing down on the sea and shore at Motobu Village. Kanbun and his younger brother, Kanso, nicknamed Hiro, used these hats to scoop up wriggling yellow, green, or blue fish in the East China Sea that stretched away into the distance below the hill town of Izumi. Sometimes, they would catch a seahorse that would encircle its tail around one of their pointed fingers extended into the tropical waters. Occasionally, a baby octopus slithered out and rolled around the water cupped in their hands when Kansho pulled them along the sandy and coral-studded shore in his fishing boat. They dipped their banana leaf hats into the salt water and then splashed the contents over their heads while giggling at the comical expression on each other's face. Kansho showed them that some fish swam close to surface, easier to see and catch, while others required more skill to reach in the deeper waters. There were some who lived out of sight deep by the ocean bottom for which the timing, bait, and luck to land had to be just right.

In the spring, Tsuru made them loose pantaloons from coarse cotton or flax material she had woven the season before. They would draw the waist in with a bit of hemp cord and then thrust bamboo sticks inside the rope pretending they were great swordsmen of long ago and race around the beach by Motobu with their bare and tanned chests panting in the hot and humid air. Most evenings, after a day on the water, Kansho would guide the fishing boat to shore, turn it over, and secure it to a large boulder with iron rings attached to its sides. He did this not out of fear that someone would use it improperly, for all the people in the fishing and farming villages knew each other and what belonged to whom. Rather, it was to prevent it from being washed away by an unusually high tide or blown out to sea by one of the typhoons that ripped across the islands. He would then walk along the beach in the sand moistened and softened by the tide toward the dry path leading the way home up the hillside to Izumi. Kanbun and Hiro followed along after Grandfather and were comforted and confident behind his sturdy and supple figure. They lengthened their strides to fit into his footprints, sometimes hopping, skipping, or digging their heels into the ephemeral markings in the soft sand. With generations of unchanging rural lives behind them bound together by tradition and geography, it would have been difficult to imagine an East Asian future that would rise up like the sea during a great storm and wash over their lives.

The Bamboo Grove

On one day, Kanbun squatted in the rocky garden of his family home splashing his hand in the clear puddles of water that formed from the spring shower that had just ended. When the water was still, he could see the cloud-filled reflection of the sky with its patches of lighter gray and pockets of bright azure, but when he slapped the puddle with his hand, it all exploded into a wrenched and twisted sea storm with crashing waves and distorted colors. For a moment the sky above him opened to let the rays of shine flood through and brighten with yellow warmth the wet and light brown soil, nearby patches of rough grass, and leafy weeds that grew here and there in the yard. Tomorrow would be the fifth day of the fifth month, his birthday and the celebration of the annual Boys Day Festival, which his family and all his neighbors in the village and beyond would celebrate for every not-yet-adult son. In the yard next to each home, they would erect long green bamboo poles straight up and adorned with cloth streamers in the shape of carp with colored paper pinwheels fixed on top. The carp symbolized perseverance and virility, as the fish was known to be able to survive for long periods out of its native water and could thrash and fight with the best when hooked or caught. Though one end of each pole would be planted firmly in the claylike ground and supported at about waist height with bamboo stays lashed to its sides, the topmost end would sway and dance widely with the weight and breadth of the cloth streamers that caught the onshore breezes that blew from the ocean and pushed the heavy air over the landscape. Today, Kanbun's mother had told him that he would

17

accompany his grandfather to the bamboo grove to cut the poles for the Boys Day decorations. Kanbun thought nothing of this, as his mother had often instructed him to assist his grandfather or other family members, neighbors, friends, and relatives with tasks whenever there was need. However, unknown to Kanbun, today there would be a something different waiting for him.

His grandfather carried two *kama* with their sharp metal blades attached at right angles to wooden handles dangling from his waist. He led Kanbun out of the yard, beyond the vegetable fields, and onto a path through the undergrowth to a flat, clear area overlooking the sea. On one side of the clearing a grove of bamboo stretched up the hillside away from the sea. Kansho handed Kanbun one of the *kama* and instructed him to cut some of the bamboo that ranged in thickness from narrow shoots around which he could enclose his forefinger and thumb to others that were too big for both his hands to stretch around. Kanbun thought this was unusual as ordinarily they needed only two long, sturdy poles to erect the Boys Day decorations and a few short stays to support them. His grandfather motioned for them to continue, and Kanbun complied. Before long they had cleared an area across which a 30 *shaku*, or about 10 meter, pole could lie on the ground. They sat on the cut and stacked bamboo in the shade at the edge of the clearing to catch their breath.

Jumping up, Kanbun said, "I'll go get us some water. My throat is as dry as pine bark."

Kansho reached up and plucked two unripe *shikuwasa*, a variety of mandarin orange, from a branch, handed one to Kanbun, and began the peel the tough skin with his fingernails until he had most of the outer layer removed. Kansho bit lightly

18

into the pulp, squinting with his eyes and twisting his lips into a pinched frown.

"These green *shikuwasa* are sour, but they help keep your thirst away," he said.

Kanbun tried doing the same and soon his face twisted from the tart juice, but it also left a slight numbing sensation inside his mouth and down his throat so that he no longer craved water. Next his grandfather picked up one of the longer bamboo staves, which Kanbun expected would be for the Boys Day decorations, but instead he cut it into lengths of about six *shaku*, or about two meters. He handed one to Kanbun and told him to hold an end with both hands. Kansho took the other end and playfully pushed, twisted, pulled, lifted, and swung the staff in semi-circles. Kanbun gladly joined in the fun holding onto his end while trying to avoid falling off balance or losing ground. Kanbun's face strained every time his grandfather was about to out maneuver him and soon he was breathing heavily and sweat covered his body. Kansho laughed and they sat down in the shade of the surrounding bamboo grove to rest a while. His grandfather was neither panting nor perspiring, which Kanbun noticed with a little disappointment.

Kanbun sensed that he should listen carefully as his grandfather began in a quiet but steady tone, "Today you will begin learning *kobujutsu* and *toodi*. *Kobujutsu* uses ordinary tools from our homes, farms, and boats in Ryukyu, like the *bo* we just wrestled with or the *kama* we used to cut the bamboo, and is an old style of weaponry and defense used by the samurai of Ryukyu. Some use horse bridle *nunchaku*, grain grinding *tonfa*, or meat skewer *sai* that Japanese mainland officials would recognize

19

only as household and farming tools. For more than two hundred years, the Shimazu Clan, the leaders of Satsuma on the southern tip of the mainland of Japan, forbade us to carry or even own swords, though they themselves have continued to do so here openly. Therefore, we learned to be better skilled at using these weapons, even though they only look like ordinary tools. We learned from father to son and from teacher to student in a quiet way, passing on our traditions and practice almost imperceptibly so as avoid the notice of Satsuma. I know only a little *toodi*, which is kind of like a dance with deeper meaning as well as practical applications. It comes from China, which we in Ryukyu also call 'Shinkoku,' the land on the other side of the western sea, and the era when it was ruled by the Tang Dynasty more than a thousand years ago. The Tang Dynasty was a Golden Era for China in which culture, society, religion, science, and government all developed to a high degree. *Toodi* consists of the two Chinese characters for the 'Tang' and 'hand,' meaning 'Chinese Hand,' and refers to the creative yet systematic way the Chinese developed their techniques for battle since ancient times. Ryukyu is its own kingdom and the Royal House of Sho has ruled for hundreds of years and has led our country for many generations from the great castle in Shuri far to the south near the other end of this island. However, we have also been indebted and protected by the Imperial Court of China, which is nowadays ruled by the Ching or Manchu people from the north and west of their wide empire. From the north to the south, the countries along the eastern edge of greater Asia and stretching out to the many island nations-- our own Ryukyu is only one among them-- that frame the continent, there are earthquakes and volcanoes, typhoons and other natural calamities that afflict the inhabitants of these areas. We are safe, healthy, and happy here in Izumi, but the wider region is unpredictable and mostly unknown to us."

His grandfather went on, "We have been subject and somewhat loyal to the Shogun's representatives in the Shimazu Clan of Satsuma, which lies on the Japanese mainland north of the island of Ryukyu. I have heard that the current generation of the Ching Dynasty in China is weak and corrupt. Our friends and relatives live in the south near the trading port of Naha, where there are exchanges with Chinese who bring us some of the news about the mainland. China itself is struggling with problems of rebellion and outside pressure for trade and had to give up some of its territory to the foreigners of Europe and America who have developed advanced and modern industry that we have never seen. They have built metal steam ships that sail across the oceans and around the world when there is no breeze or even the wind is against them. They have mechanical wagons that ride on steel tracks in a straight line from one city to another and with stops along the way. They carry great quantities of goods inland from the ports like Naha, trade across wide areas, make huge profits, and enjoy a rich and comfortable life. At the same time, the Shimazu Clan has grown stronger within Japan, while the Shogun's administration in Edo has become ineffective against the foreigners. Satsuma has helped lead a takeover of the Shogun's military government by encouraging other groups to return to power the Japanese emperor and those most loyal to him. However, the same foreign groups unsettling China are now threatening the Japanese as well with their modern ships and huge cannons. I saw several of those ships years ago when your father was a young boy. The Americans stopped in Ryukyu seeking a port to store coal for fuel on their steam ships so they

21

could have better access to Japan for trade and diplomacy. Their ships were impressive and frightening. It is hard to know if this will mean much for us here in Ryukyu over the long term," he explained, "but we will need to be cautious, listen to what they say and watch their actions."

"In any case, for today, whether learning *kobujutsu* or *toodi*, we must begin with how you stand, where you place your feet, and then develop sturdy legs and a lower body that will support your arms and upper body," continued Kansho standing up firmly. "Your midsection, which has few bones but many of your important organs, must become firm yet fluid to make the key link transferring strength and balance from your lower to upper body. Finally, you must concentrate your breath to make it short and shallow by pulling down your shoulders, protecting your ribs, and calming your mind. There is much to learn, too much in a short time, but we will take it one step at a time." Kansho then picked up the bamboo staff they used to wrestle earlier and gave one end to Kanbun.

"Now," he said, "place your feet firmly on the ground, dig the tips of your feet into the soil, and lower your hips by bending your knees slightly. This is the first and one of the important lessons I can teach you about *kobujutsu* and *toodi*, and you will hear me repeat it many times. Use your feet so that your contact with the ground is firm and strong, keep your weight forward on your toes so that you strengthen your legs, and avoid sitting back on the flat of your heels where you can be easily overpowered. Walk with the legs of a cat as if feeling for the ground with the tips of your feet. Drop your hips so your weight is lowered and you move your body firmly and steadily but lightly on your feet so that even the ocean waves driven by a typhoon cannot upend you. We will exercise until you do this naturally, and only a trained eye will be able to see that you have developed a special strength."

They began to wrestle gripping the *bo* again at the two ends, this time Kanbun did a little better than before and resisted some of the twists and pushes from his grandfather. Occasionally, Kansho would admonish Kanbun, but always with gently encouraging words, to firm his feet upon the ground or lower his hips for better balance and stability. He also taught Kanbun to drop his shoulders to keep from lifting his weight off balance and to keep his breathing down and short to avoid becoming winded. Kansho showed him how to hold his hands on the *bo* so that they were about the height of his chest but his elbows were low by his belly so that his shoulders stayed down and his breathing remained steady. He explained that with his shoulders down and breathing short he could remain calm and overcome fear or excitement in the face of frightening or unexpected challenges.

He took Kanbun to the edge of the clearing where a knee high pine was stretching up from the ground. Kansho instructed, "Stand beside the pine. Good, now jump over the pine." Kanbun crouched and sprang over the pine easily, as it was a young sapling.

"Good," his grandfather repeated, "now do it again the other way. Again... again... again!" Kanbun jumped back and forth until his legs became fatigued and his breathing heavy.

They rested a little, and then Kansho commanded "Run around the clearing and jump over the pine," which Kanbun also did easily.

"Again!"

23

Kanbun repeated this until he was winded and needed a rest. After a while, Kansho had Kanbun stand facing the little pine and told him to jump forward over it, and then backwards to where he started, and he repeated this, but fewer times until he became fatigued.

"Good!" His grandfather said again in the same steady and encouraging voice. "We will do this every day until twenty jumps become forty, and forty become four hundred! Your legs will become like tree trunks rooted to the ground."

Kansho then selected two of the longest bamboo poles they had cut and placed them on Kanbun's shoulder, while he picked up a few of the shorter pieces.

"Follow me," Kansho instructed, and they carried the bamboo out of the clearing, across the vegetable and grain fields, and back to the open yard by their farmhouse.

The next morning, Kansho called Kanbun and Hiro to help him set up the Boys Day decorations. First, with the *kama* he made angle cuts in the ends of a few of the short and thick pieces of bamboo. He drove the sharpened ends of the bamboo into the ground closely together with a wooden mallet. He lashed the remaining bamboo pieces to the tops of the stakes in the ground so that they formed two sets of four posts. Then, he tied one of colorful pieces of doubled over cloth that the boys' mother had sewn into the shape of *koi*, or carp, to the end of one of the long bamboo poles lying on the ground. The piece of cloth in the shape of a carp had a narrow opening at one end with a large black eye on either side of the narrow head and fins at the other end a larger opening so that the cloth fish would puff up and flap in the breeze. There were also some small pinwheels made of bamboo and bits of colored cloth made by their mother that their

24

grandfather placed on the ends of a short, narrow piece of bamboo that he lashed to the end of yet another long bamboo pole. He then stood up the long poles, placed them in the center of two sets of posts, and then lashed them steady. The mouths of the cloth fish opened to the breeze and their tails flapped in the wind, while the pinwheels spun colorfully overhead on the other pole. Both of the long, vertical bamboo poles bent gently with the wind.

While putting up the decorations, Kansho told them about Boys Day.

"Bamboo grows plentifully around the country. It grows tall and thin, firm yet flexible, bends with the breeze, and grows year round, but is most green and healthy in late spring when new shoots are born, just like you were. We tie the bamboo poles together with rope that is made from the branches of the mountain bushes. Some people call our Ryukyu Island chain "Okinawa," which is the Japanese pronunciation of characters that mean a 'rope out in the sea.' To the gods above in the sky, wind, and clouds these islands probably do look like knots in a rope floating in the ocean. The fish at the top of the tall poles are *koi*. They represent you boys because we wish you to grow strong and steady, even when the winds blow against you. Carp are sturdy fish because they can last a long time even away from their natural environment."

"Look up," he told the boys. "Be bright, firm yet flexible, and healthy in the spring sun. Follow your dreams but have your feet firmly planted on the ground. Only the earth, sea, and sky are greater than you."

In the following days and months, Kansho and Kanbun returned to the clearing by the bamboo grove daily. The old man taught the boy how to handle the bamboo *bo* with one or both hands, twisting, twirling, thrusting, swinging high and low, leaning forward and backwards, from one side to the other, how to move with speed, grace, stability, and confidence. More importantly, he taught Kanbun to block, sweep away, avoid, and leap over thrusts, strikes, and charges his grandfather made with his own *bo*, pursuing the boy across and around the clearing. Some days, Kansho wrapped fishnet weighted with stones around one end of Kanbun's *bo* and told him to practice swinging, sweeping, striking, and retreating first holding the bamboo firmly with both hands and then in only the right or the left. Kansho instructed Kanbun to take a short length of bamboo and tap it against his forearm and shins. Gradually, his grandfather tied several thin staves together into a bundle, and then eventually replaced that with a firmer pole. As the pounding accumulated, his arms and legs would become tough and sinewy. He taught him to swing his arms and legs in blocking and striking motions against the bamboo staff while his grandfather held it. Next, he showed Kanbun how to strike with his hands and feet, arms and legs, against live bamboo growing out of the ground that was thicker than his arm. In time, Kanbun was able to strike harder without hurting himself. Kansho explained to Kanbun that he should think about conditioning the bones in his arms and legs the way a tool smith forged metal, but he should also train his muscles to be supple and strong similar to the way they made sticky and elastic sweet rice cakes by pounding it with a wooden mallet and mortar at New Year. Kansho also used several of the tall bamboo stalks in the grove to show Kanbun how to avoid strikes or imagine attacks coming from multiple directions. On other days, they would stand on the stumps cut low to the ground at the edge of the clearing and try to knock each other off balance with their *bo*, laughing and teasing when they fell or touched the ground with their feet.

On every visit to the clearing, Kansho had Kanbun jump over the pine tree, side to side, forwards and backwards, running around the clearing and clearing the height with longer, more powerful, and higher leaps until he panted for breath and his legs shook with fatigue. Slowly, as the tree grew, imperceptibly, Kanbun's jumps became almost effortless yet with more spring, distance, and height in successive weeks and months. His legs became thick and strong. Kansho also told Kanbun to bring two *tsubo*, or ceramic jars, with them for training. Kanbun wondered what use they could be and waited for his grandfather's instruction. Kansho showed him how to grasp the tops of the *tsubo* with his thumb bent and the tips of his other four fingers gripping the lip of the opening at the top. He told Kanbun to lift the ceramic jars up in front of his face, swing them in circles out to the sides, and over his head while holding his shoulders down and shifting his body side to side, front and back. He also had Kanbun walk on the tops of the bamboo stumps holding the *tsubo* in his grasp, keeping his balance, and swinging them about as he did. On each succeeding day, Kansho dropped a small stone into the ceramic jars so they would grow slowly and steadily in weight. In turn, Kanbun grew strong, supple, mobile, and fluid handling the *tsubo* as he lifted, swung, and stalked around the clearing with the ceramic jars tightly in his grasp. His fingers too became like the claws of the hawks that circled overheard around the island hills, able to crush shells from the sea or nutty fruits that grew on the trees. Together, his fingers and hands formed a firm and unyielding grip.

One day, Kansho brought home a shy and gentle donkey foal at the end of a tethered rope leading him into the clearing around the family home. The donkey looked a little thin and timid. Kanbun plucked some sweet grass from the ground and fed it to the donkey, which nervously but gratefully accepted the offering and nuzzled against Kanbun's waist. Kanbun liked the animal immediately, leading him around the yard in a parade, patting him softly on the neck and back, and encouraging him in a soft voice. The donkey seemed at ease with the boy and accepted his attention.

"Grandfather, can I name the donkey," he asked.

"Sure," was the reply. "What would you like to name him?"

Kanbun thought just a moment and said, "Baro," which was a pun on the Japanese word for "donkey" and also for "oaf." And, so it was for Baro.

The next time Kansho and Kanbun headed for the clearing by the bamboo grove, the old man told the boy to bring the donkey with them. After they arrived in the clearing, Kansho gave Baro a taste of moist dark sugar cane that he had brought in the folds of his jacket. Next, he guided Kanbun to bend at the knees, gently slide his shoulders under the waist of Baro, and lift him until he stood up straight. Kanbun stood uneasily and Kansho instructed him to take a few steps, which he did as best he could as the animal kicked its legs and squealed. Kansho then gave the animal another treat. They did this each day until Kanbun could walk around the clearing comfortably with the donkey on his shoulders and Baro began to anticipate the sweet rewards of a bit of carrot or cucumber, and he began to trust his new friend. Gradually, over time, as the donkey gained weight and grew fuller, healthier, and taller, Kanbun also developed greater strength in his legs, back, and shoulders as he carried Baro with ease around the clearing. He became steady and confident, which Baro sensed, and Kanbun would hum a tune or sing a folk song to the donkey as he carried the animal around on his shoulders.

One morning some time later, Kansho deliberately withheld his treat from Baro, instead keeping him tied to a post outside a small shed open on one end that they had built for him. Baro squealed in complaint and became obstinate. Kanbun thought this was harsh and wondered why his grandfather was unkind to his favorite animal. However, as usual, Kansho told Kanbun to bring Baro with them to the clearing. At first, Baro expected relief for his parched mouth from Kanbun and nuzzled him warmly and expectantly, and then followed the boy has he led him away from the yard with the tether. Baro began to wheeze with frustration when they entered the clearing and started to push against Kanbun hoping for his treat and became ever more insistent and forceful. Kansho told Kanbun to push back against the animal using his legs and lowering his hips and weight slightly to the ground. It became a pushing match, with Baro holding his ground and other times slipping aside or turning away as Kanbun leaned against him. The animal was willful yet unpredictable, so Kanbun was unable to get the better of him. Kansho then pulled a small bundle of turnips from a cloth bag and handed the juicy roots to Baro who ate them eagerly.

Kansho then explained, "These are important lessons. Strength matters, but you also need to use a strategy as well as your determination and senses. You will need them all. Running or jumping, pushing or pulling, in a straight line is one thing, but you need to know how to adjust your strength, to turn or twist in different directions while you are moving. Just as Baro understands you are being friendly when you sing him a song, you need to sense when people are thinking well or ill of you, when their will is strong like yours, and whether your strategy is superior. Sometimes you will need to focus your energy and power in a single direction for a decisive strike, while at other times you will have to bend or angle your strength in a circular movement. Sometimes you will encounter a powerful opponent who comes at you straight forward, while there may be others who strike from unexpected or multiple directions."

"What's more," he went on, "animals and humans alike need rewards for their efforts. If you want to lead and for others to follow, you must be strict, fair, and reward them"

Sometimes, during these breaks in practice while they were resting, Kansho told Kanbun tales and legends from earlier times about great masters of *kobujutsu* and *toodi* or samurai swordsmen. Kanbun listened intently and tried to picture the figures and situations his grandfather described. Kanbun imagined himself in similar positions and hoped one day also to distinguish himself with extraordinary strength and skill.

During the break in training on one of these days, Kansho said, "there was a swordsman named Miyamoto Musashi who lived about three hundred years ago and was of the same samurai class as our Uechi family. He was the greatest swordsman of his day or perhaps any day. In addition to a ferocious spirit and remarkable skills, he experimented with different kinds of training and various weapons. He opened his mind and learned from other accomplished swordsmen of that era, but followed his heart, took an uncommon path, and developed his own two-sword style. He thought deeply about strategy and employed it not only with his swords but also in his daily life. He defeated all his opponents with greater strength, skill, cunning, and strategy. He also wrote that with superior strategy one man could defeat ten, or ten could defeat one hundred. Some day when you are older and will understand it better, we will read together the book he wrote called the *Book of Five Rings* and see what you think."

Thereafter, about once a week Kansho would repeat depriving Baro in the morning in order to provoke his stubborn resistance in the clearing and provide Kanbun a chance to sharpen his skills in motion and to develop a sense for when to push, pull, or hold steady. After some time, Kansho also brought Hiro along with Kanbun and introduced him also to the training in the clearing by the bamboo grove. He repeated some of the lessons for Kanbun to hear a second time but in a slightly different way and for Hiro to begin learning. Kansho used Kanbun to train his younger brother, for both boys to strengthen each other, and together to learn from him. With the passing of weeks, months, and eventually years, and the steady training of running and jumping, carrying Baro on their shoulders as the donkey grew to a mature size, and the powerful yet graceful handling of heavy ceramic jars and weighted bamboo staffs, the boys legs and backs grew sturdy and powerful yet supple. Their legs became thick and round yet springy, their arms developed sinewy muscles, their bodies stood straight and firm yet resilient, their movements were decisive yet flowing, their minds were quick yet flexible, and their senses became attentive and aware. Kansho led them in many kinds of physical training, thoughtful discussions, spontaneous responses, and strategic lessons in which he taught Kanbun and Hiro to condition and develop their bodies, to open their minds, to intuit with their senses, and to sharpen their spirits. It was training that could be called upon in a moment of distress or used as a foundation for health and balance throughout one's life.

Country Life

In the quiet hinterlands and back waters of Ryukyu, in the second half of what was known in the West as the nineteenth century, life for most had been a steady cycle of seasons-- birth, growth, death, and regeneration-- for generation upon generation. The people of northern Ryukyu tilled the same soil, grew the same crops, caught the same kinds of fish, and lived a simple and similar lifestyle to their ancestors who had lived there centuries before them. On special days of the year, such as the vernal and autumnal equinoxes, New Year, the spring family gravesite care and cleaning ritual for ancestors known as *Seimei*, and the mid-year full moon Obon festival, Uechi Kanbun and his family would tend to the memory of their ancestors, clean the stone monuments, leave some sake, set out flowers, light incense, and say prayers. There, Kanbun could see the names of each Uechi family member stretching directly back to his grandfather's grandfather, Kan'an, and still much deeper into the past. Whenever there was a birth, marriage, or death, it was duly recorded in their *koseki*, or official registry kept by local the government, so that blood lines, relations, and family histories were common knowledge. This steady and predictable way of life provided the people of Ryukyu with confidence about who they were, where they had come from, and most likely what their futures would be.

However, soon local, regional, and global pressures would begin to roil the seas, stimulate populations to overthrow governments, and provoke some nations to war with neighboring lands. They would also see the arrival of strangely foreign people, technologies, and ideas sweep across societies to change what had largely been unchanged for ages. During the reign of Sho Tai who would become the last of the Kings of the land of Ryukyu, the Ching Dynasty in China was crumbling as secret societies plotted rebellion and open insurrections occurred across the land. The British had already sailed into Canton, threatened the Ching Imperial Court, and opened trading ports by force. China was unable counter the militarily and commercially more powerful British who compelled them to accept the opium trade, which further weakened the will of the Chinese people who used the drug as well as the realm governing them. To the utter shame and embarrassment of the imperial Chinese, the British also extracted the concession of Hong Kong for 150 years into the future. In Japan, groups loyal to the Meiji Emperor overthrew the two-and-half-century-old Tokugawa military government led by shoguns. Meanwhile, the United States emerged from its own bloody Civil War to extend its territories across the American continent reaching the Pacific Ocean and beyond. They, along with the naval powers of Europe, enthusiastically colonized strategic swaths of both maritime and continental Asia, sending technologically superior ships and gun boats to explore and establish trading ports in Japan and the Far East. Commodore Matthew Perry from the United States led a fleet of steel-plated steamships mounted with cannon to Ryukyu and Japan on what were known in the region as "Black Ships" and demanded trade and concessions from the weakening Tokugawa shogun's government in Edo. Perry and his menacing ships had stopped in Shuri on their way to Japan. He requested a "Treaty of Amity" with Ryukyu in order to establish a base from which he could more forcefully open Japan. This left the King and his court in

Shuri in a quandary. They were in no position to resist the Americans, but granting portage to them would infuriate their Japanese overlords. Even the Japanese, after centuries of self-imposed isolation, had never seen such modern industrial and military power and were unable to mount a forceful response. The newly established Meiji government in Tokyo, formerly known as Edo, in a hasty effort to catch up with the fast moving American and European powers began modernizing from a backward feudal society into a unified nation with a strong military and industrial and technological expertise and organization imported from the West. Fearful of itself succumbing to Western colonization, Japan laid sole claim to the Ryukyu Kingdom soon after launching into its modern period. It changed the name of the Ryukyu Kingdom to the Ryukyu Fiefdom, remanded King Sho Tai to Tokyo where he was to stay imprisoned for the remainder of his life. A few years later, Japan officially changed the name of the island kingdom to the more Japanese sounding Okinawa Prefecture. The quiet and peaceful Kingdom of Ryukyu lay within striking distance of the Asian continent, the southern tip of the main Japanese islands, the Korean Peninsula, the naval port of Vladivostok in the Russian Far East, Formosa, so named as the "Beautiful Island" by the Portuguese and which later became known as Taiwan, the Philippine islands that 400 years earlier had been colonized by Spain and more recently had been taken by the United States, the islands of Malaya in the South China Sea, and other key posts and landfalls for the American, Russian, Portuguese, Spanish, Dutch, German, French, and English navies. The little rope of islands out in the sea, by virtue of, or perhaps by misfortune of, its geographic location dividing the East China Sea and the

Philippine Sea, became a key leverage point for the greater powers surrounding it that hoped to establish themselves firmly in the region. Before long, Prince Sho Jun, the legal heir to the now banished Shuri Court, founded the Ryukyu Shimpo, a domestic newspaper. It began circulating news every other day to inform the inhabitants of Ryukyu of current events and regional concerns related to their people and their islands.

It was in the midst of these unsettled times that Kanbun, Hiro, their cousins, neighbors, friends, and community lived in a society informed by the Ryukyu Shimpo and the stories told by traders from around East Asia who visited Ryukyu. During the summer of 1896, as the summer festival of Obon approached, throughout Okinawa families prepared sake, rice, special dishes, and rituals in their homes for honoring their ancestors. The residents of Izumi, like others across the country, also formed groups to practice music and dance and make decorations and costumes in which they would perform in the public roadways and around the village. Some would hone their skills on calf-skin drums, the three stringed *shamisen* made from the skin of the deadly *habu* snake, or a bamboo flute. Men, women, and children rehearsed rhythmic and symbolic dances or sang traditional folks songs with themes of the full moon, toil on the ocean and in the fields, separation from homeland and family, or thirst for love. The older women sewed and fashioned for young people colorful and expressive robes that stood in striking contrast to their modest yet charming demeanor. The men, meanwhile, drilled their sons and grandsons in group performances of twirling, thrusting, slipping, and defending with bamboo *bo*. Kanbun and Hiro were clear about which of these activities they would volunteer to join.

This year, a typhoon had struck the island a few weeks before the Obon holiday. The typhoons were giant hurricanes that swept across the Pacific Ocean occasionally from midsummer until early autumn bearing fierce winds and driving rain. People in the hillsides and mountain villages that were most exposed to these fearsome acts of nature would close the sliding wooden doors and shutters on their homes and stay indoors until the danger of flying debris or roofs collapsing would pass. The Uechi family spent two days inside their home waiting. When the wind finally died down outdoors, they slid opened their doors and shutters and breathed the fresh air.

"Come on Hiro, *bo* practice was already postponed and we'll be late to catch up," called the nineteen year-old Kanbun across the yard and into the open front of their farm house.

He had picked up two green bamboo *bo*, which he laid across his shoulders, and was eagerly waiting for his younger brother to finish his after dinner chores so they could join the group of teenage boys gathering in the open space in front of the village elementary school. Kanbun and Hiro, as well as their cousins and the other boys and girls of Izumi, had attended the school, learning about the intricacies of reading and writing Chinese characters, history, geography, and traditional literature of Ryukyu, China, and Japan, and some basic math and sciences. Upon graduating from elementary school, the boys joined their fathers working the boats, nets, and hauling of fish to market and helping to plant, nurture, and harvest the rice and vegetable fields. The girls, for the most part, stayed closer to home assisting with preparing meals, sewing and repairing clothing, and learning from their grandmothers about their folk ways.

Kanbun and Hiro joined their friends Matsuda Tokusaburo, Gushi Toshio, Toyama Kazuhiko, Arakaki Kiyomasa, their cousins, and the other boys from Izumi in front of their school. They formed several rows and stood straight with their bamboo *bo* held closely to their sides in the right arm pointed neutrally to the ground but with the other end reaching above their heads and directed toward the sky. The leader of group, Kobayashi Gonta, was the son of the village chief. Gonta was physically bigger and more imposing than most of the other boys, but he was also pudgy, apparently spoiled by his parents, and seemed to revel in his appointed position. He was stricter with the younger and smaller boys than was necessary using his staff to test the sturdiness of their grasp on the *bo* by whacking his against theirs, menacing them by standing right in front of their face and criticizing them loudly, and slapping the tops of their heads when he found other faults with the way they stood or looked. Gonta tried to unnerve Kanbun with a threatening stare and sharp words, but Kanbun held his gaze standing firmly on his feet and keeping his breathing steady. Kanbun suspected that someday he and Gonta would clash, but that would wait for another time and situation.

Uechi Kantoku, Kanbun's father, stepped forward and barked an order. The boys all bowed smartly, took one step backward, and held their *bo* firmly with both hands while tucking them against their hips and pointing them upward at an angle in front of them. Each of the boys looked straight forward unperturbed and set their faces in a determined gaze ready for action.

Kantoku began a rhythmic count, "One, two, three, four…One, two, three, four…," until the boys completed a routine and finished with a bow.

Some of the other fathers who had gathered in front of the school commented on the boys' movements and posture, correcting their motions by demonstrating with their own *bo*. This time Gushi Toshio's father stepped forward grunting the commands as the boys repeated the routine. Next, Arakaki Shintoku, the father of Kiyomasa, brought out a drum from inside the school and positioned it on the front steps. He beat out a rhythm that the boys followed but adjusted their motions as the pace and tone of the drum changed. Soon the boys were perspiring, though their cotton tops and pantaloons were light. Slow breezes blew across the clearing and reached the perspiration on their necks, but the evening air was heavy with heat from the day and the ever present humidity enveloped them.

At the back side of the school in another open space, some of the girls from Izumi had gathered. They were chatting in groups of two or three and commenting to each other on the different and colorful evening kimono their grandmothers and mothers had made especially light for the dances they would practice for the Obon Festival. Their hair was tied up and tucked under hats made of the same material and design as their kimono and shaped like a boat with its keel turned upside down facing the sky. Among them were Kobayashi Kazue, Gonta's younger sister, Miyagi Shige, Takamine Tomiko, Kanbun and Hiro's cousin, Uchida Shio, and other girls of the village. Kazue was different altogether in character and appearance from her swaggering and bulky older brother. She was lithe yet energetic, moved delicately, smiled easily, and always seemed to have a kind or respectful word for anyone who spoke with her. Her light eyes met others with a warm glance and slight nod of the head. She moved comfortably in the festival kimono she wore with specially colored patterns and designs.

One of the women from the village, Amemiya Saori, waved a fan and called to the girls to form a circle in the yard behind the elementary school. Next, she asked several of the older men and women who had gathered at the school to play a few tunes on the stringed *sanshin, shamisen,* and light bamboo flutes they had brought with them. Several other men and women stepped forward to sing local melodies. As the music began, Saori twirled her fan and the girls all turned to face the same counter clockwise direction. At her signal, they began slow sweeping motions with their arms, stepping forward together, sometimes dropping a step back or bending to one side, and swaying gracefully in the rhythm. The dips, sweeps, steps, waves, and twirls all imitated motions from the work of handling the daily catch from the sea or tilling the soil in their family vegetable plots. There were motions of throwing and hauling fish nets, pulling of ropes, carrying baskets of catch, swinging a hoe and drawing it across the soil, planting seedlings, and harvesting armloads of vegetables. Sometimes Saori would step to the side of one of the girls to suggest a more refined shift of the hips or turn of the shoulders and other times she would offer words of encouragement or complement the girls on their grace or carriage. All the while, the village musicians and singers continued there songs of toil, reward, and unrequited love. Even those who sat and watched felt the warm thick air turn to moisture on their foreheads and around their shoulders. The girls who danced in slow but dreamlike steps felt their breathing rise and the perspiration rise under their kimono and matching bonnets. Saori called a stop to the music and dance and ushered the girls inside the school for refreshments of tea, rice crackers, and *manju*, red bean buns. The boys had paused a little before them and were already helping themselves to the treats. All were grateful for the break.

The different age groups, old, young, and in-between, sat on the floor in the open meeting space that served at other times as the one classroom in the village school and chatted in bunches of two, three, or more. Each of the villagers knew most everyone else who lived nearby, their family backgrounds, character, habits, pleasures, dislikes, and especially their relations with each other and the community. Some were more closely related by blood or marriage and spoke with close or distant kin, while others were long time friends who had attended the elementary school, participated in the festivals since their early days, and grew up together. The latest news on the island and gossip both near and far were the common matters of interest among the different small groups.

Kazue flitted among several groups, stopping to offer greetings, chat, or exchange a smile. Kanbun watched her as he talked about *bo* technique with his friends. Once when she was nearing the layout of refreshments, Kanbun said he needed a refill of his tea cup, stood up, and walked around the room close to where Kazue was standing with two other young girls. They were about to take some of the red bean buns, but Kanbun reached in, teasingly snatched the woven bamboo plate, and held it up as high as he could over their heads.

"Oh," Shio said, "is our older brother so hungry he needs them all!"

"Maybe he is afraid he won't have enough to eat and lose the strength to swing his *bo*," teased Tomiko.

"I know how we can get them back," Kazue whispered to the two other girls. Pausing with a slight turn of her shoulders and with the hint of a smile on her lips and in her eyes, she lowered her voice and said coolly with self-assurance, "Older brother Kanbun, may we have some *manju*?"

Kanbun froze for a moment. If he refused Kazue and the girls, it would be awkward if not rude. If he simply handed them over, it would be apparent that he was embarrassed and weak on Kazue.

Mustering a steady voice and calm face, he said, "My grandmother made these buns by hand. And, I wanted to be sure you knew how to appreciate the special flavor in them."

They were about to continue their teasing, when from across the room Gonta's voice rose above most of the others, "Kazue, bring me tea!"

Kazue raised her eyebrows just slightly and turned her lips with a touch of friendly irony. She excused herself and stepped away to fetch her older brother's empty cup. After an initial silence, the buzz of conversations in the room continued among the villagers gathered in small groupings. It was not long before the Headman of Motobu Village, Gonta and Kazue's father, arrived with several of his companions. The people gathered in the elementary school made space in the center of the room for them, while the men moved a low table over beside them and the women placed tea and sweets for them on top of it.

Headman Kobayashi had just returned from one of his regular visits to Nago where he had met the mayor and learned of the latest news coming in from the South China Sea, the prices of fish at the Naha harbor market, and when the new shipment of tea would arrive from Fukken in China. After a few greetings and sips of tea, he began to talk to the men in the room. The Japanese, who had defeated the Chinese head-to-head in a war lasting nearly two years and which had concluded with the Chinese conceding defeat the year before, were showing signs of asserting themselves more pointedly in the region. Earlier, they had forced the Koreans to disassociate themselves from the Ching Empire and open ports to trade with Japan that would provide access to coal, minerals, and other resources on the Korean Peninsula. Japan joined the Western powers of England, France, Germany, America, Italy, Russia, and others in establishing independent compounds in Peking and in other strategic locations reaching down the Chinese coast to establish that they were modernizing to make a break from their feudal past. Japan had become the only Asian nation strong enough to demonstrate its might and sit at the same diplomatic table with the West. These compounds established in distant locations were free to trade, had their own laws and administration of justice, and were an obvious embarrassment to the proud and cultured Chinese whose Ching Dynasty had grown too weak to resist and was nearing collapse. To the south, Japan had taken sovereignty over Formosa and would change its name officially to Taiwan, which was another concession deeply humiliating to the Chinese. This extended the Japanese line of maritime outposts through Ryukyu to Formosa and into the island chains of Southeast Asia. Closer to home, the Japanese were replacing the native leaders in the Ryukyu islands and setting up governmental offices, mid-level regional councils, and in some localities representatives from the mainland who were military officers. Kobayashi explained that there were rumors that the Japanese Imperial Army would begin conscripting young men in Okinawa into military service. It had already done this on the Japanese mainland for those who had become twenty years old, the official age of adulthood. This could only mean that Japan was preparing for further military adventures and were willing to spill the blood of the youth of Ryukyu also to achieve their objectives. This latest bit of information caused quite a stir among the villagers, men and women alike, as the futures of their young sons, brothers, and cousins were suddenly constrained by a thick net of uncertainty. Who would be taken? How could the remaining families manage their modest means by farming and fishing without the help of their most able and needed children? Would the young men be put in danger and would they be able to return? Kobayashi was as concerned as they were, but he had no ready answers. He asked the men of the village to think of how best to prepare for this likely eventuality suggesting that they meet again as a group and with him individually as time permitted. The gathering broke up a good deal less at ease than it began and without the lively mood of Obon Festival. Families departed toward the main road with shouts of warmth and encouragement to each other, but the air was heavy with the announcements by Kazue's father. The groupings grew thinner as the way divided into sub-roads that led to smaller paths to family homes. Kanbun and Kazue walked side by side along the dirt road toward their houses. They tried to keep their thoughts and steps light after the *bo* and dance practices of the evening, but could not escape the weight of the news.

Kazue asked, "What will you do about military conscription?"

"I don't know," Kanbun replied. "It is easier to say what I don't want to do, which is to serve in the Japanese Imperial Army, than to know what I will do. I guess I will have to talk it over with my father and the others in Izumi."

They continued on a short while longer until the two families parted for the evening. Kazue smiled lightly yet steadily at Kanbun. His unsteady eyes met hers and his mouth twisted into a grin. He felt a good deal less confident than when he had responded to Kazue's teasing earlier in the evening.

In the weeks and months that followed, life continued for Kanbun and his fellow residents of Izumi at a pace familiar to those who had grown up in the easy atmosphere of "island time," but the threat of military draft and possibly an impending war were never out of their minds. There was regular news that Kazue's father brought and that appeared in the Ryukyu Shimpo. Occasionally they would hear bits of information spread by word of mouth from visitors and traders traveling from the Japanese mainland who stopped in the small port of Nago or those from the main Naha seaport in the south who put in at Nago on their way north. There were rumors that a small number of Ryukyu natives, particularly some in central and southern districts of the main island, had transformed themselves into full-fledged "Okinawans" and were actively cooperating with the Japanese. They were said to argue that it was the duty of samurai to serve and fight for one's country without questioning. Though their spoken language was the Ryukyu dialect, it was mostly based on Japanese and their written language was entirely Japanese. They also talked about how the world had changed and modernized and that as citizens of what was now part of Japan they should adapt with the new era. Others described it in terms of survival. If they did not acquiesce to the Japanese in governance, foreign relations, and especially military matters, the people of Okinawa would be unable to keep their Ryukyu traditions, culture, and livelihoods. The fruits from the land and sea, especially trade, would only be permitted by the Japanese if the island residents and merchants cooperated. The Japanese were quick to encourage and promote these compliant islanders with symbolic gifts, favored positions at social events, and even scarce but secure jobs in ports, roadway maintenance projects, postal delivery, transport services, or other government administered programs and services. China had been their patron in the past, but now it was severely weakened and Japan was the power of the future. However, the question for many in Ryukyu was whose government and country should they support. They were situated as close to the Chinese mainland as they were to the southern tip of Japan, and they had historical, cultural, linguistic, and trade relations with both, so it was a difficult choice. It was all the more a complex sentiment for those who felt their first loyalty to the deposed King of Ryukyu and their beloved islands of coral, sand, and volcanic clay, transparent light blue and green waters, and peaceful way of life. Some refused to acknowledge the changes taking place or the risks involved in non-compliance with the Japanese government. Some who lived in outlying areas, especially away from Naha and its central administrative offices and agencies, wanted to take a wait and see approach to the mood and direction of the Japanese appointed leader and whether they would continue to press their presence in Okinawa. They and their families wanted to stay in close contact with home and evade the intrusions of the Japanese, so they began exploring the caves in the many uninhabited hillsides on the main island or less populated villages in the outer islands for a suitable hideaway that they could occupy until the local conditions became clearer.

One group advocated active resistance, but they were quickly dissuaded when reminded that the Japanese had swords, rifles, cannons, new European armaments, and the backing of the central military based in Tokyo while the people of Ryukyu had only their farm implements and a tradition of secret transmission of martial training and skills in the various forms of *kobujutsu* and *toodi*. Indeed, they had no army, navy, or organized military with which to oppose the occupying Japanese. They were able to discuss their thoughts and reactions among themselves in their native Ryukyu dialect, which was a blend of coastal Chinese and mainland Japanese. This dialect was so different from anything on the Japanese mainland that the government and military officials sent by Tokyo were unable to understand the local usage and it provided security for the native speakers. Nonetheless, the Japanese administrators had heard and taken note from their local collaborators of the varying rumors among the native Okinawans. The Japanese were intently watchful for open or even latent resistance and would permit no defiance of the orders received from their superiors in Tokyo.

A few in Ryukyu took matters into their own hands by escaping to Fukken Province in southeast China. Since centuries before, there had been a lively trade in textiles, traditional crafts, tea, raw sugar, herbs, medicines, and more between Naha, the capital of the Kingdom of Ryukyu, and Fukushu, the capital of Fukken Province in China. Indeed, the tribute that the Ryukyu Kingdom paid to China passed from Shuri Castle out of the port of Naha to the city of Fukushu and then was transported overland to the Imperial Capital and Court in Peking. It was a route established during the Mei Dynasty, which was known in China as the Ming, and had opened a direct link between Ryukyu and Peking providing the additional benefits of ancillary trade along its path. The Japanese were now administering the port of Naha and closely regulating the trade between Okinawa and Fukushu. Nonetheless, it would require a native of Ryukyu to disguise himself successfully as a deck hand or merchant and secure passage from Naha to Fukushu. Those among them who could neither see themselves drafted to serve in the Japanese Imperial Army, nor offer resistance, nor acquiesce to the social changes being brought about by the Japanese, began to consider this as an alternative. The sea crossing itself would be straightforward and there were other youth from Ryukyu already in Fukushu, but those subject to the Japanese draft were by nature young, naive, unaware of the wider world, and more susceptible to deception and other dangers. In addition, the Japanese had made it clear that anyone found avoiding induction in the military draft by hiding domestically in the many islands of the Ryukyu or escaping abroad to China or elsewhere would suffer punishment and possibly imprisonment.

Despite these misgivings, most strongly voiced by his mother, Kanbun and his family decided on this last path. He would catch passage on one of the boats traveling from the nearby Nago Bay, on to Naha, and then find his way on to a larger vessel engaged in trade with Fukushu in China. He would have to make this journey alone, much as his father Kantoku wanted to accompany him to Naha, in order to escape the notice of the watchful Japanese. Kansho and Kantoku discussed their plan with village Headman Kobayashi. He recommended they wait until just before the next planting season when Kanbun could avoid questioning by the Japanese administrators. Kanbun would be come of legal age on his next birthday in May. All boys and girls who reached the legal age of 20 during the next calendar year would be feted in a ceremony at the village headquarters. If Kanbun stayed in Izumi along with other young men of Izumi born in the same year, this would be a bittersweet passage into adulthood as his age would become officially recorded by the Japanese and he would immediately become subject to the Japanese military draft. He and his family decided it would be best that he neither attract attention now, nor just before he formally became an adult. That way he could prepare for his departure and appear indistinguishable from the other young men of Ryukyu to the Japanese administrators.

Kanbun spent more of his free time in the following months taking walks with Kazue, chatting about the news and gossip they heard that passed through the village, and feeling closer to her without expressing his deeper thoughts. They talked about the excitement of Kanbun boarding a big ship from Naha bound for Fukushu, embarking on an overseas adventure, and living in a new land. Kazue's eyes glittered with a mixture of excitement, envy, and concern as together they imagined what it would be like. They also talked as if Kanbun would return the next year or the one following at the latest when the situation became settled down in Ryukyu. There were their families, their village, and their future in front of them, and this was only a temporary distraction that would take Kanbun away for a journey of adventure to the continent and the land of the great Chinese empire.

One day, as the end of the year approached, Kazue brought a gift for Kanbun. She had begged her father, the village Headman, to find a Japanese-Chinese language dictionary in Naha on one of his visits there. She didn't explain why and her father did not ask, but her older brother, Gonta, teased her whenever there was an opportunity. She held the book in a *furoshiki*, a cloth wrapping for carrying small items, which she gave to Kanbun when they walked toward the beach below the village. As Kanbun accepted the gift, which Kazue held close, he suddenly felt the need to voice his thoughts and feelings to her but somehow could not. Instead, he instinctively reached his arms around her and pulled her to him. This was the closest they had ever been, chest to chest, with only the book tucked into Kazue's hands between them. She turned her head onto his shoulder, paused to inhale, and felt his arms around her. In a few moments, they broke and both let their breath out nervously; he with an embarrassed smile and she with a small giggle. They turned and continued on their way to the sea. The waves seemed as if they were stretching out reaching and grasping for whomever or whatever lay on the shore. After reaching the beach, Kanbun and Kazue stood silently facing the East China Sea close to one another, one shoulder touching the other.

In the days waiting for the next coastal boat that would transport Kanbun from Nago to Naha, his family was generally silent, stoically aware of the changes about to take place but unwilling to express explicit concern or fear. His mother quietly prepared the few items Kanbun would take with him. On the night before his departure, the moon was full, lighting the yard in front of their home and stretching out to the ocean below. Kantoku and Kansho brought out a large clay jar full of *awamori*, an indigenous alcohol distilled from rice but more potent than sake, and set it on the veranda at the open entranceway to their home. They could hear the sound of other villagers playing music with their flutes and drums in preparation for the spring rice planting festival which they all knew Kanbun would not be participating in this year. Kantoku removed the lid bound with straw twine and set it upside down on the wooden veranda next to the jar, dipped a ladle into the liquor, and poured a generous amount into a ceramic cup. He passed the cup to his father, Kansho, offering him the first drink. Next, Kansho took a cup for himself. When it was Kanbun's turn, he leaned forward to dip the ladle into the liquid, and saw a reflection of the full moon on its surface. The moon crashed and broke into pieces as Kanbun dipped into the liquid surface, but after he filled the cup the reflection remained steady. For the first time that evening, Kantoku began to speak.

"If your heart is disturbed or lacking in virtue, your hand will tremble and the reflection of the moon will be distorted. If your mind is calm, your hand will be steady and the *awamori* will reflect a clear, round moon," he said.

The three generations quietly took turns drinking from the ceramic cup.

"Of course," he went on, "pretty soon steadying your hand is a real challenge."

Their laughter broke the somber mood, and they began to chat comfortably drinking more of the *awamori*. Kansho, Kantoku, and Kanbun continued to drink for some time talking about the journey the next day, the impending ocean voyage across the East China Sea, and what Kanbun might find in Fukushu.

Departing Ryukyu

Early the next morning Kanbun prepared to depart. His grandmother had sewn a cloth bag and his mother had put some fresh clothes and a few things to eat in it as he set out to board a medium sized shipping vessel that would be near the shore in Nago Bay a little south of Izumi and Motobu. The vessel was larger than the boats his grandfather and others used for fishing around Motobu but smaller than the ships that were too big to approach the bay and passed by further out to sea on their way to and from ports in East and Southeast Asia. The small vessels and larger ships reminded Kanbun of the flowing orbs that looked like a rope in the offing and his country's dual namesake. Whether possessed and ruled by China or Japan, or its own distinct kingdom, the islands were lush green hills floating in a beautiful clear blue ocean. The boat moored at Nago on which Kanbun would embark was on its way from Satsuma, now called Kagoshima by the Imperial government in Tokyo, to Nago and it carried fruits, fish, seaweed, and herbs. Joining him were Matsuda Tokusaburo, Uema Junpei, and Shingaki Tomohiro. There would be more who began their journey away from Izumi and other villages near Nago in Kunigami-gun by boarding boats in small groups in order not to arouse the suspicions of the Japanese officials assigned to govern the Motobu Peninsula. The captain of the boat that would transport them to Nago was beyond middle age, bareheaded in the hot sun, had dark skin and deep wrinkles, and looked at them with narrow eyes. His clothing and appearance were weathered and rough, but his demeanor was helpful and friendly. Kanbun and his comrades helped unload the boat wading in the waist deep water and bringing the boxes and bundles ashore and which would then be carried by others to market. At the shore they picked up local goods that would be traded in Naha and carried them back to the boat with small amounts of food and water in *tsubo* that resembled the ceramic jars Kansho had Kanbun train with in the bamboo clearing in Izumi. He and Tokusaburo got on well together talking in easy conversation while working near the shore and then preparing the boat for departure. The parents and families of the young men who would soon be eligible for the Japanese military draft had said their goodbyes at their homes or in the hillside villages. They resisted accompanying them to the shore in order to avoid drawing attention to the seaborne escape planned for their sons.

The ocean breezes were already warm in the spring season and they filled the sails of the mid-sized boats that would transport them out of Nago Bay, along the island coast, and south to Nago. It would be an overnight journey, the first time for Kanbun and his fellow country youth to sleep away from their homes. There was little to do other than assist occasionally with adjusting a rope, pulling in or letting out a sail, or checking their progress along the shore. It seemed strange yet exciting to travel beyond sight of Nago and Izumi, to see lamp lights in the dark where they knew the ocean met the land, and hear only the creaking of the wooden vessel as it cut through the water on its way south. Kanbun lay on the deck with his head on his cloth bag looking up at the bright stars in the sky, while the seasoned crewmen who manned and guided the boat talked among themselves. The other boys lay nearby as the vessel creaked and rolled and they felt lost in the warm breezes thinking about the villages they left behind and the adventure ahead. The boys didn't speak as they gazed outward and upward, but Junpei and Tomohiro seemed uneasy to be away from their families and homes. The eyes of Kanbun and Tokusaburo, on the other hand, shone strongly and brightly in the starlight as they were clearly exhilarated by their prospects. Before long, they all fell asleep.

Just after sunrise the next morning, they awoke to the squawking of seagulls and shouts from the docks in the port of Naha. Other boats were maneuvering in port bringing in their early morning catch. There were workmen moving about the docks, as well as stacks of boxes, lengths of rope, flags on poles, large bales of tea, and rows of warehouses at the edge of the water. The cargo that had been brought by ship to Naha, especially from China, included tea, bamboo, wooden implements, lumber, and more. There was a mix of workers, sailors, and others in the port. Most wore loose jackets and pants or were bare-chested with thin leg garments tucked up in bunches at their thighs common to local laborers of Ryukyu, while others from China with the air of merchants were dressed in flowing robes. The Japanese officials who walked about sternly shouting out orders were dressed in smartly-cut uniforms made of heavier wool material that was produced on the mainland and was probably uncomfortably hot in the thick, humid air of Okinawa. Most importantly, their leaders carried swords in their sashes, which were not only a symbol of their authority but a not-so-subtle threat. Beyond the docks were roads and paths leading uphill away from the water that were lined with fishing shacks, several storied buildings, trading offices, and shops of various specialties. The young men had never seen so much activity and congestion of traders, fishermen, merchants, and workmen. Indeed, they had never before seen any buildings higher than the single story houses of Motobu. After the young men helped the few sailors who had been on the overnight journey transfer the goods onto the dock for weighing and distribution, the captain told them they could visit Naha while waiting the next day or two for the trading ship that would take them to Fukushu. On the streets of Naha they heard shopkeepers bartering in Chinese with men from the mainland who wore long robes and their hair gathered in braids that hung almost down the length of their backs. The people of Naha spoke a variation of the Ryukyu dialect, called Shuri-ben, that sounded different and the boys listened closely to catch their conversations. They passed Kumemura, which until recent times had been a long-standing and well-respected community of local scholars and government officials as well as a center for culture and learning. Originally, it had been settled by Chinese emigrants who had arrived in Ryukyu during the late fourteenth century on a mission from Peking and were known as the "thirty-six families." They had formed a group of scholar bureaucrats who assisted in diplomatic relations between the Imperial Ming Court in China and the Royal Palace in Shuri. They also brought cultural traditions of painting, calligraphy, and the Dragon Boat Festival, more advanced technology, such as modern navigational methods and shipbuilding, and skills in papermaking and ink making. However, five hundred years after its founding, the new Japanese governor had closed the facilities and all that remained were empty and decaying buildings. Nonetheless, the history of Kumemura was a symbolic reminder to the people of Ryukyu of their long and deep relations with China and the tenuous balance they maintained between the continent and the Japanese islands to the north.

One elderly lady beckoned them into her vegetable shop, but they were embarrassed because they understood none of her heavy accent and continued on up the street. A ragged looking man in a dirty and torn jacket who carried a ceramic bottle of sake called them to role dice with him, but they continued on their way toward the center of the port town. Along the way, they stopped in front of the large windows of a tea merchant's office and looked inside. It smelled pleasantly from the bricks of tea from China that sat on shelves in the outer shop. The merchant was in the back room shielded by a *noren* curtain that hung in the doorway. The *noren* had a pale background and was decorated with flowing characters naming different varieties of tea. These *noren* helped to keep dust from spreading or flies from gathering inside. The shopkeeper was engaged in conversation at a low table with several Chinese traders who sat with him on tatami mats. He came out to the front room and in a friendly gesture offered the young men a pot of tea to serve themselves while they waited on benches that were set on the clay floor. Before long, the Chinese traders stood up, bowed clasping their hands together, left the back room, and came into the shop area without noticing the youths. With them, was a youngster with soft features and a refined expression. He glanced at the young men from Izumi, acknowledged their presence with his eyes, and moved on with the others.

"Thank you young Master Go for your excellent spring tea," said the shopkeeper. "We hope you will continue to do business with us. Please have a safe return journey to China."

After the merchant had seen off his Chinese guests, he returned to the shop and spoke pleasantly to the four youths from Motobu, "I suppose you young men are looking for work on the docks or here in the trading district."

"No sir," they replied, "we already have jobs."

Slightly impressed, the merchant asked, "Where are you from? Your accent sounds like you come from the north."

"Yes sir, that is right. We left Nago a day ago," they explained.

"These days young men are doing different things to escape the Japanese draft. Some are even boarding ships for China and plan to take their chances in places where there are others from Ryukyu, such as in Fuksuhu or other cities in Fukken Province in China," he said, drawing on a narrow pipe before turning it over and striking it against one of the benches to knock the ash onto the floor.

The boys looked at each other uncomfortably and didn't respond.

"It's alright," the merchant said. "It is probably the surest way to keep from serving in the Japanese army or navy. I understand. It is difficult for me too because the Japanese draft my best deck hands to fight wars they start, sometimes against the people with whom I do my trading. But, be careful. The Japanese military take records from the family registers in each town, city, and village to see who will become of age and eligible to be conscripted. Anyone who does not voluntarily join the military or fails to appear when called from their home is added to a list of public fugitives. Those who do not return within three months are listed as deserters. The Japanese seek out these young men who evade the draft, and then arrest and imprison them until their family pays a hefty fine or commit their sons to serving the military anyway. If the family cannot afford the fees, the young men may stay imprisoned. If you run away, you had better be sure you are willing to endure hardship and not return home for many years, maybe never."

Junpei and Tomohiro were visibly uneasy with what they heard from the merchant. Kanbun and Tokusaburo said nothing else but thanked the merchant for his hospitality. They returned to the boat where they ate a modest meal of rice, fish, and seaweed.

In the morning they awoke to the same bustle of sounds and activities in the port, on the docks, and along the shore as the day earlier. The leader of the crew that had ferried them from Nago to Naha pointed out a larger ship with characters for "Heavenly Dragon" painted on the bow and stern that had arrived from China and that would take them to Fukushu.

Before they left, the crew leader called together the young men from Izumi, "I made arrangements with the captain late last night so he will know that you four boys will board his ship going to Fukushu. The Nago crew and I will stay in port for business for a couple more days and depart after your ship leaves Naha. Take your time today and go ashore together. Once there, walk up the street and visit some of the shops, but return to the docks separately. You want to transfer to your escape ship the Heavenly Dragon without drawing the attention of the Japanese authorities."

He went on, "If you are stopped or questioned by one of the officials, state your name, age, and village clearly and honestly, but then tell them you are an apprentice seaman who is learning about transport and trade between Nago and Naha. The police in Naha are already wise to young men arriving from the countryside to escape Ryukyu and military conscription in Japan."

The four youths did as they were told and separately approached the larger vessel moored near the end of a dock. All of them boarded ship as the crew loaded and prepared for departure. The captain, who had long hair tied back, wore a rounded hat, and carried a short sword that distinguished him from the crew and the coolies on the dock, looked ominously down at them from the upper deck. He had a sturdy frame, a round belly, powerful arms, and he stood firmly. He descended the stairway to the main deck to address the boys directly. He spoke Japanese well, but in a gruff voice and with a Chinese accent.

"You are now on board my ship, the Heavenly Dragon, and you will follow orders without question," he said. "You will work hard even if you become seasick or get hurt. If you disobey, I will have you thrown overboard or return you to the Japanese authorities."

He went on, "This evening you are to return to shore and walk overnight to Kadena. There you can find the Hija River and walk along it until it opens into the East China Sea. In the morning this ship will pass the mouth of the river. If there are no other ships or fishing vessels nearby that might inform the Japanese, we will send a dingy to pick you up; otherwise, you will have to catch passage with a fisherman who will take you out to the Heavenly Dragon. Leave your belongings on board tonight when you go ashore, and we will store them below. After today, there will be no need for me to speak with you because you will get your orders from First Mate Chen," and he indicated a tall barrel-chested man standing impassively by the entrance to the hold of the ship.

Chen looked at them up and down and without other comment he ordered them in broken Japanese to follow him back to the dock. He commanded them to begin loading crates of food, ceramic jars of water, sacks of rice, rolls of the colorfully woven specialty textile from Ryukyu called *bingata*, and a variety of local craft goods onto the ship. The work was heavy, but the young men had trained long and hard at *kobujutsu* and *toodi*, so they were actually able to keep up with the older deck hands. They were grateful, however, when the crew took a break for tea. The youths were energetic and enthusiastic about getting underway, as the sailors on board the ship showed them where to store the supplies and goods. The curious youths lifted bundles of materials from the dock, boarded the ship with their loads on their shoulders, climbed up and down the steep and narrow stairs below the main deck, and stepped aside whenever one of the older crew members approached. The veteran sailors on the ship inspected and repaired the canvass sails, secured the ropes and lines that seemed to bind everything on board to the masts, decks, or side wales. They also had the young men patch cracks in the decks and sides of the ship with flat knives and black pitch that stuck to their hands and clothing. By the time evening arrived, the ship was provisioned and secured for departure. The crew on the ship gave the young men a vegetable stew with bits of fish in it, bowls of boiled rice, and cups of brown tea. After the evening meal, the sailors passed around a cup of stiff and bitter liquor to share, which the boys took turns sipping from and making twisted and squinted faces while laughing at each other. By now, the sun had fallen below the horizon, the docks were still, the warehouses were closed for the night, and they could hear conversations or an occasional song float across the water.

Chen told them to be on their way, and the four youths departed without speaking. They walked into town and then took the road north toward Nakagami-gun and Kadena. They made their way through the night by watching the stars, occasionally stopping to dip their hands into a small stream to drink, and speaking quietly only when necessary.

In Naha, the sky had turned wispy pink before the sun rose over the hills of Shuri to the east. The captain stood on the upper deck giving orders to Chen before he in turn shouted them out to the crew. Soon the smaller sails that they had raised began to catch the morning breeze, the ship edged away from the dock area, and they pointed west toward the mouth of the harbor. After the ship reached the open sea, the captain directed the vessel to tack north and travel along the coast. Within an hour they reached the area outside the mouth of the Hija River near the town of Kadena. The mouth of the river was quiet and green with trees, vines, flowers, and other vegetation. This day there was a wind blowing from the sea west of Ryukyu. The four youths called to a passing fisherman paddling in the river and asked for passage to the ship anchored in the offing. They swam out to the fishing boat, climbed on board, and then helped raise the sail to ride the breeze offshore. Before long, they arrived at the Heavenly Dragon that lay waiting for them. They thanked the fisherman and climbed aboard the ship. As soon as they boarded, the captain gave orders to Chen to be on their way westward. Junpei and Tomohiro stood at the stern looking back faintly and sadly at the river, the green hills that led up to the center of the island, and Shuri Castle atop the landscape which grew smaller by the minute. Kanbun and Tokusaburo ran to the bow. Their eyes were firmly set on the sea and the nothingness extending out to the horizon in front of them.

Escaping to Fukushu

The Heavenly Dragon tacked back and forth against the eastward wind, steadily making progress out into the East China Sea. Before long the young men caught sight of the Kerama Islands to the south, which were part of the Ryukyu chain and they had heard about but never seen before. Kerama was surrounded by beautiful white beaches at the shore that gave way to lush green land behind it. To the north was the island of Tonaki and just a speck beyond it was Aguna. They passed just south of Kume Island with its expansive flat sugar cane plantations stretching back until the land rose sharply into dramatic and scenic mountains of red, orange, and brown earth tones. And then, there was the wide expanse of the East China Sea, and nothing but the ocean on the horizon in any direction. Occasionally, they would catch sight of a passing ship or a bird would approach and land on the top of the main mast before continuing its own voyage. During the approximately ten-day journey to Fukushu, the four young men spent most of their time assisting the crew. The work was different from what they were accustomed, but they had strong grips for handling the ropes and firm but flexible stances for balancing themselves when the ship would pitch or roll. The crewmen spoke with each other in Chinese and occasionally would give instructions to their helpers so that the youths began to pick up some of the language, including everyday words and parts of the ship. In the evenings, Kanbun would make a list of all the Chinese words, phrases, and expressions he could remember from that day, look them up in the dictionary that Kazue had given him, and carefully write them down in a list that grew longer every day. Before falling asleep, he would review the list, try to remember the meanings, and then think about how he could use the word or phrase in a conversation the next day. He found that he could hold onto more Chinese in his head if he spoke the words as part of an exchange with the crew of the ship. At other times, he would speak a Chinese word to himself when he touched a corresponding part of the ship, adjusted the cargo, or ate his meals.

The young men sat together with their hosts and elders at meal times and tried to engage them in conversation to the extent that their common knowledge of Japanese and Chinese would permit. They learned that like Ryukyu there were different dialects spoken in China. One of the friendlier crewmates who had learned some Japanese explained that the city to which they were pointed was known as Fujou, Fuchu, Foochow, or locally as Hockchew, depending on the dialect, but not Fukushu, which was the Japanese reading of the Chinese characters for the name of the city. They told the youths that their island country was known in China as Liuchiu or Loochoo, rather than Ryukyu. It was also better to call it Liuchiu or Loochoo, or even Ryukyu, rather than Okinawa, the name the Japanese had recently given to the small island chain. The Japanese had just defeated China in a short but significant war and the Chinese were sensitive about it. Another of the crewmen asked the young men to write their names, which they did with charcoal on the wooden deck, but his faced turned grave. He said he didn't know why people in Ryukyu had so many characters in their names. In China, most people had a surname of one character and a given name of one or two and that there was balance in this configuration, especially when it was a total of three, which stood for stability and strength. However, most people from Ryukyu had four characters in their names, which was plain unlucky, and five or more was just too many to remember. At this, Junpei and Tomohiro, whose names contained four characters, looked disappointed and a little scared. They knew that "four" had symbolic meanings. It could refer to the four points of the compass, but it was also synonymous with death because it had the same pronunciation. Kanbun's name also had four characters, but he suspected the crewman was trying to take advantage of their age and lack of experience to frighten them about China.

After several more days at sea they caught sight of Formosa to south and soon after that the Chinese mainland directly to the west. This was the first time for the young men to see the continent, which stretched from right to left, north to south, as far as the eye could. The sun set over the continental horizon, which had the effect of making China appear like a giant magical kingdom floating just above the ocean and under a broad and crimson sky. Early the next morning, as they drew closer to land, they could make out green hills, fishing boats off-shore, and eventually buildings and even people. The Heavenly Dragon moored by an island at the mouth of the Min River that would provide access to Fujou. If the port at Naha was filled with more noise, commotion, and confusion than they had ever seen in Nago or Motobu, the harbor area of Fujou was of even grander scale and activity. There were several piers with wooden booms extended out over the shipping vessels and the water. They had wheels of rope, gears, metal hardware, and several men working each of them as they loaded or unloaded large parcels wrapped in thick nets. Behind the piers there were huge stacks of shipping equipment and ocean gear in front of long rows of wharf houses and warehouses that reached several stories into the sky. Compared to Ryukyu, everything in China seemed so much bigger and grander in scale.

As the four youths surveyed the scene, there were people shouting everywhere, some arguing, others directing crews carrying loads of goods, and still more shouting calling back and forth as they worked the decks, masts, riggings, sails, and sides of the ships that came in all different shapes and sizes. There were others sitting on sacks of grain drinking tea or wine, smoking tobacco in long thin pipes, or dozing in the sun. There were workmen, foremen, merchants, accountants, officials, shopkeepers, and onlookers who all wore different shades and shapes of clothing or almost none at all. They could distinguish the Chinese merchants, shippers, and officials by their hair styles, clothing, or manner of expression, while others were unlike the locals and completely foreign to the youths from Ryukyu. Some had Asian features, but with different skin tones and clearly were neither Chinese, Japanese, nor from Ryukyu. Perhaps they came from Korea, the Philippines, or somewhere in Southeast or even South Asia. In addition to the great variety of people, goods, sounds, languages, and smells that this port of call drew from around the Asian region, the magnitude and complexity of operations surprised them. Some of the ships were larger than any they had seen before. In Naha, the stacks of cargo had been big, but here some looked like small mountains. The area was so congested with vessels that one could traverse from ship to ship without touching either a wharf or the shore.

They spent the next two days unloading, organizing, and accounting for their cargo, which they carried up from the hold of the Heavenly Dragon and onto the pier. They then transferred the seaweed, vegetables, herbs, spices, *bingata*, and other tradable goods to smaller boats that would ferry them up the river to the city center and then take them to market. It felt good to be doing familiar physical labor on dry land after dipping and swaying across the ocean. The captain of the ship gave the youths from Ryukyu a folded map of the city of Fujou and each several coins of Chinese currency.

The captain explained, "You can board with one of the smaller transport boats and help the oarsman pull upriver against the current to Fuchu. The map shows the city waterfront and the market where you might find work, as well as the location of what you call the Ryukyukan Jueneki or what we know as the Loochooguan Jouyuanyi. You have been responsible for yourselves since we left Naha, but now you will be completely on your own and must find your own way. Don't come back looking for help or for return passage to Loochoo."

The young men had heard about the Ryukyukan Jueneki, or the Ryukyu Fellowship Hall, from their fathers who had made the arrangements for their escape to Fukushu. The Jueneki had been established centuries earlier and maintained by traders, merchants, and travelers from Ryukyu. With the support of officials and commercial dealers in Fujou, the foreign residents from Ryukyu had constructed a building to provide assistance for those arriving from their homeland. It was an administrative as well as social center for the Ryukyu immigrant community in Fujou. After paddling with an oarsman up the Min River and arriving at the city, they helped to unload the cargo onto the docks. As they made their way from the Min River into Fujou to find the Ryukyukan Jueneki, the young men felt awkward and out of place and they were amazed by every new sight, sound, and smell. The streets were congested with pedestrians, carts, hawkers, wild birds and animals in cages, and peddlers. Those not trying to sell them an item or service paid them no attention. They encountered men and women approaching from all directions, walking alone, in small groups, or carrying heavy bundles, but who were quite willing to bump into them rather than step aside to yield in their path. The youths slowly made their way from one street to the next by dodging, ducking, and obliging the people they encountered along the way.

At one point, they also saw something none of them had even heard about in Ryukyu. It was a white almost pinkish looking man with golden hair and a full red beard. He was wearing a black robe, had a wooden amulet around his neck that looked like the two stroke, cross-shaped Chinese character for the number "10," and he was holding a small but thick black book in his right hand. He had a smile on his face, but looked straight forward neither acknowledging nor deterred by the foot and cart traffic in front of him. Kanbun had heard from his grandfather about the Western ships that had arrived in Ryukyu decades before. The ships were made entirely of metal, which made them heavy and he didn't understand how they could float, but they moved through the water with great round paddle wheels on both sides, noisy engines inside the hull of the ship, and sent out sooty smoke from metal towers that stood up on the decks. The admiral of the Western fleet, his captains, officers, and crew all were very pale and tall, hairy but of all different colors, and were said to be dirty and smell badly if you got close to them. As foreign as the people and streets of Fujou were to them, the sight of this strangest of strangers in an Asian city was the most exotic to them. Compared to this yellow haired Westerner, the Chinese faces in Fujou seemed familiar and comforting.

Unsure if they were headed in the right direction because they seemed to be reaching one edge of the city, they tried to stop a passerby to ask a question but he ignored them completely. Another person did stop, but without looking at their map made an unpleasant face and moved on. They referred to their map again and decided to try their luck in the hopes of discovering the location of the Fellowship Hall. Before much longer, however, they saw the vertical characters for Ryukyukan Jueneki on a painted board hanging beside the double doorway of a wooden building that was on an undeveloped lane with trees, bushes, and fields. They approached, but before entering, they noticed a small cemetery with familiar shapes next to the Jueneki. In it were mostly very old but also some new stone markers for the graves of their countrymen who had crossed the sea, spent some part of their lives, and the last of their days in Fukushu. Kanbun was struck by the irony of his fresh arrival in Fukushu when compared with the fates of those who would never return home to Ryukyu. He clasped his hands together and said a silent prayer for their souls, whoever they were, made a solemn vow to someday return to his family in Izumi, and entered the building.

There was an elderly woman with grey hair tied in a bun wearing a neat yet subdued kimono seated behind a low desk on a raised platform of tatami mats. Behind her was a *noren*, or split curtain, dyed with the familiar *bingata* pattern that hung in the doorway to a room leading from the reception area. Her face was worn but the skin was soft. She smiled and greeted them with "*mensoore*," a friendly welcome in the dialect of their language

71

from home. They immediately felt more at ease and crowded near her.

"*Obaachan*," they called to her affectionately. "We just arrived in Fukushu and have to find work and a place to live," they added hopefully.

"Yes, yes, there are more young men like you arriving these days. There have always been merchants who did trade here or married local women and settled down. Some of us from Ryukyu have never found a way to return as you probably saw from the graveyard you just passed on your way. These days more young people seem to find us since the Japanese expanded their military conscription system to Ryukyu, which they are now calling Okinawa. I am afraid there is not much we can do because we are really best at helping to find trading partners, arranging for laborers on Ryukyu-bound boats, or getting parts and materials to repair the ships that arrive in the harbor. We do have some social events and exchange news between China and our home islands. For the short term, you can stay in one of the empty rooms in the back building and we can give you one meal a day until you find a job and a better place to live."

They responded with an eager chorus of "Thank you."

The elderly woman set out a tray with a ceramic pot of tea, which she poured in small cups for the travelers, and a few rice crackers. Then, she called into the back room, and an even more ancient gentleman who nonetheless had clear and alert eyes shuffled out to the counter. He looked at them warmly from behind spectacles, which made him look comical to the boys who had never seen anyone wearing glasses before. His hair was healthy, white, and cropped close to his head. He wore a grey robe in the fashion of the Chinese passersby they had seen on the streets of Fukushu, but he also had on broadly striped and loose fitting pants familiar to them from Ryukyu. All in all, he made an odd sight to the four visitors from Ryukyu who had just arrived literally from across the sea.

"This is Nakaima-ojiisan," she said, "maybe he can point you in some helpful directions."

He said in a soft yet clear voice, "I am Nakaima Tadahiko, but most people call me Old Nakaima, and I am from Nakagusuku in central Ryukyu. Perhaps you have heard of it?"

The youths replied that they were from Motobu and recognized Nakagusuku. It was a well-known town for cultural activities in the middle section of the main island on the Pacific Ocean side of Ryukyu where there was an old castle.

"Yes, that's right" the old man replied. "How can I help you?"

The boys chuckled, and then Tokusaburo asked, "Old Nakaima, what are those pieces of glass attached to your face?"

"Ah, these help me to see better. I can see that you haven't been out in the world much," he replied with a droll face.

They laughed in a way that made all of them feel more at home.

"We need to find jobs so we can live here for a while until it is safe to return to Motobu and not be prosecuted for avoiding the Japanese draft," Kanbun explained.

"What can you do?" asked the old man.

"We know how to farm and fish, but we don't know much else," responded Tokusaburo.

"I see." said the old man. "There are plenty of fishermen in Fukushu," he went on, "both on the docks and in the fishing boats, and the other fishermen won't be happy to see you taking their jobs. There is a better chance of finding work in the fields or helping at the farms outside of town. There are also some shops in town that I know that might need an odd helper or two. I see you have a map."

The young men laid their map on the tatami mats.

"Hmm, let's see," murmured the old man. He made small circles on several locations on the map and wrote the names of the shops in Chinese characters. "You probably can't pronounce these names, but you should be able to recognize the shop signs. Do you read enough Chinese characters, and can you use an abacus?"

"Yes, sir," they replied, "we all went to school."

"Good boys," he said. He then wrote his name at the bottom of the map. "You can show this map with my signature to the shopkeepers and they will know where it is from. Some of them speak pretty good *Naha-ben* from back home, but you may need to use more Chinese with others. It would be a good idea to learn some Chinese, especially the local Fukkensho dialect."

"You are always too encouraging," muttered the elderly woman. "I don't want to frighten the young men, but it is more difficult than that." She turned to the youths and added, "Our Ryukyu is known as the Land where Courtesy Reigns, but you will find very little of that sentiment here in Fukushu. And, you had better start learning as much of the local Chinese as you can. There are secrets upon secrets. Even after living here for more than forty years it is hard for me to know who I can trust. Anyone who makes a promise to you or agrees to do something on your behalf may have a deeper loyalty to someone else or may change their mind. All of that is hidden inside, especially to foreigners like us from Ryukyu. These are unsettled times in

China. They just lost a war to Japan and people might mistake you for Japanese citizens, even spies trying to infiltrate their communities. People are very suspicious of outsiders, especially foreigners, and they are unfriendly before they become civil, if ever. Be sure to tell people that you are from Ryukyu and you have always admired China."

The images of the tough captain of the Heavenly Dragon that had brought them to Fukushu and the unfriendly passersby that they had just approached for help with their map on the way to the Ryukyukan Jueneki surfaced in Kanbun's thoughts.

"Most people won't bother with you, but some will try to take advantage of you. You have to watch out for gamblers, thieves, tricksters, and others who will lead you down the wrong path. Some are loyal to the Imperial Court in Peking, while others are members of secret groups trying to overthrow the government. These clandestine groups are sworn to secrecy among themselves but battle each other over which is the most patriotic, who has the purest intentions, or simply over territory. Some call themselves the White Lotus and some go by the general name of Boxers. Other groups are just plain criminals disguised under the flag of patriotism. They rob, swindle, bully, threaten, and even murder to control the flow of goods, services, or taxes in some districts. There are stories of immigrants from Ryukyu who have been bullied or worse by the dispossessed acolytes and former temple workers who were scattered by the break-up of the Shaolin Temple. Bandits or pirates will trick you into joining their gangs and make you as guilty as they are, and then they will threaten to kill you if you try to leave. You had better be careful," she added.

75

"What about Chinese *kenpo*?" asked Tokusaburo. "We learned some *toodi* in Ryukyu and want to learn *kenpo* while we are here."

"Ah yes," replied the old man, "what we call *kenpo* or the "fist method" is known here by other names, such as *chuanfa* or *wushu,* and mean something like "martial skills." It is something that is taught in many different forms here in Fukkensho, however you had better be careful with this, too. The Shorin Temple system, called *Shaolin* here in China, has been an important organization for this kind of activity for centuries. The priests use this training method to develop physical, mental, and spiritual discipline among their apprentices. Somehow, in recent times the Boxers, who are also known as the "Righteous and Harmonious Fists" and by other names, became mixed up with these priests. Now, it is hard to tell who is loyal to whom or whether they uphold the peaceful teachings of the Buddha. The Ching rulers in Peking got very upset with the Shorin Temple branch here in Fukkensho and destroyed it. Apparently, they feared the Boxers and the priests were plotting against them. In any case, they burned down the temple buildings, but most of the priests and apprentices got away. Now they are spread out more widely, preaching their Buddhist ideology, and expanding the teaching of their kind of *wushu* to ordinary people in many districts. I know of a local Buddhist temple southeast of here, called the Gushing Spring Temple, where there are priests who will even teach foreigners. In fact, there are some people from Ryukyu there already."

The youths, especially Kanbun and Tokusaburo were excited by this news and eagerly asked for the location of the temple and an introduction to it.

"I can tell you where it is," replied the old man who became slightly reticent, "but I don't know anyone there well enough to give you an introduction. You can try approaching them on your own, but use your good sense about who they are and what you can learn."

The youths warmly thanked the two elderly people at the Ryukyukan Jueneki and added they hoped to be able to repay their kindness one day. Kanbun and Tokusaburo were eager to find the temple where they might learn *kenpo*. They hoped that if they were permitted to join the training sessions they might also find work as laborers on the temple grounds. Junpei and Tomohiro argued they should find jobs nearby the Juenenki, where they would be staying for a while, before they went off on adventures. In any case, it was getting late in the day, they were hungry, and it would be better to see the room the old woman had offered and store their belongings. It was indeed a plain room with a hard dirt floor and a couple of posts in the middle to support unfinished beams. They could see bits of the sky through cracks in the roof and there was one window looking out over a brambly area that was bounded by an old clay wall. A little while later she brought them some miso soup with tofu, boiled rice, seaweed, stir fried vegetables, and cups of tea.

"I'm sorry," she said, "this is all we can give you, because fish and meat are expensive."

They thanked her heartily and ate the simple meal hungrily. That evening Kanbun took out the dictionary he had received as a gift from Kazue. It had been several days since he had used the dictionary or written down notes about new phrases he had learned. He paused to look at the book and caught the faint scent of island flowers in the cloth *furoshiki* with which Kazue had wrapped the gift. Was it the scent of flowers, or the fresh memory of Kazue, or was it both?

In the morning, they decided they would divide into pairs and meet back at the Jueneki and compare notes. Kanbun and Tokusaburo drew a rough copy of the map of Fukushu writing in the place names and directions Old Nakaima had shown them as well as the outline of the Min River. Together, they set out for Gushing Spring Temple, crossing a bridge over a tributary of the Min River on their way. Lacking knowledge of the city or its roadways, but with the help of the map they were able to find the temple grounds in the afternoon. The temple had been founded at the beginning of the 10th century just after the end of the Tang Dynasty, the era of great flowering of Chinese art, culture, society, philosophy, and traditions. Among other things, the temple was noted for its collection of precious relics, such as antique scrolls of Buddhist scriptures, delicate pottery from the Song Dynasty that followed the Tang, and its ancient cycad trees that were said to have been planted at the time of the founding of the temple nearly a thousand years earlier. There was a stream outside the temple that was fed by small flows from openings at the base of the temple walls. The water splashed over blocks of granite, down sluiceways, and joined the stream that gurgled away from the temple. They entered through a massive wooden gate that had a stone foundation and pillars on either side with a tile roof over it. Inside the gate there was an ancient walkway of flat granite blocks and many other small earthen paths that diverged under giant cryptomeria trees, towards small buildings, or disappeared up a hill or into a bamboo grove. One of the main trails pointed toward Drum Mountain behind Gushing Spring Temple. The trail was known for its long ascent of stone steps, poetic inscriptions carved into rocks, maze of caves, and numerous prayer pavilions along the way up the mountain. They walked further into the temple grounds, but saw no one. It seemed empty. They heard the scratching sound of twig bristles on stones from the other side of one of the small buildings, and went around it to see whom they might find. A man in his late twenties or early thirties, shaved completely bald, and wearing the plain robes of a Buddhist apprentice was sweeping the flat area in front of a veranda that extended from what looked like the back of the building.

Not knowing what to say or how to ask directions, Kanbun tried, "*wushu.*"

The Buddhist apprentice straightened his posture, looked at them without expression but with chilly eyes, turned his head over his right shoulder toward one of the other buildings, and said in Japanese, "*atchi da,*" meaning "over there."

The young men were shocked to hear him speak in their language, because he looked Chinese, but they nodded their heads and firmly thanked him with "*arigatou*" before moving on.

They found the building had stout wooden doors on the front, sides, and back, but they were all shut tight. Tokusaburo called out, "*nihao*" or "hello" in Chinese a couple of times, but no one replied. By now, it was late afternoon and it would become dusk soon. Kanbun and Tokusaburo were mindful of the warnings from the old woman at the Ryukyukan Jueneki about thieves and gangsters, so they decided to return and try again the next day. Once back at the Jueneki, they told Junpei and Tomohiro about their visit to the Gushing Spring Temple and their lack of luck in learning anything.

The two youths who had sought out jobs at shops in Fukushu, on the other hand, were more successful. Though it would be tough work that paid very little, both of them had found something to keep them going. Junpei was able to get a position in a fish shop, which meant filling, carrying, and loading barrels of daily catch, and then disposing of the mixture of fish guts and sea water into the river. Tomohiro spoke with a tea merchant who would take him on as a leaf gatherer at one of the many plantations outside the city. Tomohiro's family had a small plot of tea bushes in Motobu, so he knew that he would have to rise early, pick as much of the tea leaves as the other more experienced gatherers, and carry it in large baskets from the fields to a drying house before returning to the tea shop in the evening. What had surprised him was the length and breadth of the tea fields in Fujou, which stretched over the sloping terrain near the base of the mountains. He had never seen so much agriculture in one place. Both he and Junpei were optimistic about their opportunities and planned to leave the Jueneki early the next morning to live with the work crews at places arranged by their employers. Kanbun and Tokusaburo were also hopeful, but a little less cheerful about their lack of success.

The youths woke to the sound of heavy rain drumming the rooftop of their back room shelter. Rain was leaking through the cracks in the roof and they moved their straw mats out of the way of the dripping water. Junpei and Tomohiro were disappointed but eager to get started in their new jobs and didn't want to miss the opportunity because of the weather. They gathered up their belongings, promised to let Kanbun and Tokusaburo know how they were doing after they settled down, said goodbye, and stepped out of the shelter into the chilly grey rain. The young men who stayed behind lay back on their reed mats in silence and looked up at the inside of the tile roof.

"Kanbun, what do think of the Gushing Spring Temple," asked Tokusaburo after a while.

"There isn't much to know so far," responded Kanbun, "but the place seemed unfriendly. I suppose it is better to wait until the rain stops before we go back."

"Yea, that's true, but we can't expect more. We will be lucky if we can join the *kenpo* training group and learn something," replied Tokusaburo.

Later in the morning, the rain lessened and the young men headed back to the Gushing Spring Temple. The streets had puddles and there were ruts of water running beside the roads that eventually fed into vegetable fields and rice paddies. The ground that had seemed dry and dusty the day before was now soaked with a cleansing wash over the houses, shops, buildings, trees, and fields. There were few birds, except for the occasional caged pet outside a shopkeeper's door, cooing doves that were kept for their eggs or stir fry, and hens and roosters that clucked or crowed in the narrow alleyways that cut off from the streets. By the time they reached the temple it was afternoon and the rain had stopped completely, though openings for water to flow through the base of the temple walls were roaring with life and the outside stream had risen up and spilled onto the roadway. The granite walkways inside the temple were also wet and slippery in spots. They found the building with the heavy wooden doors and once again called out "*nihao!*" They waited a few minutes, and one of the great doors opened slightly. A heavy set man naked to the waist, carrying a thick bamboo staff, sweating from his forehead and shoulders, and bald like the ground sweeper they met the day before stepped outside. He had a round face, a thick neck, bulky shoulders, a muscular waist, meaty arms that ended with fat wrists and chunky fingers, and solid legs and ankles with stubbly toes. He glared at them from the landing at the top of three steps leading to entrance to the building.

"I suppose you are the two vagrants from Ryukyu who came here yesterday," he said in a gravely voice of Ryukyu-accented Japanese. "Are you so timid that the Fukushu rain scares you indoors," he challenged.

Their eyes noted the sturdy bamboo pole in his right hand, which encouraged them to speak.

"Please sir," replied Kanbun, "I am Uechi Kanbun and this is Matsuda Tokusaburo from the Motobu Peninsula in Ryukyu. We heard that we might learn *kenpo* here. Of course, we are willing to work at anything to earn our way. We will work hard, we promise."

"There are a lot of Ryukyu runaways who come here these days," he grunted. "They think they know some martial arts, but they are green and what they know is only basic techniques. Come back at sunrise tomorrow, and we will see if you can handle the training."

The gruff man from the temple turned to leave, but they called out again, "Please, may we ask your name?"

He turned squarely toward them holding the bamboo staff firmly and said with a tight face, "I am Makabei. You won't forget who I am." Saying no more, he re-entered the building and closed the big wooden door.

On the way back to the Ryukyukan, the young men talked about their visit to the Gushing Spring Temple.

"Do you think Makabei is a priest or a guardian devil for the temple," asked Tokusaburo with a smile.

"He sure wasn't friendly to us, even if he sounded like he was from Ryukyu," said Kanbun. "He looks tough enough."

"Anyway, it's our chance, so we had better make the best of it," replied Tokusaburo.

They continued their conversation during the walk back to the Ryukyukan, looking forward to the next day with both hope and questions. The went to bed early that night and barely slept because they wanted to be sure to rise with time enough to reach the Gushing Spring Temple as Makabei had directed them. They rose in the dark and arrived in time, but the building with the heavy wooden doors was closed and there was no one in sight. Kanbun and Tokusaburo decided to sit down and wait, which they did for what seemed like a long time. Towards late morning when the full sun was showing through the tree trunks, Makabei strode up holding his bamboo staff.

"Uh, you're here," he said. "Today, we will begin with maintenance work around the temple. If you do as you are told, you may be able to move your things from the Jueneki. Is that where you are staying?" But, he did not pause for a response.

He went on, "I am not a priest, but the abbot at this temple has given me some of the rights and responsibilities of one, so I can do as I please. They taught me their *kenpo*, which comes from the Fukkensho Shorin Temple and it is my duty to pass it along to other foreigners who are worthy of staying here and learning its secrets. There is no need for me show Buddhist compassion to anyone, because I am not a priest. Do as I say, and you may survive to pick up something useful. Now, go and clean out the water troughs so the flow from inside the temple to the outside stream will not be blocked. If I see you resting or loafing today, I won't let you come back tomorrow."

He looked at them with a short glare, turned, and left. Kanbun and Tokusaburo looked at each other somewhat disappointed that they wouldn't begin *kenpo* training yet, but they knew the work they were instructed to do would have to come first. When they returned the next day, Makabei ordered them to tend to the medicinal herb garden in a shady section of the temple grounds, pulling weeds, and watering the plants. This continued for about a week and a half until Makabei told them they could bring their belongings from the Ryukyukan Jueneki and stay in a hut in the back outer area of the temple near where a mountain rose behind them. He neither scolded nor encouraged them, but was brief and direct. After they had settled into their routine of working from early morning until sundown, when they would eat a simple evening meal and return to their hut before dark, Makabei told them they should come to the training hall the next night. This filled them with excitement and expectation. When the time came the next evening, they finished their chores as quickly as possible, ate their meal, and went over to the training hall. The building was dark, but one of the great doors was unlocked. They looked inside and saw only Makabei. He stood at one end of a wooden floor holding his thick bamboo staff. The room was large, open, and had a high ceiling with beams that extended from one wall to another, but it was nearly dark because the doors and windows were closed and the air was stuffy.

"Light the lamps and sweep the floors," Makabei commanded.

When they finished, he told them they would have to arrive every evening before their seniors and clean and light the training hall. Next, he told them to sit in a kneeling position to one side of the great room. They wondered what he meant by "seniors" because Makabei and they were the only ones in the hall, but soon others in dark or grey or drab robes entered through the one opened door. Kanbun and Tokusaburo recognized some of them as priests in training or workmen like them at the temple, but others they had never seen before. Makabei closed the heavy door and began leading the men in conditioning, strengthening, and stretching exercises. He used his heavy bamboo staff for rhythm or emphasis striking one end against the smooth wooden floor. Sometimes he would divide the men into pairs or small groups for drills, conditioning, or different levels of training depending upon ability. Most of the activity appeared to be routine to the students under Makabei's instruction, but at times the training, particularly the striking, blocking, and counter moves, became quite rough with the collision of flesh upon flesh, bone upon bone, and grunts from the participants.

Kanbun and Tokusaburo sat at the edge of the room and took it all in. Some of the training was familiar or intuitive to them, but some of the forms were completely different and incomprehensible. They watched with determined interest. When the practice session ended, they waited until all their seniors had left before they closed the great door and walked the darkened paths lit only by the night sky back to their hut.

"We can do that," said Tokusaburo. "Some of them are pretty tough, but so are we."

"Yea," replied Kanbun. "I can't wait to give it a try."

The next night was a repetition of the previous session, and so it went for some time. Makabei told them that during the day they should learn from the other apprentices about which herbs were good for different ailments, conditions, or injuries. They learned not only how to select herbs from the garden, but how to harvest plants, twigs, leaves, mushrooms, berries, mosses, and even insects and snakes they found outside the temple grounds along the streams and on the hillside. They also took turns, as they learned was customary for new students in the training hall, selling the herbs and medicines outside the gates of the Gushing Spring Temple. All of the modest cash they received from selling their products was to be strictly handed over to the temple. Kanbun continued to note new words and phrases that he heard. For verification, he looked them up in the dictionary Kazue had given him, wrote down the context in which he had learned them, and then would try to use his fresh knowledge whenever he could. Each night before sleeping he would review his jottings and commit to memory the new words. The next day he would try to insert his recently acquired knowledge in a phrase or expression to see if his usage or pronunciation were correct.

One evening, with a stern face, Makabei pointed his stout staff at Kanbun and Tokusaburo and then to the training floor. The young men jumped from their kneeling position and joined the group exercises. They imitated the movements of the others in the training hall, and some of the seniors gave them pointers on positions and practices. Makabei ignored Kanbun at first and only gave instruction to Tokusaburo with grunts or by pointing or prodding with his bamboo staff. Eventually, Makabei did respond to Kanbun's efforts, but only with disparaging remarks and groans of disappointment. At times he would push Kanbun with the tip of his staff to knock him off balance or make his stance and posture seem weak. Kanbun wondered what he was doing wrong, but Makabei gave no indication. A few weeks later, after the apprentices entered the training hall for the evening, Makabei announced that they would train with a staff. He stood in the middle of the floor and demonstrated a set routine of wide swings, pointed strikes, firm blocks, sweeping moves, and avoidance stances with his own thick staff. He was not only clearly skilled with the *bo*, but he was strong, forceful, and menacing. He ordered the apprentices to pick up a staff from a stack of bamboo of varying thicknesses and flexibility along the wall. Kanbun and Tokusaburo were particularly enthusiastic because of their training at home in Motobu and their familiarity with the bamboo staff. Makabei demonstrated his form once again but more slowly and then told the group to practice the set routine. Some of the apprentices had already learned the routine and were quite good at it. They in turn helped the novices to walk through the motions. This training continued for several weeks in addition to the strengthening and conditioning exercises they had been doing earlier. Makabei began adding sample applications to the practice showing the apprentices how to place their hands when blocking so their fingers would not be injured by an opponent's bamboo staff. He put them through drills in pairs and small groups with actual strikes and blocks pushing them not to hold back and to make the attacks and defenses realistic.

One evening, in an unusually sullen yet verbal mood, Makabei lifted his staff firmly over his head and reminded the apprentices, "In an actual conflict an opponent will try to penetrate your defense to cause serious damage or worse. If you stifle your aggression in training or do less than try to hurt each other, you do no one any good. You will lose the first contest you face outside the temple. These are light bamboo and can only do minimal harm, while an actual opponent will be carrying a *bo* made of hardwood that will be lethal."

He turned to Kanbun, "You, stand at the middle of the hall."

Kanbun did as he was told, standing in a neutral but ready position with his bamboo staff by his right side.

"Attack," commanded Makabei.

Kanbun hesitated but he could see the anger and impatience rising in Makabei's eyes. He thrust his staff toward Makabei's belly. The instructor, still holding his own staff steadily in both hands, turned to the side so that Kanbun missed.

"Again," he demanded.

Kanbun swung his staff around toward Makabei's head, but the latter ducked and again the apprentice missed.

"A single thrust is useless. More!" exploded Makabei.

This time Kanbun put several different strikes together in succession, but Makabei circled to the right and the result was the same. When he swung his staff low to strike the ankle, Makabei lifted his left foot and stepped on the end of Kanbun's staff with a scratching sound of bamboo against the wooden floor. Kanbun tried to retract his staff, but Makabei scowled and pinned it to the floor with his foot.

Next, shifting his position resembling a snake, Makabei slid sideways slightly and swung his thick staff in a circle towards Kanbun's waist. Kanbun instantly took a step back to hold his staff firmly with both hands spread in a vertical position away from the side of his body. This happened in less than a moment, but in a single smooth yet rapid and powerful motion, Makabei's staff crashed through Kanbun's defensive position, splitting the bamboo into strips at the middle, and struck squarely against the young man's kidney area. Kanbun crumpled to the floor clutching his side. Tokusaburo rushed to his friend while the other apprentices stood with wide eyes and twisted faces.

"Leave him be," said Makabei. "He is not good enough to stand in this hall."

Kanbun struggled to the side of the hall and sat dazed and in pain. The apprentices continued with their practice, but no one spoke. Makabei's intent was clear. Kanbun would no longer be able to train or learn with the others in the temple. It was also clear that there was something unusual about Makabei's staff. Normally, bamboo was flexible and yielded against pressure or even a well delivered blow. Makabei was ignoring them and examining his favorite staff. He threw it to the floor with a crash that filled the hall.

In disgust, he said, "Ah, now it's no good," and walked out the door.

One of the senior apprentices walked over to the where the staff was on the floor and reached to pick it up. He needed two hands to lift it, and then he said in surprise, "Look at this!"

The other apprentices crowded around and could see splits in the bamboo, but instead of being hollow on the inside it was filled with lead. He passed it along for the others to hold. Again, they were surprised and shocked. It was heavy to lift with one hand and difficult to control even with two.

It was the end of the session. Tokusaburo lent Kanbun his shoulder and helped him limp back to their hut. The next morning, Tokusaburo brought him some tea with ground leaves of *itadori*, the knotweed that grew wildly in Ryukyu and Fujou, to help with the pain. Tokusaburo was filled with youthful anger.

He said hotly, "That is no way to treat a student. Who does he think he is?" After a pause he added, "When you recover, let's get real hardwood staffs and together teach him a lesson."

Kanbun, dazed but knowing they were beaten, said, "It's no use. I can't study or stay here without his permission. Besides, did you see the way he handled that staff of his? He carried it all this time and wielded it like it was something we cut from a grove when we were kids. He is heavy on his feet but he moves as lightly as a cat. We would come away worse a second time against him." They continued to talk for a while until Kanbun fell asleep. Tokusaburo lay awake, eyes wide open, and staring at the ceiling.

Kanbun felt a little better in the morning, but there was blood in his urine. Even though he had no appetite, he drank some more of the tea Tokusaburo gave him. He got up, moved about with pain, and gathered his things for departure.

"Tokusaburo," he said, "it would be better for you to stay."

"To tell you the truth," his friend replied, "I was thinking about what to do last night and I hadn't decided what would be best."

"If we both leave, neither one of us will have a place to stay or a way to get along," Kanbun offered. "I see now that it was me that Makabei disliked from the beginning. You have a chance to stay on, learn what you can, and take your time before you decide whether to stay, return to Ryukyu, or do something else. There is no reason you should suffer my misfortune. Besides," he added with a slight smile, "I want to hear from you some day when a bigger bully takes care of that bastard."

"Ok, but let me know if things don't work out. I will help whenever you need it," he replied. Then, he added, "Here, take some herbs and medicines that will help your kidney." Tokusaburo gave him several containers and bags of plants, medicines, and materials, far more than he would use himself.

"Kanbun, you can support yourself for a while selling the extra like we have been doing until you are able to get back to good health," he said.

Tokusaburo walked with Kanbun to the temple gate and they remembered the day they had entered with optimism.

Before they said goodbye, Tokusaburo warned, "You had better find another temple gate to stand in front of and sell the medicines. I heard that Makabei is unkind to anyone who lingers after they have been told to leave."

The young men nodded to each other, turned, and departed in opposite directions. As Kanbun walked along the road with no particular direction or objective in mind, he was struck by the irony of his position in a strange land. Up until then, he had dealt mostly with people from or familiar with Ryukyu. The kind old Granny and the elderly Nakaima at the Jueneki had been friendly and helpful, but unable to offer much support. Makabei, on the other hand, could help Kanbun considerably by accepting his work at the temple in exchange for meals and a place to stay, but was ill-tempered and threatening. Kanbun wandered from street to street and eventually wound up in the neighborhood of the Ryukyukan Jueneki. Granny welcomed him with a sigh and offered him the room he had stayed in before. Kanbun sighed too as he entered the room with the dirt floor carrying a straw mat the kind lady had lent him again. Here he was, back where he had started, and no prospects for making his way.

For the next three days, the wind blew and it rained incessantly. The winds weren't quite as strong as a typhoon, but the rain was heavy and intense. Kanbun huddled in a corner, drank the hot miso soup the kind old lady brought him in the evenings, and chewed the rice, seaweed, and pickled vegetables. Tokusaburo was probably staying busy clearing the drain culverts, keeping the herb garden from flooding, picking up debris, and training with Makabei and the others at the temple. He missed his friend. At last, the sky cleared, but the wind died down and he could see stars overhead. The next morning, Kanbun felt better. He awoke early, washed his face in a ceramic crock that was used to catch rain water outside the room, gathered together his herbs and medicines in bundles, once again thanked Old Nakaima and the kind Granny from Ryukyu, and walked off toward town.

There were puddles, ruts, and mud everywhere. He had to duck aside people carrying bundles to avoid slipping in the mud or watch out for carts that would send waves of dirty water onto him. After a while he found a large intersection of roadways with shops at three corners and some kind of official building at another. It was a large building that extended down the street with a gate at the far end. Around the building was a wall of brick and clay that was more than eight *shaku* high and obscured the view of what was inside. He had no idea of what it was, but it seemed like some kind of institution or government building. He set down his bundles in front of the wall and began to call out to passersby with a few words that he knew in Chinese to those who might purchase his herbs and medicines. Most paid him no attention, but some would stop, look, and ask a question or two. He understood little of what they were asking, so he said nothing and they left muttering.

When he had arrived in Fujou he could read clearly most signs and printed instructions because written Japanese also employed Chinese characters, though the spoken language was a different matter altogether. The tones, dips, and rises in pronunciation in standard Chinese sounded like a mish-mash of grunts and spits to him at first. Fortunately, though the official language of Okinawa was Japanese, the spoken language in Ryukyu was somewhat similar to the Fujou dialect of Chinese. Upon listening closely to some of the shopkeepers and merchants in Fujou who had commerce with his homeland, he had detected words, phrases, and even common expressions that sounded much like the conversation in Ryukyu that his grandfather and elders spoke when they got together in the evening or at festivals to trade stories and discuss the ways of the world. In his first few weeks in Fujou and at the temple, whether it was merely a stranger in the street of whom he had asked directions or someone more familiar to him, the listener would stare in blank apathy or burst into a fit of laughter and Kanbun would know his tone was off or what he had actually said was something quite different from what he had intended. However, little by little, day by day, he had developed some workable expressions in the Chinese language. He also learned like others picking up a new language; he understood a great deal more than he could actually speak.

At that moment, a young man crossed the intersection and walked directly towards where Kanbun was standing with his wares. The young man voiced some awkward sounds and then pointed to the herbs. Kanbun tried a few words of his own, but it was as if the man wasn't listening until he realized his prospective customer was deaf and mute. Kanbun held up two fingers in front of the man's face. The man responded with one finger. After some thought, Kanbun nodded. The man then took some of the herbs, paid Kanbun with a coin, smiled, and left. Kanbun was happy and confused. After a while three men who appeared a little older than Kanbun and wearing rough clothes walked past where he was selling the herbs and medicines. Their whiskers had not been shaved in days and they had dark faces. They even smelled unpleasantly. One of them was carrying a wooden staff and stopped to pick up and inspect one of Kanbun's small jars with medicine in it. The three of them lingered a while and the first one with the medicine jar asked a question. Kanbun said nothing, but held up four fingers. The young tough made a threatening face and dropped the jar breaking it on a rock and spilling the contents in the dirt by the road. He then said a stream of things to Kanbun, none of which was apologetic but among which Kanbun recognized clearly the word for coins. The other two young men circled into a menacing position in front of Kanbun, whose back was to the high wall surrounding the long building inside. All four of the young men were now tense, but Kanbun was clear-minded that they were challenging him and he would have to respond quickly. As the first young tough raised his staff, Kanbun turned and took a quick step toward the wall, crouched his short frame like a tightened spring, thrust himself upward, and grasped the top of the nearly three-meter high brick and clay wall. In one flowing motion, he swung his legs up, scraped himself up onto the top of wall, set his feet on the narrow tiles, ran a few steps, and, as a few of the weathered and loose tiles slipped under his feet, fell into the bushes on the other side. The young men who were about to accost Kanbun were open-mouthed at first, but then began shouting and pointing.

Kanbun sat in the bushes ignoring the young men on the other side of the high wall at the street corner, not knowing whether he should be happy or embarrassed. He was safe, but he would have to do better than this.

After a while, the shouts on the other side of the wall stopped, and Kanbun walked along the edge of the inner garden until he reached a corner at the far end of the wall. He climbed a tree and looked at the street on the other side. The young men had apparently left and there were other people walking along road. Kanbun reached out, put a foot on the top of the brick wall, and jumped down to the grass and weeds on the street side below. He quickly looked up and down the street, thought about going back for his herbs and medicines, but then walked away briskly along one of the roadways. He pointed himself away from the direction of the Ryukyukan Juneneki and the Gushing Spring Temple beyond it. He could tell from the sun that he was heading southwest toward the edge of town and did not stop as he found a road leading out to fields that were broken by streams of running water and clumps of pine, bamboo, or poplar trees. He pressed on, not knowing where he was going or what he would find. The scale of the roads, the fields, the rivers, the countryside, the buildings, and even the size of some of the houses astounded him in comparison to his quaint and simple life in Izumi and Motobu. He could see along great stretches of the brown rivers flowing by swiftly. In other places, there were fields upon open fields in which workers with carts drawn by donkeys on the far side seemed to have shrunk in size due to the distance. The roadway along which he walked was congested with people carrying loads, hand drawn carts, and others mounted on horses.

He felt small and insignificant in the vast mass of nature and people around him.

Kanbun wandered along until he came to the edge of the great Min River of Fujou, where a group of workmen had gathered. There was a dock with goods and equipment laying on it and a ferry boat part way out into the river. More people arrived and there was a commotion on the dock with several people shouting and pointing. Apparently, the rain had raised the level of the river and the current was too strong for the ferry boat to cross. Kanbun hesitated. He could not cross the Min River, but he did not want to go back to Fujou. Without much thought, he climbed a slight rise to the side of the dock area and sat on a flat rock to survey the area and ponder what to do. Ants and spiders busied about the top and around the rock, but Kanbun paid no attention to them.

Encounter along the Way

Jou Tzuhe sat with a group of friends sipping from delicate porcelain cups in a corner tea house whose opened warm weather windows looked onto a main street in Fujou. The Fujian Oolong tea they drank had been picked and dried in the late spring and now was steeping in a pot on a table in front of them. They were discussing the unstable political situation and court intrigue of the imperial government in Peking. Its corrupt officials and weak leadership were barely holding together the Ching Court, which had been established by the Manchus that had invaded from the north two and half centuries earlier displacing the Ming Dynasty that had been established more than two hundred years prior to that. The current Ching Court was divided by competing factions who with differing motivations were loyal to the declining imperial institution, an inept government, a military of uncertain allegiances, restive groups in the provinces, or others. There were open insurrections in various locales, not to mention clandestine groups that operated out of sight and plotted the overthrow of the government. And, these were merely some of the internal threats to sustaining the Ching Dynasty. Externally, the military had recently lost a significant engagement with the Japanese, resulting in an enfeebled Ching Court ceding to Japan some of its continental territory in the northeastern Liaotung Peninsula, Formosa to the southeast, and the strategically significant Ryukyu Islands in the offing between Formosa and Japan. The Western powers had for decades been moving aggressively into East, Southeast, and South Asia with advanced technology, industrial strength, military power, and modern finance to support their seizure of trading rights, diplomatic outposts, and outright hegemony over vast maritime and continental areas. China had also been humiliated by similar encroachments on its territory and many felt the country was in danger of becoming divided, plundered, or colonized.

Jou sat with his back to the far wall that was facing the open window that looked out onto the street corner in front of the tea house. He listened to his friends talk, quietly weighing their arguments with his own experiences and impressions. He was younger than the others, but sophisticated in his thinking and well acquainted with the contemporary world. Though well-bred, he also had an earthy sense of humor that sometimes would surprise those close to him. He had been born into a clan of landowners, which formed a small but influential group in Fujou society. They collected rents in the form of produce from their farmlands, which they leased to local families and laborers, and prospered in cooperation with merchants and traders. Though still young, Jou was well schooled in calligraphy and painting as well as Chinese philosophy. Indeed, his commercial acquaintances greatly admired his skills with a brush and requested that he draw signs for them that could be seen here and there outside their shops in the streets of Fujou. He had read and studied the classical texts of Confucius, Mencius, Lao-tzu, and Buddhism. Among them, his personal preference was for the balanced and nuanced understanding of man, nature, and the world as described by the proponents of Taoism. What his circle of friends did not know about this young man was that he was also an accomplished student of *wushu*. It was in part his stature within Fujou that had provided him access to the best teachers and to meet other *wushu* specialists in the Buddhist temples and secret societies of Fujian, exchange ideas, and learn as much as he could.

Among those sitting in the tea house was Chen Paoshen, a highly literate, classically educated, and out-spoken supporter of the Ching Court. He argued that though the imperial institution had obvious shortcomings, the same could be said for the previous great Chinese dynasties after governing under a Mandate of Heaven for several hundred years. However, Chen's argument was more nuanced than mere conservative support for the status quo. Despite its shortcomings, the Ching should not be automatically dismissed from consideration for governing and leading, he asserted. Indeed, as unstable as it was, weak governance was preferable to anarchy, which would serve no one, certainly not those sitting in the tea house. Furthermore, with the pressures exerted on China from outside the realm, as well as the instability within, the Ching Court was the only institution with the legitimacy, if not the capability, to rule the land in these turbulent times. Everyone knew that Empress Dowager Tsu-hsi, the widow of the former emperor, had given birth to a son who had assumed the throne at a young age, but had died while in his late teens. She had schemed and manipulated, bypassing the normal rules of succession, installed her nephew on the Imperial Throne, and had continued to control him from behind the scenes. Chen suggested that the rightful heirs to the Dragon Throne should eventually replace the current imperial line and the Empress Dowager should be sidelined. He believed firmly in the classical model of civil governance with the Emperor at the pinnacle of all elements of society. Little did anyone among the small gathering know, nor might they have predicted, but their eloquent friend would one day in the near future be appointed by the Ching Administration the first President of the Fujian Railway Company. Later still, in reward for his persuasive oratory, broad and deep learning, and civic accomplishments, he would be called to serve in Peking. Once there, he became the tutor to the young heir to the Dragon Throne, the guardian, mentor, and confidant of Aisin Goro Puyi, the twelfth and final ruler of the Ching Dynasty and the last Emperor of China.

The group of friends in the tea house argued the pros and cons of Chen's ideas, as well as the current economic, political, and social situation. Some agreed with Chen, while others were in favor of modernizing, which controversially meant westernizing, as quickly as possible for survival of their homeland. The group was fundamentally divided over whether to preserve and restore the greatness of China's long and illustrious history of conservative Confucian rule or to adapt quickly and catch up with the West so as not to be overwhelmed or swallowed by it. Jou listened carefully, but kept his thoughts to himself. He had his own preferences and planned to act upon them, but did not want to reveal them openly, especially to such a talkative group. He was engaged in a clandestine group that was biding its time to see which way the political storm developed. As a landowner who derived his income from his lands, he stood much to lose if the prevailing sentiments blew in the wrong direction. He might need help one day and he kept a sharp eye out for potential talent that could serve his purposes.

Across the street, Jou noticed that a young itinerant had chosen a spot in front of the city government guest house to sell his wares. The high wall surrounding the guest house was sturdily built but, like the current imperial dynasty, had decayed in recent years. The buildings within were no longer well kept as the city rarely welcomed important visitors and had little budget for suitable entertaining. Rather, the city leaders had begun to make it a practice to host important but infrequent guests in a famous local restaurant and lodge them in the home of a senior official. After a while Jou perceived that the young peddler was about to be accosted by three ruffians who had stopped to look at his goods. Jou sat with keen eyes, curious as to the outcome of the impending encounter. His eyes and mouth turned upward into a satisfied chuckle as the youth outwitted the other three by escaping skillfully over the wall, rather than standing his ground to fight against long odds and unknown assailants. A couple of his compatriots looked at him surprised at his amusement amidst a serious conversation. Jou quickly recovered, coughed, and spat on the floor.

An early lunch was being served, which Jou ate quietly and then excused himself saying that he had already been delayed by the recent three-day downpour and would return home that afternoon for important business. He said his goodbyes, bowed respectfully, and exited out the back door to the stable where his horse was being kept. He mounted his grey and white horse and entered the road that led southwest out of town to his family estate in the outskirts of Fujou. As he rode to the edge of town, he surveyed the damage that had been done by the heavy rains and flooding of the past three days from the height of the narrow road that had been built up between the rice paddies. It was an unusual torrent that had come in mid-summer and caught the villagers unprepared. It was not so much the rush of the water that they feared would wash away the plants already nurtured to knee high, for they were sturdily rooted in the thick mucky soil, but the silt deposited around the stems of the rice shoots would choke the plants and cause the lengthening ears of grain to shrivel and die before the autumn harvest. He watched farmers scurrying about under their coolie hats redirecting the little currents away from the fields with dams of sod and sticks toward the tributaries that flowed into the broad Min River which cut the road up ahead. Others were busily digging away with their bare hands, makeshift wooden spades, boat oars, or anything that would do to separate the plants from the wet, thick soil around them. Today the sun was bright and the sky clear. The downpour had erased any hint of clouds from the heavens and the wash of water gave the air a fresh and clean smell. Jou took in a deep breath and his long, slow exhalation seemed to relieve his head, neck, and shoulders of the stress accumulated from the rainy period of inactivity and the conversation with Chen Paoshen and his friends earlier. At this moment, it was a day free from worry. Before him lay a smooth road over which his horse gently ambled along. Beyond the river the road would become coarse with stone and gravel and split into myriad little dirt paths branching into vegetable fields, rice paddies, and the innumerable farming villages that lay on the outskirts of Fujou. One such village was the location of Jou's home and birthplace. On maps and in the common language of the Mandarins who ruled in the northern capital of Peking it was pronounced Nanyu. To the natives of Fujou it was known as Nanyoi or Nanyu, but to Jou and the people who spoke the country dialect of his village it would always be home. There he would be with his family, his servants, and his lands. For some reason in Nanyoi the air always smelled fresher, the vegetables tasted sweeter, and the roads and pathways were clear of the dust and grime that seemed in Fujou to kick up simultaneously from the wagon hardened streets and fall from the charcoal burning tenement kitchens. In Nanyoi the perspiration that first glistened and then flowed from his body felt clean and healthy. His skin would become relaxed over the taut but smooth muscles beneath. His very pores seemed to welcome and breathe in the abundant nature that surrounded his country home.

From his seat atop the horse Jou could see up ahead the ferry boat landing that had been built at the intersection of the road and the river bank. Years before, a thick rope had been stretched across the broad expanse of the Min River connecting to a dock on the far side, which was only partially distinguishable in the distance. The rope was tied to sturdy posts that had been erected in several piles of stones that had been ferried out and dropped into the current. The tops of the stone piles were now just visible in the flooded river and the posts with the rope attached stood above them. Loops had been tied in the cord at intervals of about 20 meters and a much longer second rope had been strung through them. A ferry boat had been secured at the midpoint of this second rope to prevent the vessel from being swept away in the swollen current. Normally, the ferry boat men would pole their way across the river using the first rope as a steadying guide. But today, as in the rainy season, coolies had been hired on either bank for extra support to pull in and let out the slack of the second rope. The rains of the past few days had been particularly heavy so that the drag of the swiftly flowing river had broken one of the frayed loops on the connecting cord about 60 meters from the dock Jou was now approaching.

"Shit," muttered Jou.

Men with long poles aboard the vessel were trying desperately but unsuccessfully to push their way against the onrush of the water and reconnect the ferry to the securing line

103

that stretched across the river. The ferry boat listed in the current as passengers moved about holding onto their possessions and agitatedly tried to avoid being thrown into the water. Two dogs that had fallen into the river and a horse that had stumbled overboard could be seen swimming in the downstream flow trying for shore.

As he drew closer to the river, Jou noticed a stir developing at the water's edge. Three coolies were engaged in a tug of war with the ferry boat that had been pulled away from the securing line and was threatening to break free altogether to be carried away with the rippling waters. A man, who apparently was the dock master, exhorted them to pull harder while five or six rough looking characters sat on the dock drinking wine from ceramic jugs and both cheering on and jeering at the three coolies. As Jou approached, he realized the group of ruffians was gambling with small amounts of money over whether the coolies or the torrent would prevail. He saw several men from the jeering gang raise their hands and vigorously slap down sums stating the odds on their gamble as the ferry wavered and the toiling workers made no headway. A slightly larger group, consisting mostly of merchants and onlookers, stood at the river bank peering anxiously at the ferry boat. After hesitating, a few men from among the merchants joined the wager with even larger bets when the coolies managed a foothold and secured the end of the rope through a ring in a post on the dock. The three coolies, sweating profusely and breathing heavily, collapsed onto the dock, but they still held onto their end of the rope. The previously somber group of merchants raised a holler and slapped themselves on the knees and each other on the back in congratulations.

Jou rose up slightly in his saddle at the sight ahead of him and urged his horse to move on more quickly. The corners of his mouth lifted slightly as he sensed the excitement of the crowd up ahead. He arrived at the landing to hear both sets of gamblers cursing and spitting in anguish; one side chastising the coolies for not getting up and carrying out their task, and the other betting the ferry would break loose and be carried away. Jou alighted nimbly from his horse and strode with strong yet easy paces to the scene by the river. The small crowd of other coolies, stragglers, and shopkeepers, which had grown up around the disturbance quieted at his approach as he appeared to be a man of means. His dark blue robes flowed from the barrel of his torso and stretched in a trail that reached out to his heels. His hair had been freshly washed and combed. Though his hands had a powerful look usually associated with years of manual labor, they were clean and smooth. And, there was something more. His carriage had the indefinable poise of one who had been well bred, was confident in himself, and had earned the respect of those who knew him. His features were youthful, but his expression was mature, unlike the faces of the spoiled younger generation well-to-do who filled out the ranks of offspring of prominent government officials and prosperous merchants.

A pack mule standing at the edge of the dock was tethered to a post near the road and was absentmindedly looking toward the river while chewing wet grass. The three coolies pulled and stretched the end of the rope that was threaded through the ring in the post at the dock and tied it to the saddle of the mule. The coolies tried to encourage the animal to pull on the rope, but he paid no attention and continued to chew. A man wearing a shopkeeper's apron picked up a thin wooden rod and began beating the neck, sides, and haunches of the obstinate animal. The mule brayed, turned its head from side to side, but refused to move.

After briefly looking from one set of gamblers to the other and surveying the scene with eyes that seemed to see much but say little, Jou announced, "I will wager five silver pieces to one with any man who, with or without the aid of that ass, can return the ferry boat to the dock."

Jou's motives were not purely for entertainment, though he enjoyed the game as well. The ferry was his only means of reaching the other side of the Min River and he hoped to arrive at the far bank and continue his journey into Nanyoi before nightfall. There were other more important things on Jou's mind, but at the moment no one present would have guessed. For one, the swollen Min River and its rapidly flowing current caused a slight feathery feeling in his stomach. Though he told no one, he could not swim and did not want to risk a dangerous river crossing. Second, he kept an eye out for young recruits-- youths with potential who would grow into men of talent to train with him in *wushu*. He might need competent assistance to protect his family, his livelihood, and his lands should the political situation take a turn for the worse. Even if he found no green aspirants to power, fame, or fortune today, he would have some fun with this motley bunch.

By now the two groups of gamblers had given up their original bet on the fate of the ferry boat still wavering in the offing. They muttered to themselves or each other about whether it would be worth the risk of a silver piece for the fortune with which the elegant stranger had so plainly tempted them.

"Come now," urged Jou, "there must be at least one among you who has some measure of confidence in his own strength. My wife," he went on, though he was unmarried, "gets more of a fight out of the chickens she slaughters for the summer holiday than I see in the flock of squawkers scratching and clucking about here."

At this a murmur arose from among the gamblers. One, who twisted his sweaty torso and face turned pink with alcohol into a sneer and puffed his chest with more than a little injured pride at this last remark, stepped up and said, "I can haul in the ferry boat these three weaklings let get away without that pack of old bones you call an ass, but how do I know you'll pay up?"

"Yea, how do we know your bet is payable," echoed a few of the more vocal gamblers.

"Very well," replied Jou. "We will entrust our cash to a worthy person who will hold my five pieces to your one while the wager is on. But, don't waste any more of my time with fairy tales. Show your piece of silver and just how much of your words can be matched with deeds."

The ruffian, who had gone so far as to call what he thought was the stranger's bluff, could not back down now without a loss of face among the other gamblers. He stepped forward digging a coin from a pocket in his worn leather legging and said rather insolently, "Yea, here's my cash. Now let's see yours."

At this Jou turned away from the foul smelling lout and again surveyed the crowd before him, which by now had grown larger and closer than a few moments earlier. He inhaled deeply through his nose, and the corners of his mouth lifted slightly into the same expression that had come over his face when he first spied the gambling party from a distance. He looked about for an honest face, one with integrity that trusted in the good judgment of its owner. His eyes traveled across the mix of unemployed gamblers, coolies, and day laborers who had come up to see what all the excitement was about. He looked closely at the merchants, who sold tea, rice cakes, and provisions to travelers departing and arriving or were hoping to have goods transported across the river from the busy ferry boat landing. Earlier, the merchants were eager to see ferry service renewed. Some had joined in the wager and sided with those betting on the three men pulling the rope because the lack of ferry service would mean a decrease in the day's income, and this coming at the tail end of torrential rains during which there was no business at all. As Jou attracted a crowd about him, the merchants gleefully began to register the profits in their heads from the resumption of regular commerce. They liked this eloquent stranger. But, Jou was not inclined to return the sentiment nor feel he could entrust his purse to one of them. He was looking for something more. He looked hard until he discovered a smallish young man sitting on a rock on a rise above and to the left of the landing.

"You there…come here," he ordered firmly yet respectfully.

Uechi Kanbun had been gazing out over the rapidly flowing waters of the great Min River before him. Though he had grown up near the ocean, he had never seen such a broad stretch of fresh water with its racing current. His mind had drifted to the sweep of hillside stretching down to the clear azure sea behind his home where the land was covered with leafy vegetation and blue skies yielded to a warm sun over the little village of Izumi in northern Ryukyu. He wished this dirty brown torrent would be Motobu Bay and the muddy hillside were carpeted in green like the hills of home, as homesickness welled up from his heart to

108

his eyes. He had wandered without destination from the center of Fujou to this isolated spot away from the bustle, dirt, congestion, and discomfort of the city. By now, his stomach was quite empty and his clothes were still damp and stained from the extended downpour. A shiver ran across his shoulders and down his spine as he shook with a sneeze. He was sick of being tired, hungry, bullied, and dirty, but worst of all ignored. If only someone would notice his existence. He might just as well be one of the miserable insects that crawled around the top of the rock upon which he sat. At least they had food and family. He missed his mother and the warm call of her voice when her simple but fulfilling meals of grilled fresh fish, steamed rice, sautéed vegetables, dry seaweed, miso soup, and crunchy pickles were ready.

It was at this moment in the midst of his daydreams that Kanbun became aware that someone was calling in his direction. He hadn't noticed the swell of the crowd at the ferry boat landing and the ruckus they were making, but now he could feel eyes upon him. Instantly and unconsciously he rolled his shoulders back and down as he straightened from the hunch of his private thoughts. His eyes caught the fixed stare of a swarthy man waving an imperious hand calling him to descend to the crowded dock. Kanbun's expression turned to an embarrassed and puzzled look as he unconsciously lifted his forefinger and pointed at his own nose in the way he would identify himself in his native country.

"Ah," thought Jou disappointedly, "another of those runaway foreigners."

But, there was something different, almost recognizable, about this ragged looking refugee. If past experience with these "masterless warriors" as they called themselves had not taught him otherwise, Jou would have guessed the subject of his attention to be warmhearted and reliable. The little fellow obviously was alone, but there was something in the instant glare of his eyes that told of greater depth. Apart from his crude and foreign expression, he seemed to possess an inner strength.

"Come," beckoned Jou again, and said to himself in a lower voice, "Hmm...Perhaps I will find someone of merit here today after all."

Kanbun ducked his head and slid off the rock on which he had been sitting. Though he felt timid and unsure whether this would be simply another opportunity for one of the local toughs to bully him, there was something in the voice that called him to inspire his confidence. While Kanbun picked his way down the rocky and gravelly slope, Jou pulled a leather pouch from the sash around his waist and gently tossed it in the air in front of him so all present could hear the jingle of his store of cash. Kanbun threaded his way through the gathering and slipped into the open area of the semicircle that formed around the ferry boat landing. He approached Jou, but stopped several paces short not knowing what to do or whether to proceed.

Jou turned, approached Kanbun with an extended arm, rested his hand upon the younger man's shoulder, and said, "Come, my man, I want you to hold this money for me for a while. Will you do that?"

Kanbun looked up at Jou. Though Kanbun was solidly built, he was shorter than the robust figure now addressing him. Physical stature was not all that made Kanbun feel small at this moment. He was naturally shy, particularly when dealing with strangers. What's more, despite the several months he had spent on the continent living in Fujou, there were plenty of gaps in his understanding of Chinese that further undermined his confidence.

When Jou placed a hand upon his shoulder and showed him the money pouch, it was through the spoken words and gestures that Kanbun was able to comprehend what was asked of him. Shaking off his diffidence, he gave a decisive nod of his head and held out his hand to receive the purse. Jou grunted approval and turned to the slightly more sober but still pride puffed gambler.

"Give your piece of silver to this fellow and we shall soon see who goes to sleep a richer man tonight," said Jou with a flourish.

The tough covered the distance to Kanbun with an exaggerated stride. Lifting the palm on which sat his one piece of silver, he spat on the coin and slapped it into Kanbun's free hand.

"Don't worry, runt. You're not gonna hold this long," he said with a sneer.

Kanbun wasn't sure what the gruff words were, but he caught the gambler's menacing intent and held his ground. Something in the pit of his stomach hardened as he found the strength to stand face to face with the dirty and foul breathed gambler. Kanbun met the man's stare with an even gaze that neither threatened nor backed down.

"Hmph," thought the gambler," after I take the bet and shut up that big mouthed dandy, I'll teach this worm a lesson."

Immediately, those who had neither won nor lost their original bet began laying odds with each other on the newly established wager. The crowd shifted its attention back to the dock where the pathetic mule now sat on its haunches with its neck stretched by the rope away from the direction of the drifting ferry boat. The rough cut gambler kicked through the straw and dirt on the dock searching for sturdier footing among the wooden planks. Finding a place to pitch his battle, he rubbed dirt on his hands, set his heels, and took a firm grip on a section of the rope between the river and the post on the dock. Clenching his teeth, screwing his face into a grimace, tensing his legs, and grasping firmly the taut rope, the gambler strained and grunted against the pull of the river current. When he succeeded in gaining a step, and then eventually another, the crowd began to murmur. The mule sat unfazed. However, try as he might, the struggling gambler could make no steady headway. Heaving a mightier grunt, he shifted his position so that he stood parallel to the rope and set his legs in what Jou recognized as a "horse stance," a strong side defensive position used by men who practiced *wushu*.

"This man has had some training," thought Jou in less than a blink of the eye, "but I wonder how much and who his teacher is."

The gambler slid his hands apart so that the rope lay across his shoulders and both arms were completely outstretched. Panting heavily and red faced, he was able to rest while he gathered strength and plotted his next strategy. The gamblers, who had been watching intently, hawked and changed the odds with every exertion of their confederate. The ruffian gathered his strength and attempted to rotate his body drawing the ferryboat closer with a twisting motion, but this too failed. When he could no longer bear the strain, he dropped in a heap. With heaving lungs and head down he sat defeated on the dock. Those who had wagered against him raised their voices and collected their bets from their disappointed opponents.

112

Jou walked over to the exhausted man and said, "An impressive try!" while extending his hand to lift the gambler from the ground.

Rather than accept the offer of assistance, the humiliated gambler leapt to his feet and pushed his menacing face in front of Jou's. In an instant, almost imperceptibly, Jou lowered his center of balance by slightly bending his knees, put his hands against the gambler's waist, and shoved him away. The thrust sent the gambler sprawling across the back of the seated mule and onto a pile of dung-filled straw that lay to one side of the dock. After his initial surprise at the ease and power with which Jou had dispatched him, the gambler became infuriated and picked up a wooden spade, but then thought better of it and slinked off into the depths of the crowd. Once again Jou raised his strong throated voice and addressed the crowd around the dock.

"This is your last chance. Before the ferry boat captain gives up for the evening, isn't there one man among you who will try his luck here."

"But sir," offered a rather feeble and hopeful looking merchant, "you look strong enough to pull in the boat yourself. Won't you at least give it a try?"

At this, Jou replied in exaggerated surprise, "Oh, he was drunk and I was just lucky. Besides, I am not really made for this."

Kanbun, who had been standing at the edge of the crowd closely observing the goings on, was neither impressed with the gambler nor was convinced that Jou lacked strength. Apart from the fine clothing and glib talk of Jou, there was something about this man who one moment sounded fully confident and the next backed away from praise for his evident stature and strength.

Kanbun sensed there was a current of energy that existed beneath Jou's smooth surface. It appeared to be a flow of power, like the rushing waters of the river that swelled before them, but much more regulated. Kanbun stepped forward and nodded humbly and held out Jou's purse.

"Oh yes, my young friend, thank you. Here is a reward," he said handing Kanbun a small coin.

Though Jou was openly big hearted, his motives ran deeper. He wanted to see if the youthful foreigner would snatch the cash and run off with his new found treasure or be motivated to think on his feet. Kanbun stood wavering in surprise and bewilderment at Jou's unexpected generosity. After his rough and tumble experiences in Fujou he had not anticipated even a "thank you" for his part, not to mention this bonus. Instinctively, Kanbun bowed deeply and in a moment of inspiration nodded toward the ferry boat waving in the offing.

With feigned astonishment, Jou asked, "Oh you think you are powerful enough to rescue the ferry boat, do you?"

Once again Kanbun nodded, but this time a little more cautiously. "Do you have a piece of silver with which to wager?" asked Jou jingling his bulging purse.

Kanbun could only drop his eyes and murmur, "No sir."

"Well then," said Jou putting on a thoughtful face, "I will reward you this one piece of silver I gained today if you can fetch the ferry boat," as he pointed to the place where the mule still sat.

Kanbun looked up hopefully, comprehending quite well. He accompanied Jou to the dock where once again the eyes of the crowd followed. However, the gamblers who had profited by the earlier wager could find no takers this time. There were no odds given on the diminutive foreigner being able to recover the boat.

Jou stood back and said, "Okay my little friend, let us see what you can do."

Kanbun surveyed the scene from the ferry tied to the rope and drifting in the current to the line secured through the ring on the post and back to the mule on the dock. He walked over to the animal and squatted down patting its forehead and ears. Some in the crowd muttered, the mule looked nonplussed, but Kanbun continued by brushing the dirt and straw from the back of the mule and gently running his hands over where the shopkeeper had beat him earlier. The animal shifted slightly and seemed to appreciate the sympathy. Indeed, until a few moments earlier Kanbun had felt as unappreciated and hapless as the animal. After a few more minutes of soothing massage and gentle words of encouragement Kanbun managed to get the mule to rise to its feet. The crowd began to take notice and some gamblers were at it again, but still no one would accept a wager. Jou watched silently, but there was a look of satisfaction in his eyes. Kanbun continued to work the animal into a position where it was facing away from the danger of the river and toward the safety of the road. Kanbun nuzzled his chest against the face and nose of the mule and hummed the little song from his childhood that he had sung to Baro in Izumi as he stroked the forehead of the animal. He picked up the thin wooden rod that lay beside the post and with a warm and sympathetic brushing motion rubbed it across the haunches of the mule. The animal gave a jerk forward and Kanbun deftly slipped the rope around the tether on the post. As the ferry boat turned slightly in the swift current, the crowd began to stir. With gentle but determined swishes of the rod, Kanbun succeeded in coaxing the mule as he used his strength along with the animal and wound more of the rope around the post. By now the ferry was out of the swiftest flow and strongest pull of the current and floating without distress in the shallower water closer to the river bank. Kanbun pulled the boat all the way up to the dock and secured it with the aid of the three coolies. The passengers jumped off the ferry and warmly thanked Kanbun. The crowd pushed forward around him shouting their support and clapping him on the head and back.

Jou walked up throwing his arm across Kanbun's shoulders and said, "Come my little hero, you must be hungry after such a splendid effort."

He led Kanbun over to a teahouse and ordered bowls of noodles, roast meat, and sautéed vegetables for himself and his new companion. During the course of the meal Jou chatted affably with the shopkeeper and the small crowd that had followed them into the teahouse. Kanbun spent most of the next half hour devouring whatever was put in front of him. Indeed, he hadn't realized he was so hungry, despite the fact he had not eaten since the night before leaving Fujou. After Kanbun had finished eating, using simple words and a mixture of gestures, Jou invited Kanbun to accompany him along the road of his journey. Kanbun knew not where the kind stranger would take him or how long his generosity would extend, but somehow he felt his fortunes had turned and he was about to make a fresh start on life in China.

Jou had the shopkeeper fetch his dappled mare and together they boarded the now manageable ferry boat at the landing. With the three coolies holding the boat firmly in place and the ferry master directing the men with the long poles, Jou and Kanbun crossed the broad and swollen current. During the slow ferry ride Jou opened a conversation with Kanbun.

116

"Though I feel I already know you in some measure," he began, "I have yet to introduce myself. My name is Jou Tzuhe, but in the dialect of my home town I am called something different. I am pleased to make your acquaintance, but tell me your name and why have you come to Fujou?"

Kanbun looked at his somewhat senior companion and answered as politely as he could in his broken Chinese.

"I am Uechi Kanbun, son of Uechi Kantoku and Tsuru, of the village of Izumi in the Kunigami region of the land of Ryukyu. We are simple farmers living in the mountains on the northern end of our island nation. In recent times, the Japanese have been harsh and I decided to escape to your country. In my village I learned a little of how to handle a staff and I have heard of a Chinese martial technique using no weapons called in our language "toodi." The "too" character stands for the Tang Dynasty and "di" is our dialect for "hand," so I suppose it could be translated to mean "Chinese Hand." I hope to meet a teacher of this technique and devote myself to its study."

"Hmm," said Jou thoughtfully, "perhaps I do, but you speak more Chinese than I thought."

"Actually," replied Kanbun, "I have only learned very little since coming here a few months ago, and I have been hoping to speak with someone from Fujou, but never seemed to have the opportunity."

Indeed, it had been Kanbun's shy nature as much as his lack of knowledge of the local dialect that prevented him from speaking more freely.

"I am afraid I cannot express much more than what I just told you now. I have been thinking for some time how to say what is in my heart and I have repeated this little speech to myself over and over."

"I see," said Jou, impressed with Kanbun's simple honesty as well as his words. They chatted on a while and Jou was able to elicit from Kanbun how it was that he came to be seated on the rock by the river when Jou had asked him to hold his cash pouch.

"Tell me," Jou continued, "what are the characters of your name?"

"Uechi means "upper earth" which is my family name," he replied, "and Kanbun means "completed writings."

"I see, you write it like this?" Jou asked picking up a twig and drawing imaginary characters on the ferry boat railing.

"Yes, that's right," said Kanbun, "I think in Chinese it's pronounced Shandi Wanwen."

"Yes, yes," replied Jou.

Soon they reached the dock on the far side of the river and upon disembarking the ferry captain presented Jou and Kanbun each a little gift packet of sweet rice cakes cleanly wrapped in bamboo leaves. The captain told Kanbun, though he was not sure the little foreigner completely understood, if he ever wanted to cross the Min River, he would transport him free of charge. Kanbun bowed wordlessly and turned to join Jou on the road away from the river.

Through the Gate

Jou rode atop his horse, which ambled along with a gentle step. Kanbun followed on foot a few paces behind. The sun that had shone brightly since morning was gradually drying and warming the damp and dirty garments Kanbun wore. It was getting late in the afternoon, but Jou knew if they made no other stops along the way they would reach Nanyoi by nightfall. The road was narrower and bumpier than the one that led up to the ferry boat landing on the other side of the Min River, but nonetheless it was distinguishable as a traveled pathway different from the small trails and lanes that diverged from it and split up into farming compounds or craftsman's communities to the left and right of the winding roadway. Whenever Jou and Kanbun encountered one of the local townspeople, they would step aside to let the two pass, but Jou did not stop to exchange more than the simplest of greetings and pressed along the way. There were stretches of rice paddies and fields of vegetables, millet, flax, and buckwheat broken only by clusters of thatched roofs made of sticks and straw to cover the mud and brick homes. Today it was particularly muddy and rutted with the tracks of wagons loaded with firewood, charcoal, vegetables, or small livestock carried to slaughter. As Jou and Kanbun passed through the villages a grey mutt might rise up and bark at their approach or a dusty red rooster would crow at their arrival. Sometimes young boys and girls would peak out from inside a wooden shuttered window or rusty hinged kitchen door, giggle at the passersby, and then duck behind the earthen walls or their mother's apron when Kanbun would glance up in their direction. It seemed to Kanbun that

119

most of the people knew Jou as they greeted him, but Jou kept riding upon his steady horse and would only grunt some response or take no notice at all. As for Kanbun, apart from the girls who giggled or the young boys who stared when he walked by, no one paid him any more attention to him than the horse his host was riding.

After passing one small village they entered a level roadway that cut cleanly through an expanse of yellow fields filled with grain bent and ripening in the warm, late afternoon sun. Jou's mind drifted with the golden glow of the natural beauty that made up the Fujian countryside. The sky was clear, the air was fresh, and the residual moist sensation from the unexpected downpours earlier gave the earth a rich, musky odor. Jou signaled for Kanbun to draw up and take the reins of the horse to lead the animal along.

"Yes Master Jou," replied Kanbun in his clearest and politest Chinese.

At this, Jou who had been until then in a solemn mood burst into laughter. Somehow, this young foreigner seemed even more prompt and courteous in responding to him than his hand picked servants were at his rural home. Indeed, Jou did feel masterful today, and this unexpected pleasantry reawakened him to the bright prospects he felt for his new charge. After resettling his thoughts, Jou began slowly and deliberately so that Kanbun could grasp the meaning of what he was about to say.

"Wanwen, my friend, I have important things in mind for you. However, you will need to learn more Chinese. You will have to show initiative, to work hard, to apply yourself, to adapt to life here, to dress like a native, to nurture the mannerisms of a man from Fujian, to think as if you are Chinese. You will find that in this country there is virtue in the philosophy, religion, teaching, and in the hearts of the people. However, you must always remember your background, and that you come from Ryukyu. You may wear the garments of China, but you must retain the heart of your homeland. Only those who put virtue to practice keep the faith of the matter. Remember the goodness of your native soil and open your eyes, ears, and mind to the great qualities of the ancient and splendid history of this country that we call China. Finally, you should call me 'Jou'."

Kanbun listened attentively for it took all his concentration to gather the meaning of what his Chinese speaking host had to say. From time to time Kanbun would nod his head in assent or murmur a "Yes sir" as Jou continued his recitation, but a "Pardon me sir" or an "I'm sorry sir" would elicit from Jou a simpler, easier to understand rephrasing of the remark just made. Though Kanbun had many questions, out of deference and politeness to his benefactor, he listened without asking. Jou proceeded, this time paraphrasing the Daoist patriarch Lao-tzu.

"Like the flow of water, man is at his best when he serves the course of nature. Each seeks its own level. Close to earth it is a common level of life: clearness of heart, kinship with neighbors, words that ring true, evenhanded governance, fair and profitable dealings, and the right timing for good deeds. If egotistical men block the flow of the river, eventually they meet with overwhelming pressure and invite disaster. The little man who channels a portion of that current to bring nourishment to his rice fields sustains his family and contributes to society."

Jou paused to dismount, stood in front of some weeds, and both men relieved themselves beside the road.

In a mischievous and inspired moment, too short for contemplation and only arrived at instinctively, Kanbun offered, "I see... the noodle soup we ate this afternoon flows back to nature.

"Ho, ho, ho," laughed the lecturer from his belly. "That's good."

Though he had been told before he was given to unsolicited sermonizing, not many had made Jou laugh at his own preaching.

"You know enough Chinese to make a joke of Jou, ha-ha, don't you," returned the jovial elder of the two.

A tension had been broken and the two now walked along together leading the mare toward the village that had come into view up ahead. They chatted lightly back and forth about the coloring and shape of the sky, the lay of the houses, fields, and hills, and the road on which they walked. After a short time, several coolies in neat but loose fitting clothing and long braids on that backs of their heads emerged from inside a large wooden gate in a sturdy looking brick wall fronting a sprawling and clearly well-maintained mansion that was two stories high and sat on the high ground to the left of the road before them so that it looked even more imposing. The coolies hurried to where Jou and Kanbun were walking and threw themselves upon the dusty road.

"Welcome home Master Jou," they said in chorus, "we are happy you have returned safely."

"Mm," replied Jou, barely noticing them.

To the right of the road on a lower level lay a cluster of mud brick houses from which narrow columns of smoke rose above the evening cooking fires. A stout foreman, field workers in shortened black britches leading draft animals attached to carts, and groups of half naked barefoot coolies bearing hand tools were steadily making their way back to the village from the expanse of farmland that seemed to stretch off into the distance leading away from the extensive manor overlooking the flat plain. Not only were the fields rich with the abundance of the ripening crops, but along the little lanes and avenues that led into the peasant villages were flowering leafy plants and thick green grasses bent under the weight of nearly full maturity. The air began to feel cooler at the base of Kanbun's neck and along the back side of his bare upper arms as the day turned to a shadowless dusk. Jou led Kanbun through the main gate to the mansion. Inside was a courtyard and garden where servants were sweeping the walk and picking up clippings from the day's trimming of greenery. Luscious looking pears and other fruits unknown to Kanbun hung heavily from the boughs of the trees sprinkled here and there in the garden. To the left was another walled area separate from the main house, but still within the brick compound of the manor.

"That is where you will sleep," said Jou pointing to the obscured section of the grounds, "but first we'll have some food and drink."

They entered the great house through a tall and narrow double door with moon shaped trim on either side. The entrance seemed to dead end, but stepping to the right Jou led Kanbun down a long passageway past several doors with hanging curtains screening the contents of the inner rooms. He stopped at one and turned left into a square dining room lit with oil lamps. A round table sat in the center of the room with high backed chairs placed around it and embroidered cushions on the seats. Dishes had been set out with colorfully decorated porcelain cups, ivory chopsticks, and brass spoons sitting on lacquered rests. There were polished dining trays, porcelain teapots, glass decanters, and cloisonne vases arranged on a side board.

Kanbun had never seen such opulence. Matching pieces of ebony furniture, as well as large painted wooden boxes, sat against the walls. Brocade covers with scenes depicting animated characters, some looking like contorted demons or fantastic and unbelievable creatures, with colorful scenery were draped over the edges of the furniture. The walls were bare save for two dramatic scroll paintings hanging opposite each other: one with a tiger fiercely portrayed to look as if it might burst into the dining room at any moment, and the other of a lofty mountain range with the speck of a meditating hermit sitting by a trickling stream. The ceiling was of carved wooden beams and ornamental panels, while the floor was plain slabs of granite. Jou sat at one side of the table facing the tiger painting, to his right was a small reflecting plate hanging on the wall and to his left was the door through which they had entered. Jou motioned for his companion to sit by his right side, which he did rather uncomfortably. Kanbun was thoroughly unaccustomed to such luxury, not to mention the square wooden chair. At home in Izumi everyone sat, slept, studied, worked, and conversed on firm but flexible straw tatami mats. One supported the weight of the upper body with the small of the back and the pit of the stomach. In Jou's dining parlor, Kanbun either had to slump to reach the floor with his feet to support himself or sit stiffly in the hard chair with his elbows on arm rests while his legs kicked limply beneath him. Instinctively, he crossed his legs in his chair as if he were sitting on the floor.

Jou brought his hands together in two resonant claps and turned to Kanbun and said in a gentle voice, "Now we shall feast a little."

A servant opened a door leading to a passageway to Jou's left and two others entered each carrying a tray. The servants placed wine cups before them and poured out a dark liquor from a glass decanter.

Jou raised his cup and said, "Welcome, Shandi Wanwen, to Nanyoi." The Chinese accented pronunciation of his Ryukyu name struck Kanbun as cute and even a little comical, but he said nothing as Jou continued.

"In the local Nanyoi dialect, 'Shandi' sounds more like 'Chingli.' And, when in China one needs a Chinese name, so I will distinguish you with something appropriate to the Fujian countryside to commemorate our auspicious encounter along the way. Let me see... you are good hearted and a good fellow."

At this Kanbun could not resist adding, "And good for nothing."

Jou roared his approval at Kanbun's self-effacing humor.

"Actually, some of my friends call me 'Sanra,' which when written is the characters for 'three goods," explained Kanbun.

"And, so it shall be," said Jou with mirth in his eyes, "that in Nanyoi you are also called Sanra. And since good luck often comes in threes, I believe ours will be a fortunate association. I can think of an additional significance to the meaning of 'three goods,' but I will leave that for another time."

After a brief pause Jou completed his toast with, "May you profit by your stay in Nanyoi."

Kanbun nodded and lifted his cup to his lips. A small taste of the bitter liquor seemed to burn his throat increasing in heat and potency as it reached his stomach. He felt his temperature rise as perspiration formed on his upper lip, forehead, and temples. His eyes widened and teared up as he fought to suppress a cough. In Izumi he had tasted *awamori*, the strong spirits made from millet and rice grain that his grandfather and other village elders liked to sip in the evening. It had a noxious smell, but it would glide down his throat and make his belly feel warm and relaxed. The liquor Jou had given him shocked his system. Seeing Kanbun's reaction Jou broke into a knowing grin.

"This is Moutai, made from sorghum and wheat, and it is delicious but takes some getting used to," he said.

Without turning away Jou uttered the single word "tea" in a deep voice. The two servants who had been waiting by the sideboard poured Oolong tea from a large porcelain pot. Kanbun gulped the liquid, and though it was hot and almost burned his mouth, it cleared his eyes, and he gave a sigh of relief. Jou's smile burst into a howl and he ordered the meal to begin. The servants stepped into a back room that Kanbun guessed was the kitchen. Soon they began bringing in little dishes of delicate shellfish bathed in a clear broth. Kanbun eagerly wolfed down the dishes and sipped at his freshened cup of tea. Next came plates of vegetables with sliced roast duck, stacks of thin pancake-like baked dough, bowls of rice, a whole steamed fish topped with a delicious and crispy brown sauce of a kind that Kanbun had never tasted before, braised pork, seasoned chicken, bowls of fried noodles, and a cool wine to wash it down.

Kanbun paused only to realize that he had eaten and especially drunk more than he would have believed possible. The servants set a steaming fresh cup of Fujian Oolong tea in front of him. Slowly, as he sipped from this cup, the special tea seemed to gather the cooking oils he had ingested and settle the food in his stomach. In Ryukyu, Fujian Oolong was considered the best Chinese tea available and was reserved for honored guests and often used in the Royal Court. The servants re-appeared bringing with them steaming plates of shrimp and green vegetables, beef with plant roots, dishes Kanbun had never seen before nor could guess what they were, and set them down before the two men. There were so many flavors and sauces, each different, and all tasty. The servants poured a thick wine into his ceramic cup until at last Kanbun could accept no more of the lavish hospitality. Unconsciously, he slumped in his chair fatigued from the enormous quantities of food, the drink he had consumed, and his long, stressful, and eventful day.

"Well, how was that for beginners," asked Jou with a twinkle in his eye. "I think I'll go wrestle an ox for a while to rekindle my appetite."

With that he rose from his chair and unceremoniously left the room. Kanbun sat dazed for a few minutes not knowing or wanting to know what he should do next. He was exhausted from the stresses of this unusual day, not to mention having to listen closely to every word spoken to him and to think how he would respond in Chinese. Presently, an elderly servant entered the dining hall and motioned for Kanbun to follow him. With the assistance of another servant, Kanbun stood and followed unsteadily after the old man. The aged servant shuffled out the door through which Kanbun had entered, down the hallway, and outdoors into the evening air. The cool moisture outdoors refreshed Kanbun's face and he felt some control return to his limbs as his lungs breathed in the cleanliness that followed the drenching rain of the previous few days. The guide led him to the enclosed area Jou had indicated earlier and pausing before a narrow doorway pulled a set of keys from his robe. The servant opened the door and showed him through the darkness across an open stone courtyard to a wooden doorway in the wall and an attached room just outside. The servant pointed the way with a lamp into the room, which had a table, chair, and bedding on the floor by one wall. Kanbun entered, dropped heavily onto the straw filled cotton covered pallet, and lay down to what he thought would certainly be a deep asleep.

In the brief span of a just a few minutes as Kanbun was falling into the depths of a dream that he was back at home in Izumi in the cozy sleeping room he shared with his family, he recognized the first hints of consciousness. Instinctively, he reached for a quilt to pull over his chest and shoulders, but found only the thin coarse blanket that had been left for him. Now, his face was tight and the taste in his mouth sour as he lifted his head slightly, which immediately sent a sickening feeling from this eyes down his neck and into the base of his stomach. His head fell back on the pallet beneath him and a slight groan escaped from his lips. After resting in this position a while, he first rolled onto his side and then to his stomach. Next, crouching his forearms and legs under him, Kanbun pulled his body up and off the floor, still keeping the blanket material over him. Opening his eyes to the darkness in the room he could see the light through the doorway was still dark in the evening sky but the stars shone over the Chinese countryside. He shuddered and bent his neck so that his forehead met the floor with a thud. However, the dull sound he made was followed by stronger one, and then another coming from somewhere outside in the courtyard. In fact, there was a muted mix of noises that sounded like pecks, wraps, and slaps.

Kanbun listened with pained concentration as he could feel muffled and shuddering shocks-- thump-bump, thump-bump-- of something butting against the supporting pillars of the second floor landing he had seen earlier inside the courtyard walls.

Instinctively, his shoulders rolled back and his elbows clung to his ribs as his ears perked and he heard even less distinctly a noise similar to the dragon breaths he and Hiro made when imitating wild animals in their back yard in Izumi. Listening more closely, he could make out the short hissing exhalations of someone or several people engaged in regulated exertion. Kanbun slid off the matting on which he had lain down, crawled to the wooden doorway of the courtyard, and put his eye to a narrow opening between the wooden boards. Visible in the dim light, two youngsters were engaged in some form of *wushu*, lifting their slippered feet in turns and kicking a solid wooden pillar that supported the second floor of the great house. They wore thin material tucked in around their waists and the sweat that formed on their backs and shoulders had an eerie grey glow in the dull evening light. Across from them, standing by a second main column supporting the upper floor, another pair was rhythmically pounding the pillar with their forearms, shoulders, and chests. A few others stood facing the inner walls of the first floor striking padded beams with their fingertips and hitting wooden slats with their bare hands, wrists, and elbows. Kanbun crawled gingerly back to the small room and then dragged the blanket with him, for he was chilled and weakened from the feast earlier in the evening. He made his way to the doorway and then onto a ledge that let him see over the top of the sturdy wall and look at the stone paved yard. Peering over the edge he could see other youths practicing *wushu* under the guidance of two young men

129

who were apparently more skilled and experienced than the others. The higher ranking *wushu* men wore clothing of a thicker material that covered from their forearms down to their lower legs. Though the loose-fitting garments seemed wrapped around their bodies more than pulled over their arms and legs, there was a sash tied about their midsections that held the flowing material in place. One was adjusting the foot position and posture of several younger students standing upright with knees bent slightly and hands placed upward in front of the torso. Perspiration slid down their tensed bodies as they hissed with powerful exhalations. Another man stood unperturbed with elbows bent and palms outstretched against the concerted push of two sweaty, nearly naked students exerting all their might but unable to budge the senior man. Some younger students stood paired together chafing and pounding at each other's forearms as Kanbun watched. Kanbun stared at their practice in silent fascination as pink and purple light stretched across the western sky and reached the ledge where he stood. The atmosphere here was altogether different from the Gushing Spring Temple and the practice sessions of the bully Makabei who carried on there. The more experienced trainers he was now watching were firm but helpful to their younger counterparts. Those of apparently similar level worked in silent and courteous consideration of each other. The stone yard below was still in the shadow of the surrounding brick and earthen walls, but the activities of the *wushu* practice became more clearly visible as his eyes adjusted to the fading light. Soon, several of the students had lit oil lamps that hung along the walls of the enclosed area. Sometimes, at the grunted command of one of the instructors, the composition of a pairing or group in an exercise would shift and a different regimen would

130

begin. Occasionally, the seniors would chat with each other, but the activities of the toiling students continued without respite. Kanbun began to wonder if Jou would be willing to introduce him to the teacher so that he could formally apply for instruction under his tutelage in this group. Surely, he thought, there must be some connection between the leader of this *wushu* activity and the master of the house. He leaned against the wall with his elbows resting on top, gazing in excitement, and formulating in his head just how he could best phrase his request.

Before long the booming voice of Jou could be heard entering from somewhere above and to the back of wooden platform that Kanbun could see to the right.

"Jiang, Lee," called Jou, "it is the peak of the day."

The younger students maintained their pace without pause, but the two seniors who had been singled out by name turned to greet him with a "Good evening, Master Jou." They continued to oversee the activity before them, but with somewhat greater attentiveness as Jou strode up stoutly in flowing robes and sat facing the setting sun on a stone platform diagonally opposite the place where Kanbun peered out onto the scene in the yard. Jou surveyed the practice carried on before him and occasionally called over Jiang or Lee to make a point. His instructions were simple and unelaborated. After a while he called a halt to the activity and signaled the group to sit before him. They saluted Jou in patriarchal respect while the two seniors stood at the back of gathering. Jou addressed the gathering before him.

"You have worked the fields for long months and we have been blessed, except for the past three days, with overall favorable weather so the crops are plentiful this year. Soon the autumn harvest will begin and your daily burden will become heavier still. Put your best effort into your jobs and all our families shall prosper with the fruits of our labor. Among the villagers you have a special position because you are the few who have been accepted into tiger style *wushu* training. However, this special consideration requires extra exertion and vigilance. There are those who will fear the skills we are developing and conspire against us. Train hard daily but keep our activities confidential! Those who persevere shall become men of strength. But remember, no matter what your level or ability, first you are a man and second you are a *wushu* practitioner. *Wushu* is like a water jar. It is the vessel with which you carry the flow of your heart and soul and it is what makes you a man. The jar merely provides form and finish for what lies within. Bear your responsibility to yourself, your family, and to society as a manly man. Show no one outside this group what you have learned, unless you are suddenly called upon to defend yourself or a family member. If you reveal the extent of your knowledge, someone else will take advantage of you and perhaps overcome you," he added forcefully.

"Even a tiger can be hunted and killed." Jou paused gathering himself, and then seeming on the verge of expressing another thought, simply nodded and grunted in self-satisfaction.

"That is all for this evening," he said.

The younger students rose and filed out leaving only Jiang and Lee standing close to where Jou still sat. "Come," said the teacher, "let us study *wushu*." With that Jou led the two senior students to the wooden platform and disappeared behind a door in the back wall. Kanbun was confused by Jou's last remark. If the group had been practicing *wushu* earlier, what was the *wushu* Jou and the two others would do now? Kanbun shook his shoulders and head as a chill ran up his spine. Gingerly, he straightened his back and stretched his shoulders, still feeling the effects of overeating and drinking, and made his way back to the pallet to sleep. He lay down and rested his body, but his mind was busy with the images of the *wushu* he had just seen and he wondered how he too might join the training. Before long drowsiness came over him and he fell off to a deep sleep.

When Kanbun awoke, the air was heavy as the sun had already risen in the sky. He sat up and only a trace of the ache and dizziness of the night before remained. He shook himself, stretched, and went outside to face the brightness of the day. He looked onto the empty training area from the open wooden doorway, but now all was silent, and there was not even a hint of activity. He had a strong urge to relieve himself, but did not know where it would be appropriate. After crossing to the stone courtyard and peering around the open space, he found a latrine in a back corner of the enclosed area. He walked out of the practice area into the larger treed garden of the compound. A couple of workmen lay dozing in the shade of the far wall. Though his tongue felt pasty and parched in the dry heat of the summer sun, Kanbun was still too shy and considerate to break in on the resting workers and ask where he might get a drink of water. The great wooden gates of the estate were open, as they had been when Jou and Kanbun had arrived the day before, so he strolled out onto the roadway in front of the grounds. He looked from left to right, and everywhere in the village there was stillness and silence. Coolies, women, children, and even farm dogs were taking their midday nap. Kanbun wandered about the village kicking stones and sticks in front of him as he walked along the narrow paths between the houses. He looked for a friendly face, but found only those dozing obscured by straw hats or quiet infants held in the arms of a sleeping mother. Even the farm dogs did not rise to bark, but merely lifted their eyes and wagged their tails while they lay in the shade of the midday sun.

Kanbun returned to the mansion hoping to find Jou, but the great house also seemed empty of activity. He found a narrow hallway that led him back to the training area, this time from the rear entranceway. The walls were of a light colored plaster that had been painted with clusters of Chinese characters composed into pithy sayings or obscure poems. One such phrase read something like, "All is contained within three battles," attributed to someone else. He pondered the meaning, but did not understand the reference. Other walls were decorated with scenes of rugged countryside and lofty peaks divided by narrow streams. Kanbun wondered who the artist might be. It was one thing to purchase artful creations to hang in one's home, but another altogether to commission the artist to come in person to decorate one's home solely for private use. Apparently, these were high quality works. The folk craft items adorning Kanbun's home in Izumi paled in comparison, but then again they had a simple charm that suggested modest and simple beauty. Upon turning around, Kanbun noticed the elderly servant who had helped him to his room the evening before coming in his direction down the hall.

"Good day, sir," said Kanbun, "may I ask for something light to drink," lifting his hand to his mouth in an imaginary drinking from a cup. The servant turned wordlessly and led him to the kitchen where they sat together and sipped a cup of yellow herbal tea. The elder man still kept his silence, and Kanbun wondered if he had offended him in some way. Reluctant to press the matter, he said nothing. Suddenly, several iron pots that had been left to dry beside a washing basin behind where the old man was sitting shifted and fell to the floor with a great clatter. The dull expression on the face of the aged servant changed not even slightly as he waved a fly away from his temple. It was then that Kanbun realized the old man was deaf but could speak. Kanbun smiled broadly, and for the first time the servant responded with a smile and an audible "hao, hao." The old man lifted the pot to pour Kanbun some more tea, but Kanbun dipped his head and waved his hand over the cup in refusal. Kanbun stood and gestured as though he would like to use the toilet as he felt the heavy quantity of food he had eaten the day before working its way through his system. The old man chuckled and led him out the back door of the kitchen to a small shack attached to a woodshed. Like most toilets in rural or agricultural communities there was a pot to catch the night soil that would be used later for fertilizer in the fields. Kanbun turned to settle himself when he noticed painted on the opposite wall a savage bull with its enflamed snout lowered and shoulders arched as if it were about to plunge its weight into a mighty charge. Something echoed in Kanbun's memory to one of Jou's obtuse statements. He laughed to himself as he recalled the comment at dinner the night before when Jou mentioned something about wrestling an ox to prod his digestion.

Afterwards Kanbun went for a stroll to the top of the short rise behind the great house. From this vantage point he could see more of the broad fields dotted by laborers tending to the crops. In the distance a river cut a swath with meandering tributaries bordered by high grass and branching off here and there supplying water to the maturing vegetable and rice fields. To the west beyond the irrigated farmland, the earth rose up into craggy hills with stony cliffs and evergreen trees. Kanbun saw the stretch of flat roadway he and Jou had taken the day before that led to the neighboring village just barely visible in the distance to the northeast. Directly in front of him was a small orchard of peach and pear trees with dark green leaves and whose fruit would be ready before long to be picked. At his back was a bamboo grove of green stalks and delicate branches swaying, bending, and shifting whenever a breeze would pass through their upper branches. Kanbun sat with his legs crossed in front of him and his wrists resting on his ankles. His mind stretched and pushed to the limit his knowledge of Chinese as he slowly composed the humble but earnest request he would make to Master Jou.

He must have been daydreaming longer than he realized for when he looked up from his thoughts he noticed the farm workers were already making their way back from the fields. Kanbun jumped up and walked back down the hill to the compound. He was beginning to feel a little hungry, but Jou was nowhere to be found and he was unsure whom to ask about something to eat. He also wondered if Jou's kind hospitality of a place to sleep would be extended beyond a single night. He found himself at the base of the platform Jou sat on in the training area, but there was no one in sight, so he returned to the room in which he had slept. On the table beside his rough pallet, there was a plain wooden tray with a bowl of rice, some dumplings and vegetables, a cup of tea, and a new pair of cloth slip-on shoes. He sat on the cotton quilting on the floor and munched thoughtfully on the food that had been left. Before long he heard the sound of people entering the open area on the other side of the courtyard wall and chattering in the dialect of Nanyoi so Kanbun understood very little of what they said. Kanbun went back to the ledge on the wall and watched the students striking at the wooden posts, lifting ceramic jars with their fingertips by the lip at the top and walking with short steps, stretching their legs, torso, and neck, or using sections of bamboo sticks to pound at their forearms and legs, and rolling a stone wheel up and down their shins. The group included students Kanbun had seen the night before, and some of the training reminded him of his daily instruction with Grandfather and the sessions with Makabei, but particular movements and methods were new to him. The youthful banter continued until Jiang and Lee entered and began making corrections in the low postures or adjusting the position of the elbows or knees of their students. The group fell into silence as training continued in earnest and the two seniors guided their charges through breathing exercises, strengthening drills, and two-man parrying techniques. Apparently, Jiang was the most senior among the group present. Like Jou, he was a large man, built firmly, and had long hair that was tied loosely back around his head. He had no whiskers, but his face was rough. His loose clothing seemed to fit him and his personality just right, so he had an air of comfort and confidence as he moved among the younger students. Sometimes he would work with an individual, at other times with a pair, or step back and observe the overall activity. Kanbun watched with deep fascination until Jiang called for the training to halt. The two seniors stood in front of the group with legs slightly parted but firmly planted as Jiang addressed them. He complimented them on their effort, but urged them to apply themselves with greater initiative and the spirit of a tiger at the next training session. With that, all left the training area. Kanbun felt uneasy that Jou had not appeared. He was beginning to feel lonely again as it seemed hardly anyone knew he was there. He returned to his room and lay on his bedding facing the ceiling. It had already grown dusky outside and the lack of windows in the room made the atmosphere heavy and dark. His mind drifted over the training exercises he had just seen. Soon his thoughts led him to a gentle and silent sleep.

For the next few days, Kanbun continued to watch silently the nightly training sessions taking place on the other side of the wall from where he stayed. He was disappointed that Jou did not return at all and was beginning to wonder if he had left the district. In the mornings, Kanbun would go to the kitchen where the elderly but kind and deaf servant would be directing the preparation of a simple breakfast consisting primarily of rice porridge, soup, and vegetable pickles for himself, the other household help, and Kanbun. The other servants ignored Kanbun and chatted or joked among themselves. However, the kind man seemed to take a grandfatherly interest in Kanbun and would smile broadly as he handed him a dish of hot broth or a bowl mounded with white rice. For his part, Kanbun would help with washing the dishes and kitchen utensils after meals. Sometimes the deaf man would give Kanbun little chores to do or take him along when he went out to pick fresh vegetables from the garden or herbs used for flavoring. From what he could gather of the other servants' conversation, the elderly man was called Old Wu, and though he was quite deaf, he seemed to know when someone called out his name to get his attention. One day, using his index finger to draw imaginary characters in the palm of his hand, Kanbun asked Old Wu for some paper and a writing instrument. Old Wu went to a sideboard and produced some sheets of rough paper, a well worn horsehair brush, an ink stone, a hardened stick of compressed ink, and a ceramic tumbler of water. Kanbun poured a little water on the stone and rubbed the ink stick across it until it produced a dark black liquid. He dipped the brush in the ink and then wrote in script, "My name is Uechi Kanbun." At this Old Wu looked perplexed until Kanbun wrote beside this in larger characters, "Sanra."

"Ah, ah, Sanra," nodded the old man and he smiled.

In this way, Kanbun and Old Wu communicated writing simple phrases for each other. After Kanbun had written such things as "thank you for the new shoes," "my country is Ryukyu," and "I hope to learn *wushu*."

Old Wu took up the brush, but did not respond to what Kanbun had written. Instead, he wrote, "I present you these writing tools." The elderly servant laughed warmly at the surprised and pleased expression on the young man's face. Kanbun lifted the materials to his forehead as he bowed deeply in gratitude. Old Wu picked up the brush again and wrote, "Now, I go" and with that he shuffled out of the room.

Kanbun took his collection of writing apparatus to his sleeping room outside the training area and sat down at the table beside his bedding. On a fresh sheet of paper he continued composing his collection of words and his diary of information that he had recorded on bits of paper saved from the days, weeks, and months earlier. First he wrote the Chinese character for "home" and then in the Japanese phonetic alphabet the pronunciation in both standard Mandarin and the Fujian dialect next to it. He followed this with "grandfather," "father," "mother," "younger brother," and "lonely." His next grouping included "*wushu*," "tiger," "strength," "effort," "posture," "stance," "breath," "spirit," "eyes," "stomach," and "perseverance." He went on this way through the day until he had exhausted most of his Chinese vocabulary and had quite tired himself out, too. Finally, he wrote "Kazue" and pronounced softly how it might sound in Chinese. There were many gaps in his list of Chinese pronunciations and even more for that of the local dialect. But, he was pleased because he knew that he could ask to have a single or compound of Chinese characters pronounced for him in the Fujou dialect, and then he could transliterate it into the Japanese phonetic alphabet for a close approximation of the sound. In time he would expand his notebook to include phrases, expressions, and sayings as he learned them. He fell back on his sleeping pallet and closed his eyes while a vision of strings of Chinese characters danced inside his head.

Jou did return several days later taking Kanbun aside for a conversation. Kanbun had thought long and hard and was anxious to make his formal request to Jou for instruction in *wushu*, but he waited patiently for the older man to begin. Much to Kanbun's surprise, it was Jou who raised the topic at the beginning of the conversation.

"Sanra," he began with the local name he had given Kanbun. "Come to the stone courtyard on the other side of the wall from your room this evening. I have a couple of students, Jiang and Lee, who can start teaching you some of the tiger *wushu* we practice. I have already told them you will come, so there is no need to be shy about joining the training session. I know there are different kinds of *wushu* that the people of Ryukyu do, and my friends who are merchants that trade with your country have told me about them. I also understand you have done some training

140

yourself. Now that I think about it, you were the guy I saw jump on top of the wall outside the Fujou government house to escape those three ruffians who attacked you the other day. You didn't know then, and I did not know it was you, Sanra, but I was watching from the tea house across the street."

Kanbun nodded, but didn't interrupt.

Jou continued on, "I am only a couple of years older than you. I am twenty-three and you are twenty, so we are both quite young and need to learn and experience much to become more mature, especially in *wushu*. What we do here at my residence is a form of the tiger style of *wushu*. I have learned a few fundamentals from experienced teachers and put that together with some of the traditions passed down in my family and others I have picked up locally. Jiang and Lee have potential, but the others are merely rough material. Even though they won't develop into much, I have my reasons for letting them practice here. This will be a good way for you to get to know some of the people in the area of Nanyoi. Learn from them, not only *wushu*, but the way they think, express themselves, and interact with each other."

Kanbun thought Jou was, just as he had done at the ferry boat landing, speaking more modestly about himself than was the actual case. Jiang and Lee, the two top students in Jou's group, appeared skillful and equal to most of those who were skillful at *toodi* in Ryukyu. He had felt certain that this was the *wushu* he wanted to learn. However, Kanbun was seeing *wushu* with an inexperienced eye and in truth had very little with which to make a more sophisticated comparison. Kanbun felt a creeping disappointment that he would be lumped together with the "rough material" that Jou had just mentioned. However, Jou surprised him even more with his next statement.

"Kanbun," he said, "there are highly skillful men in Fujou whose depth and understanding in *wushu* are far greater than mine. I have made arrangements for you to train in the morning with Hsu-sabu who lives nearby. '*Sabu*' is the local dialect for '*sifu*,' which you probably know means honored teacher. He is a rather odd character, keeps to himself, is not well liked by the neighbors, and has had only a couple of followers. But make no mistake, there is no one in this area who is as advanced and expert in *wushu* as he. He and I are acquainted, I respect him a great deal, and the way that others misjudge him is their misfortune. He rarely shows anyone what he can do, but I have seen him do things that I doubt I will ever be able to duplicate or perhaps understand. The practice you will do at my home will supplement what you will learn from Hsu-sabu. He is to become your true teacher. You should know that this is a rare opportunity. Hsu-sabu hardly ever teaches anyone anything about what he knows. I had to persuade him that you have a worthwhile background and prospects, and eventually he agreed because of our friendship."

Kanbun was excited, but his mind raced because he was also confused by Jou's arrangements. In Ryukyu, it was customary to have one teacher. Anything else would be insincere on the part of a young hopeful; besides, no two teachers would impart anything meaningful to the same disciple. As he thought about this, he remembered that so much was different from his homeland. In China, he had seen, heard, and experienced people as if they were from another world. He realized that this was one more way in which the culture and customs were distinct. In the instant it took

142

for these thoughts to pass through his mind, Kanbun kneeled and touched his head to the ground in gratitude.

Jou went on, "Master Hsu practices a *wushu* that is an amalgamation of different styles that were originally taught in the Shaolin Temple of Fujian. Principally, they are the tiger, crane, and dragon. The tiger is powerful yet light on its feet. It is stealthy and cunning, taking its prey by surprise with bursts of power. When defending, it is quick, spirited, and makes little room for an opening. Master Hsu teaches tiger style that bears some resemblance to what I and my students practice. The crane is graceful, focused, and yet elusive. It is able to leap high into the air and leave its attackers clutching below, like you did against those three amateurs in Fujou. It uses both wings at once, which you can learn to do with your two arms and legs, for smooth defensive measures. No one has ever seen a dragon, though some fools and fakers say they have. As an imaginary creature, it is distinguished by its fiery breath, slivery maneuvering, and unshakeable grip. Our breath is the essence of our life, and with it you can dominate your thoughts, your passions, and your opponents. It helps you understand timing, which is crucial in most things. You can learn much about someone by merely watching their breathing, and the breath of the dragon is fearsome. It has fire in its eyes and breath. The dragon also moves in unpredictable ways, which you can learn, too. Once a dragon has caught hold of something or someone in its grasp, there is no letting go. Of course, Hsu-sabu's forms mimic the movements of these three animals and there is overlap in the characteristics and strengths of them, as well as others. These are just the physical manifestations and there is much more. I teach my students as best I can, but Master Hsu will address the heart of the matter, which you will learn over time."

"I see. "I will do my best and follow his instruction with dedication."

"Good," replied Jou, abruptly turning away and entering the manor before Kanbun could rise from the ground.

Kanbun returned to his room excited and hardly able to wait for the evening practice. He was the first to arrive inside the stone paved courtyard. He waited a while until a couple of students arrived and began stretching and exercising, but they only conversed with each other and ignored him. Later, after more students had entered the enclosed space, Jiang and Lee also arrived. Lee was smaller and thinner and he wore his clothing in lighter shades and trimmed more closely than Jiang. His movements and instructions were also more compact and precise. There was an air of aloofness about him and he seemed to say less than he knew, but it was clear when he did act that there was speed and power behind his reserve. Lee gave Kanbun a bamboo broom and told him to sweep the area, which he did. When Kanbun finished, Jiang and Lee called the group to attention and began instructing in the same way Kanbun had observed on the nights earlier. They said nothing else to him, so when he finished he set the broom against the wall, sat in a kneeling position, and began to watch the activities from eye level. This continued for several weeks. Sometimes Jiang or Lee would tell Kanbun to do other chores or bring tea from the kitchen after a particularly vigorous set of exercises. At these times, the instructors would engage the students in small talk or tell them stories. Most of this was in the Fujou dialect or about people or places Kanbun didn't know, so he understood very little of what they said. Trying to catch some of the conversation or make out what people were saying with his limited Chinese was mentally tiring, but he was able to piece together some of what was being said from the context and their gestures. He did, however, clearly recognize words or phrases here and there and began to remember the names of the other students and the terms they used for their movements. After the practice sessions, Kanbun returned to his room, would try to remember new expressions, and then write them down.

One evening, Lee approached Kanbun.

"Sanra," he said, "stand like this," which Kanbun imitated. "Now move your hands like this. Move your left foot forward and plant it like this. Extend your hands in front of you and raise them up like this, but keep your shoulders down. Roll your hips under and firm your belly. For now, breathe naturally. Don't worry about understanding yet, for now just try to do as I do."

As Lee indicated, Kanbun did not understand, but he did as he was instructed. Kanbun continued to do these movements over and over until the session ended. The next night was more of the same, except Jiang told Kanbun to join in the stretching, strengthening, and conditioning exercises the other students were doing. Occasionally, Jiang or Lee would stand in front of Kanbun, observing, making corrections, or encouraging him to apply more strength and spirit into his repetitions. Kanbun was young, strong, and physically and mentally well conditioned from his training sessions with Grandfather in the bamboo grove in Izumi, so he was an apt student who learned quickly and applied his energies to developing his new skills. Though Jiang and Lee allowed him only to progress slowly from one sequence to another, Kanbun trained enthusiastically and was polite to the others in the group. The students began to accept him, regularly involving him in their routines, helping him when needed, and including him in their greetings and eventually in conversations. Occasionally, Jou would stop by to observe or comment at the end of the sessions, but Kanbun saw him only on those occasions and only from across the courtyard.

In the meantime, his morning sessions with Hsu-*sabu* were something else altogether. Kanbun felt a little apprehensive about learning from Hsu. Invariably, he arrived as early as possible, because there was no appointed time. Sometimes Hsu would rise at his leisure and come out of his home, which was more of a hut than a proper house, after breakfast and a cup of tea. At other times, Hsu would be waiting impatiently for Kanbun no matter how early he arrived. In the beginning, Hsu was vague and brusque in his teaching. He would demonstrate simple movements for Kanbun and say, "Now repeat. This is called *sanchin* in the Fujou dialect and it is the most basic and at the same time the most important thing you will learn here. It is early for you to understand this, but in time you will see that all lies within *sanchin*," he added.

There was something familiar to Kanbun about what Hsu said, thinking that it sounded vaguely like one of the sets of calligraphy on the walls inside Jou's home, but he put the thought aside for the time being. While Jiang or Lee would be more precise, often correcting his position or form, Hsu was general with his guidance and comments. It was also clear that Hsu expected Kanbun to summon his inner spirit and practice with fire in his eyes, breath, and belly.

Still a little unsettled and curious about the different styles of training morning and evening, one day Kanbun asked, "Master

Hsu, I am confused. How do I follow your guidance while paying attention to the instructors at Master Jou's house? They are focusing on the tiger style, while I understand that we are also employing the motions and advantages of the crane and dragon. What if they teach me something different from what you do?"

Hsu chuckled and responded, "You are getting some of both worlds, and you will have to decide if one is more beneficial and useful than the other. You can call what we do *"pangainoon,"* which is local dialect, but the Chinese characters mean half hard and soft. It is the two together that create something balanced and complete."

Kanbun pondered this for a while. It seemed that his host, Jou, and the teacher, Hsu, were suggesting complementary approaches to training in *wushu*. In Ryukyu, it was customary for there to be one teacher for any student and anything more would result in contrary objectives. It was a question that he would save for another time.

One day, Jou came to see Kanbun during the mid-morning. He said, "Sanra, I want you to do a couple of things."

"I will do anything you request," replied Kanbun, "and I want to thank you for allowing me to join your students and for your kind introduction to Master Hsu to learn *wushu*."

"During the day, between your morning and evening training, I want you to help Old Wu with gardening. He doesn't hear well, but he knows a lot, more than I do about growing plants and herbs. More importantly, he knows how to apply them or mix them together so that they can be used for health, illnesses, treatments, and injuries. He can teach you the cures for almost any kind of ailment. He also knows where to look for plants, bark from trees, berries, mushrooms, and other

147

ingredients that you can't cultivate and only grow on their own in the wild. Listen and learn from him. He can teach you about medicines and treatments that have been developed over the centuries and contain the accumulated wisdom of many generations."

Kanbun listened intently to understand as best he could and because he wanted to show his interest and gratitude to Jou.

"And, be careful what you say," said Jou.

"I'm sorry," replied Kanbun with surprise on his face.

"I have heard you offer to do anything on other occasions," Jou responded. "You have to think before offering to do 'anything' for someone. You don't know what might be asked of you."

Though Kanbun was sincere about his offer, he realized that this was a direct translation of what he might say in Ryukyu as a standard response to someone to whom one is in debt. This was a valuable lesson from Jou about whom he could trust and exercising discretion in his relationships. He also made a mental note of the differences in culture, communication, and implication. Even though words in Chinese and Japanese sometimes could be interchangeable, how they were used and intended might be subtly different.

Kanbun nodded, Jou went on, "Tomorrow morning early, when the daylight begins and before you have breakfast, come to the training area."

"Yes sir," replied Kanbun, curious as to what this could mean.

The next morning Kanbun woke extra early, before daybreak, waited for a while in his room, and then went outside to the stone courtyard when he saw the first grey light in the spaces around the manor. He waited for Jou who arrived soon afterwards.

Jou greeted him and began by asking, "How are the *wushu* training sessions going?"

Kanbun thanked him again and replied that he felt his progress was slow, but he was eager to learn what Master Hsu called *pangainoon*.

"Ah yes," replied Jou, I think *pangainoon* is a particularly good fit. You see, though the lessons and wisdom of Buddha and Confucius are dominant in the way most Chinese think and live, Master Hsu and I, in addition to valuing these sensible and spiritual traditions, are also Daoists. There is a balance to most things in nature and under the heavens. *Pangainoon* is a general term that expresses that balance.

Jou went on, "I think you understand that it takes time and there is much to learn here and to discover on your own. Jiang and Lee have been with me for over five years, they are Chinese so they understand our ways instinctively, and they are skilled and strong. I work with them later in the evenings on *wushu* that I don't show to the other students. They, in turn, help me to improve, though they may not realize it. There are secrets in technique, in training methods, in developing power, and in relations to others and society. They have pledged to keep these secrets for there are risks and dangers in this world, especially these days in Fujou, Fujian, and greater China. This applies even more so to what you learn from Master Hsu. As I said, I don't understand all that he does, because there is great depth to his learning and abilities. He has the very soul of the deep. Would you like to try to learn about some of this?"

"Yes sir," replied Kanbun enthusiastically.

"Good, you are to continue in the mornings with Master Hsu. The practice sessions with Jiang and Lee will balance what you and he will do in the morning. Study and learn from Old Wu during the day. In time, there will be more to say about that.

The next morning, Hsu said he would like to see some of what Kanbun learned from the evening practices. He did as he was told, and Hsu watched carefully. Hsu explained that that shape, form, and method framed his practice, but it was his internal will, his spirit, that would be much more important. Hsu then showed Kanbun some new exercises. They did push-ups on their finger tips, fists, and bent under wrists. Hsu put flat stones on Kanbun's lower back to make him work harder to push himself up. Kanbun adapted to these exercises quickly because of the training and strengthening exercises Grandfather had taught him by holding, lifting, turning, and rotating ceramic jars with stones in them in Izumi. Next, they did squatting exercises, which were easy for Kanbun because of his sturdy legs. Again, Hsu taught Kanbun not only to boost the power in his legs by carrying large stones on his shoulders, but also to strengthen them while in motion. During a short rest period, Hsu explained that these were simple exercises and there would be others as well as more developed training and practice for Kanbun in due time.

"Sanra," he said during one of the rests, "you will learn to be powerful and graceful yet ferocious like a tiger, but you also need to develop a delicate touch and be light on your feet."

Kanbun thought a moment and said, "Master Hsu, I think I understand, but I am sorry I have only read stories or seen pictures of tigers. I have never actually seen a tiger anywhere."

"Ah," replied Hsu, "Watch the house cats that come to the kitchen for something to eat in Jou's home. They are small, like miniature tigers. They are delicate and gentle, but they can also be ferocious. They can jump from the ground up to several times there own height onto a counter top or window ledge. Most humans cannot do that. Tigers are fast and focused so that they can catch a speedy animal or a fluttering bird with the swat of a paw. You want to be able to move like a cat or a tiger, but there is more to learn than mere movement. It is a way of thinking, or better yet a way of not thinking at all. We will come to that in good time."

Kanbun took this all in as best he could. He was excited by what he was learning, but he had many questions and wondered what would come next. He kept his thoughts to himself and did as Jou suggested, helping Old Wu during the day, and putting his energy and concentration into the training sessions in the morning with Master Hsu. He continued to refer to the dictionary Kazue had given him and treasure its presence in his room. At night, before falling asleep, both thrilled and tired, he expanded his collection of new information into a kind of journal of things he had learned from Jou, Master Hsu, Old Wu, Jiang, Lee, the other students, the house helpers, and even the people in the village. He noted his thoughts and impressions, and drew pictures when he felt visually inspired or a drawing would depict more than his words. The next day he would try to insert his recently acquired knowledge in a phrase or expression to gauge the reaction of the listener to see if his usage or pronunciation were correct.

This cycle of rest, distinct yet related and balanced tutelage in the morning and evening, and learning from Old Wu became Kanbun's routine. In addition to the special exercises he practiced in the evening, Hsu taught him about learning and practice, what it could lead to and how it could be applied. In Taoist terms, Jou used examples from nature and society to illustrate his points, while Hsu prodded him to summon his inner self. At the same time, whenever Kanbun learned something new from Old Wu about the qualities and characteristics of an herb, mineral, liquid, or medicine and how they could be combined together for differing effects, he would write it down in a Cures and Remedies section he had created in his journal. He noted with words and pictures what the materials looked like, where or how they were gathered, the best times of year for harvesting them, the methods for mixing them together, and to what ailments they could be applied. In fact, there was so much to learn so quickly that Kanbun soon composed many more pages about these Chinese medicines than about his *wushu* training. The progress under Jiang and Lee and with the other students was slow by comparison, but he was becoming as skillful as the other students who had trained for a longer time in Jou's courtyard in the evenings. He got to know them all by name, the types of work they did in the fields, and where they lived. Some evenings he joined them in conversation after the training sessions had finished. By the end of the day, he was exhausted physically and mentally. He could piece together parts of the conversations he heard, but there were also gaps that left him wondering. He concentrated and listened as closely as he could, but sometimes the topics were out of his range or he missed key words and he stretched his mind to try to understand if what he missed was important. Besides, there was so much that was new and different. The way that people related to each other, their sense of humor, what they valued, what was important or insignificant to them could be quite different from what he was normally used to in Ryukyu. At other times, it seemed like the Fujou dialect and the Ryukyu dialect had natural cognates and similarities that he could only wonder why some things were so different and others just the same. The whole effect was at times baffling and often tiring to think about. It was stimulating to learn and think in new ways, but it was also so much that he felt fatigued and ready to sleep even during the day. The midday siestas, a custom of southern China, were also new to him but as welcome as the straw pallet when he lay down at night and easily fell asleep.

One day after his early morning practice and training with Hsu, Jou told Kanbun to join him on a visit into Fujou. He said, "Bring some of the herbs and medicines that Old Wu has taught you to use. While I am meeting with my friends, you should sell them on the street as you did when I first saw you in the city. You are making progress, but your Chinese is still limited and rough, so I want you to talk to as many people as possible even if you don't sell them anything. Speak with them, learn from them, not just the words, but how they communicate with each other. You apologize too much, which may be fine in your country of Ryukyu, but Chinese will not respect or like you if you say you are sorry so many times. Save your apologies for when you have done something obviously wrong or made a mistake that is clearly understood by others and you truly want forgiveness. This is different from being polite and respectful, which you are, so you will be appreciated by those you meet or know you because of it. Words are important, but in China it matters more how you carry yourself. Listen to what people say, but watch what they do."

Kanbun was puzzled. He was sincere in his apologies and he wanted to be thoughtful with others. However, he took it as fact that the people, language, and society were different in many ways here in China, and he would try to learn.

Jou went on, "The people you meet while selling herbs and medicines, indeed all the people in Fujou, are a resource for you. They are living, breathing, and thinking dictionaries, encyclopedias, reference books, and works of philosophy and literature. Learn from them all. If you want to know something, ask. If you don't understand something, have them repeat it. If it is hard to remember, write it down. They are all your teachers of language, customs, culture, society, politics, history, literature, philosophy, and much more. Whether they know it or not, whether they want to or not, they can give you knowledge, help you learn, and lead you to understanding and perception. Don't worry about being too polite or apologetic to Chinese, they will let you know quickly if you are a nuisance. The next person you meet may be more helpful."

On the boat ride across the Min River on the way into town, Kanbun asked Jou about the paintings and inscriptions on the hanging scrolls and the walls in his mansion.

"Master Jou, you have a beautiful collection of art and calligraphy in your home," he began. "I have never seen anything like them in Ryukyu. There must be famous artists in Fujou and they must have come all the way to Nanyoi to paint them for you."

"Ha," said Jou firmly, "I don't know anyone famous, except maybe my teacher who taught me how to look at an object and how to draw it, but I like to scribble as a hobby."

"You mean you are the artist," said Kanbun in surprise. "You are amazing, and the paintings and scrolls are beautiful."

154

"Brush work is worth learning, if you have an eye and talent," replied Jou, "but there are other things I want you to learn first."

As they entered the city, Jou began pointing to shop signs and illustrations here and there that he had painted. Kanbun was even more impressed. His respect and appreciation for Jou grew and he wondered how he had been so lucky to encounter such a talented man who was also generous and supportive of a poor foreigner from an undistinguished country. Jou guided him to the same tea house as before where he had arranged to meet his friends, and told Kanbun to set up his display of medicines across the street. While Jou was in the tea house, which was quite some time, Kanbun sold herbs and medicines and did his best to engage his customers or anyone who would speak with him. This was challenging for him because he was naturally shy, but he listened, learned, and later wrote down as much as he could remember.

In the next morning training session back in Nanyoi, Hsu began building from basic practice and training to the next level for Kanbun. He locked hands with Kanbun at chest level when doing lower body and leg strengthening-- pushing, pulling, and turning to build power and sturdiness in his stance and posture. He taught Kanbun to root himself to the ground, to draw strength and stability from the earth. If someone or something pushed against him, it should feel as if the energy flowed through his body to the ground beneath his feet. In that way, he would become as firm and steady as the ground on which he was standing; indeed, as if his opponent were trying to move the earth. Kanbun recalled the pushing, pulling, and wrestling with his donkey Baro in the bamboo grove in Izumi and put his effort into the exercises. Kanbun couldn't even budge Hsu, but he always felt his teacher was urging and leading him on to greater power.

Hsu, in an unusual session of spoken instruction, went on to explain, "you will develop your own strength with these exercises, in fluid, liquid, rolling, flowing, and dynamic motion and power. Linear strength and speed, which are straight back and forth or up and down, are useful at times, for work for example, but they are also one dimensional. Exercises that develop strength that result in powerful yet static muscles appear impressive or fearsome, but they are bulky and awkward when applied. Liquid power is subtle. You must develop strength and speed from any angle and any direction to be able to change or adjust part way through a motion when defending or attacking. You will be powerful yet supple, stable yet adaptable, strong yet flowing. Even more importantly, you also must learn to understand the strength of your opponents and the sources of their power. These exercises of pushing and pulling to test our balance and stability will help you measure your opponent so that you will know better how to respond. You may block, counterattack, sweep away, avoid, or simply escape depending upon how you sense the skills and positioning of your opponent when compared to your own."

That evening, Jiang and Lee had all the students work on drills strengthening their arms. They instructed the students to stand upside down on their hands with their feet against the courtyard wall. It was relatively easy for everyone to hold their balance while supporting themselves with their hands and arms. The students soon realized, however, that it was another matter to be able to sustain this position. It became a contest to see which student could hold up the longest. One by one the students gave up grunting and exhaling as their feet tumbled down to the ground and they sat on the stone floor. Kanbun was among those who could keep the position the longest. Jiang and Lee then demonstrated the same position, but they did push-ups on their hands, fists, and fingertips in this inverted posture. They invited the students to try as well. Most of the students were already fatigued, especially in the arms and shoulders, so they tumbled to the floor, laughing at themselves as they did, as soon as they tried bending their elbows in an upside down position. Kanbun and a few of the other more senior students were able to manage a few, but their arms were shaking and they could do no more.

"We will add these exercises to our routines so that your arms, hands, fingers, and fists become firm and steady like branches of hardwood," said Jiang.

Next, Lee paid particular attention to the arm and leg pounding and conditioning exercises they did in pairs or small groups. They began in a basic stance, rubbing their forearms against each other to warm up the muscles, stimulate the blood, pull down their shoulders, and strengthen their posture and foot positions. Next, in circular and striking motions, they pounded up and down the forearm of each other, from the wrist to the meaty part of the arm while moving back and forth in the same basic stance.

"Do these conditioning exercises after your arm and leg strengthening exercises," instructed Lee. "Pound your arms and legs like you are making rice cakes with a wooden mortar and pestle. The more you pound steamed sweet rice, the more it becomes thick, sticky, and malleable. Like rice cakes, your limbs will become firm yet flexible."

The next day, Hsu helped Kanbun develop the training from the night before to another level. Hsu showed Kanbun how to strengthen and stabilize his blocking, striking, and kicking still further.

He explained, "When you block with your arms, it is the stability of your stance that matters most. When you kick, it is the support of the other leg that determines how strong and effective the kick becomes. When striking with one hand it is always important to balance the position and strength of the other. Indeed, it is the action away from the center of activity that often determines the outcome of an encounter, because rarely does a single parry end anything. It is often the follow on or the follow through motions that carry the day."

One morning Hsu led Kanbun back to the courtyard in front of Jou's stately home. He had Kanbun kick with his toes the wooden posts that supported the second floor, as well as with the flats, sides, and heels of his feet. Kanbun felt and heard the thud reverberate up the posts, through his body, and down to his other foot. Then, as Kanbun lifted his right or left foot to kick, Hsu struck Kanbun's supporting foot or leg with his own kick. Most times Kanbun was able to stay on balance, but Hsu's kick forced him to concentrate on the supporting leg and subsequently his own kicks became more solid and the wooden support post sounded with a deeper thud. Next, Hsu grabbed or pulled at the arm Kanbun wasn't using when he struck the padded beams and wooden slats on the courtyard wall. Again, Kanbun had to concentrate on the still hand while using the other. Hsu explained that this was the meaning of Daoism, of inaction as well as action, the pushing and pulling of energy and its flow, forward and background and around in circles.

He went on, "Jou told me about how you met at the flooded Min River several months ago. Perhaps you did not realize it, but you demonstrated some of the flow of energy that day when you used the power of the donkey to assist you."

Hsu continued training Kanbun in this way while employing his spirited energy. He had Kanbun practice blocking, striking, kicking and moving forward, back, and to the sides and at angles. Kanbun began to see and feel how his breathing, his whole body, its connections to the earth, and his interactions with others were linked together in action and inaction, motion and stillness. He became aware of himself, gravity, and the forces he felt from Hsu.

As the autumn harvest, changing of the leaves, and the cool winds came and went, Kanbun continued his daily training with Hsu in the morning and Jiang, Lee, and the other students in the evening. Winter started with colder mornings and evenings, more than any Kanbun had experienced in Izumi. He began wearing cotton undershirts and long underwear beneath his outer clothing and wore padded jackets to keep his upper body warm when going out. The weather and temperature made no difference to the training routines. The strenuous training warmed him to perspiration, heavy breathing, and fatigue just the same. Jou took him on visits to Fujou, sometimes staying over night in an inn. At first, Jou showed Kanbun several temple gates and street corners where he could sell the herbs he had collected or medicines he had mixed together with Old Wu. Kanbun was able to fulfill his modest needs with the income he earned from selling the Chinese remedies and he practiced his Chinese by encouraging customers to purchase his wares, asking questions, and engaging in conversation with whomever he could. Old Wu gave Kanbun a metal pot in which to put coals to warm himself when he sat in his room writing, which he refreshened in the evening after *wushu* training when it was time for sleep. They continued to gather dried seeds, leaves, bark, juices from plants, and even insects, storing them in marked boxes or grinding and mixing them together with water, milk, or alcohol into concoctions. Kanbun recorded what he learned in his journal as they went along, noting both the methods for making the medicines as well as the applications Old Wu taught him.

When early spring arrived, Old Wu took Kanbun for long walks pointing out the angle of the sun, the color of the sky, the direction of the wind, and the moisture in the soil. He showed Kanbun delicate shoots that had sprouted beside rocks, in the forest, and between the rice paddies and vegetable fields that ordinarily no one seemed to notice. Some grew best in the shade, others liked the morning light, while still more lengthened and blossomed in the full strength of the sun beside rocks that collected and radiated heat. Old Wu talked as if each plant had its own personality and mission in life. He showed Kanbun where to find fruits and berries that were normally inedible. They gathered bits of nuts and shells, twigs and leaves, and even the dried droppings of rodents, animals, and birds whose materials might be added to a recipe to increase the potency or change a mixture into a different medication altogether. They collected snake skins, turtle and insect shells, fish scales and skins, and much more to add to their stores of materials and to employ in caring for, treating, and healing Jou's students, farm hands, servants, and neighbors. He didn't always understand Old Wu's reasons or

160

explanations, even when he asked the elderly gentleman to repeat something that was beyond his knowledge in Chinese. However, as Kanbun learned more and became surer of his ability to speak in Chinese with others, he was able to sell greater quantities and varieties of medicines in front of the temple gates and in the streets of Fujou. By now, Jou no longer told him where to set up his moveable shop, instead simply arranging to meet later at a given time at the teahouse where he first saw him.

By early summer, Kanbun was approaching his first full year in Nanyoi. He had learned the combined movements of a basic form called *sanchin* from Hsu. As at the beginning, Hsu pushed his pupil to generate spirited activity rather than focus on particular movements. Jiang and Lee encouraged him to train as hard as the other students in the evening classes. They tested his strength, stability, and breathing, and he worked hard with his fellow students to develop even more. Just as Grandfather had shown him in Izumi, they picked up ceramic jars holding the lip with their finger tips and bent thumbs, lifted them front and back, and swung them in circles. Jiang and Lee put water in the jars to increase the weight depending upon the skills of the student and gradually added more to develop greater strength and mobility over time. They did other training exercises with different kinds of equipment, too. Jiang and Lee tied a small grind stone with a length of rope to a hardwood pole. At different times during the evening, the students would take turns holding the wooden staff horizontally in front of them and rolling and unrolling the rope around the pole while lifting and lowering the stone. Their arms, wrists, and grips became like iron. At other times, the instructors would take just the hardwood pole and place it on two wooden boxes, and then have two students face

161

each other standing in position at either end of the staff. They would then have the students push their bellies against the ends of the staff to see who was stronger and more stable and to help each other develop further. Sometimes, for fun, the instructors also rolled wooden barrels into the stone courtyard where they were leading the training. While rolling the barrels, they would have the students run, leap, and land on top of them. Their objective was to stop the barrel from rolling, to maintain their balance on top, and to develop agility on a shifting surface. They also used the hardwood staff for other applications. Lee fastened a couple of metal disks to the end of the pole. Then, Jiang showed the students how to lift the pole straight out in front of them with one hand but without bending the wrist. In time, he taught them to tap back and forth in repetitions on small drums fastened to the posts supporting the floor above the courtyard. If the tap were too strong or heavy, it would pierce the drum. The objective was to have the wrist, forearm, back, and stance strength to swing the weighted staff but also to control it and have a delicate touch. Lee instructed them to hold the pole in one hand extended vertically out in front of their body, and then twisting their arm to the right and left without letting the weights touch the ground. And yet differently, they had the students hold the staff beginning the same way, but then swinging it around in a wide circle keeping their elbow straight until bending it and holding the end of the pole against their chin. Frequently, Jiang or Lee would take the small drums from the posts and beat out a rhythm with wooden sticks commanding the students to swing and control the weighted staff in syncopated motions. They explained that the training hardened the body, but the drum beat and rhythm soothed the mind. If they had the fortitude to repeat these exercises 10,000 times, they would achieve physical strength and mental confidence, and they would be able to apply their skills as if they were a natural part of who they were. Kanbun was reminded of Makabei and how strong and confident he was with the lead-filled bamboo staff, holding, swinging, and controlling it as if it were hollow. The memory motivated Kanbun to work harder putting his mental concentration and physical conditioning into these exercises every night.

One evening, Jou came to the evening training session while Jiang and Lee were instructing. Jou told the students to lean thick wooden planks against either end of the courtyard enclosure so they could walk up and onto the top of the wall, which he had them do one time completing a circle. Next, he had each of the students fill two ceramic jars with water, hold them at the lip with their thumbs and forefingers, and then walk the same course. He encouraged them to grasp the jars firmly, roll their shoulders back and down, lower their hips and center of balance by bending their knees slightly, and move with steady steps and their feet close to the ground, but also not to let the ceramic vessels drop and break on the ground. He explained that they needed not only to develop strength in their hands and feet through exercise and conditioning, but also to combine skills and be able to concentrate so they could engage in multiple demanding challenges at the same time. Some weeks later, after the students had improved at grasping the ceramic jars, mounting and descending the slanted planks, and balancing along the top of the courtyard wall while moving in a circle, Jiang and Lee had them dig a pit in the ground into which they poured the water from the containers. At this time, Jou arrived carrying a wooden bundle. The bundle was made of five or six small logs about a meter long and each 8-10 centimeters thick. They were tied together tightly at either end with a firm rope. He dropped the bundle into the water in the pit and told the students that this evening they would be practicing balance and lightness of foot, as opposed to the heavy stances and slow movements of walking while grasping the ceramic jars. This was the sturdy yet agile movement of the tiger style they were learning. To demonstrate, he set a foot onto the log bundle, walked across it to the other side of the pit, and stepped lightly back onto firm ground. Jiang and Lee followed by doing the same. The next most senior student tried and succeeded though not confidently. A few more, including Kanbun, were able to cross the pit of water on top of the bundle reaching the other side somewhat awkwardly. Kanbun remembered playing with Hiro in Grandfather's fishing boat and rocking it from side to side in the waves while trying to keep balance and from falling overboard. One student stepped onto the end of the bundle, which sunk under his foot and he slipped ending up knee deep in the water. The rest of the students laughed but encouraged him by saying he would do better the next time. Another student set his foot lightly on the bundle, but it spun around in the water so that his full body fell into the pit and he was completely soaked. Yet another took a running start and tried to skip across the pit of water, but the opposite end of the bundle lifted out of the water and soaked his chest. The students laughed even louder and cheered each other on as they tried their skill one by one. Many of them ended up slipping into the pit filled with water, splashing around, and getting soaked from falling off balance. Jou explained that in order to maintain balance while not sinking or slipping into the water, they needed to learn to be light on their feet, centered with their weight evenly distributed in their stance, and move their body as a single unit, rather than leaning heavily one way or the other. Jou, Jiang, and Lee demonstrated once again. The students also tried again, and the results were much the same. Jou told them that like other types of training that it would take repetition, time, and concentration to improve, but they could and would become better.

The next day when Kanbun arrived at Hsu's house, his teacher was waiting for him. Hsu guided him back to Jou's mansion where they met him. He led him to the pit with water in it. This time the logs were separated and lay floating apart in the water. Hsu told Kanbun that crossing the water on bundled logs was easy, and he would have to learn more to improve his balance and skills. To demonstrate, Hsu leapt with his sturdy body nimbly into the air and landed gently but evenly on one of the small logs. He held his balance for a few moments, bent his knees, and then leapt back onto dry ground. He went on to explain that not only was it necessary for Kanbun to be light on his feet, but he should land on one of the small logs with his legs spread and balanced from one end to the other so that his weight would be distributed uniformly along the entire log. If he did so, he could use the buoyancy and surface of the whole log on the water to sustain his weight. Then, he instructed Kanbun to try crossing without falling in the water. Kanbun surveyed the pit filled with muddy liquid and the small logs floating in the middle. He took a step back and with a quick leap cleared the water and pit completely. Jou roared with delight and threw an arm across Kanbun's shoulder.

"Oh ho, Sanra, you understand strategy better than I thought. Good for you. You jumped over the water in the same way you escaped those three thugs in Fujou," he added.

They all paused for a while sipping hot tea in the cool morning air. Hsu then returned to the training, "Now let's try crossing by actually stepping on one of the logs."

Kanbun tried, but he slipped toes-first into the water, which quickly swallowed his ankles. Kanbun stepped out of the water and tried again. This time the log skated away on the surface of the water and Kanbun fell flat on his backside. Thoroughly soaked and heavier than when he started, Kanbun tried again and again, but landed in the water each time. Hsu and Jou told him to add this training before his morning practices, but he should bundle up the sticks with a rope when he finished so that the other students could practice as usual in the evening. Hsu explained that Kanbun must learn even greater balance and delicacy to cross the water by stepping on the logs.

Hsu continued, "The transition of first going from dry land to balancing and walking on the bundle of logs to performing the same feat on the separated logs was merely the refinement of technique."

He elaborated, "If you merely accomplish a level of competence by reaching your initial goal, you have only achieved mediocrity. You must take the lessons you learn from your first struggle, apply the knowledge you have gained from the process, and then seek, make a goal of, and finally attain the next level of ability and comprehension. The way of natural balance is to perceive, strive for, and then achieve the next step."

Kanbun had marveled at the fineness of Jou's stroke with a brush on paper. Step by step Jou had polished his skills, and

Kanbun realized that his brush stroke was delicate but supremely confident and powerful, like the tiger subject in some of his paintings or the pithy phrases he chose for his scrolls. He realized that Jou's brush work was analogous to landing lightly on the floating logs in the water pit. There was definite power, even weight in the movements of Jou's hands and legs, but there was also nimbleness and subtlety. This thought led Kanbun to consider the depth of Daoism, the meaning of *pangainoon*, and their paradoxical yet complementary dynamics of hard and soft.

Kanbun also realized that what he was learning was a major step. While studying spirited *wushu* from Hsu, he now understood that he must also develop his character, think on his own, and apply himself to new challenges and not merely repeat what his teacher had taught him. Almost imperceptibly, Kanbun was beginning to feel more confident in his comprehension of Chinese, though there were times when the language of older folks or young children was difficult to understand. As he learned new words, phrases, and ways of expression, be began to practice by talking to himself in Chinese. He found that if he practiced patterns of speaking in Chinese by himself he would be more fluid in real conversations. He also began to dream at times in Chinese, but the sleeping world rarely made sense. Sometimes, in a dream, his grandfather would be encouraging or guiding him in *toodi* training, but he was speaking in Chinese, which Kanbun knew he could not do. Other times, a pretty girl from one of the nearby villages in Nanyoi would smile and offer greetings in Japanese, but there was no such person and no one there spoke his home language. He continued to keep a record of his impressions, new expressions, medicinal remedies, and *wushu* training. From time to time, he would re-organize his collection of writings, re-writing parts when he reached some new level of ability or comprehension after reflecting on his notes from pages he had composed months earlier.

One day, Jou took Kanbun into a curtained room that he had seen from the hallway the first evening he arrived at Nanyoi. There were paintings and inscriptions covering the walls, stacks of unfinished works sitting on tables and benches, brushes in hollow bamboo holders, loose drawings, and collections of different colored inks, some splattered on the floor and furniture. Kanbun looked around unable to absorb with his eyes more than a couple of the paintings and objects he saw. On the other side of the room were shelves and cases of books, some old, others new. Jou ignored the paintings at first and guided Kanbun to the book shelves against the wall and began handing volumes to Kanbun.

"Here," he said, "these are the *Analects* of Confucius as well as later commentaries about the sage philosopher. You know a lot of Chinese characters that are used in Japanese and your knowledge of our language is improving, so you should be able to digest something from these classics. Take them to your room and see if you find them useful. If you have questions, let's discuss them when we can."

Next, Jou dug out among a row of books the *Way of Life* according to Lao Tzu, tracts on Buddhism, Mencius, legalism, and even folk wisdom and superstitions. "These are more difficult, except for Lao Tzu, whom I find the simplest and the most helpful," he went on. "You will see that the teachings of Lao Tzu are deeply related to *pangainoon*, the category of *wushu* you practice with Master Hsu."

Jou also showed him such classics as the *Tale of the Three Kingdoms*, the *Water Margin*, *Monkey*, the *Dream of the Red Chamber*, and other traditional tales. He pointed out works by Li Bo and Po Chu-I, the great Tang Dynasty poets, and told Kanbun he could borrow them anytime. He also took out a slim volume on one of the book shelves and said, "This is an excellent work on strategy written originally in Japanese but is a Chinese translation. I don't know how you pronounce the surname of the author in Japanese, but the characters have the meaning of 'the base of the shrine.' He was a great swordsman and strategist who lived in Japan 300 years ago. His thinking draws from Chinese philosophy but his approach is wholly original. The meaning of the title is *Book of Five Rings*, and I recommend it. Perhaps you are already familiar with it. My good friend the tea merchant Wu Hsienkuei who does business with Ryukyu and Japan and whom I will introduce you to one day, gave it to me as gift from his travels. Kanbun recognized it immediately as the work of Miyamoto Musashi that his grandfather had talked about. Kanbun also remembered the tales and legends about the feats of strength and cunning of great martial men of Ryukyu. He knew that centuries earlier the imperial envoys from China who came to visit and stay at the Royal Court in Shuri had brought with them sophisticated knowledge and advanced training in "Chinese Hand" to Ryukyu. Some of those in Ryukyu who had been privileged enough to engage with these envoys had learned a great deal and over time some of it had spread to other martial men in the island country. Kanbun was amazed. He had never seen or heard of such a library of works related to philosophy, life's path, and martial ways. He stacked up a collection of books and carried them back to his room delighted to have them as companions.

Finally, Jou lifted a brush from among several in a hollow bamboo stand on one of the tables, dipped it into a tin of opaque black ink, and quickly and gracefully began to write on a sheet of rice paper. He composed a poem.

Whether it is clear
Or it is misted
The shape of the mountain
Is always a drum

"Here," he said, "this is to commemorate today's lessons. They are merely a first step and will have more meaning for you over time.

In time, Hsu led Kanbun to new and more developed training routines to complement his sessions. He instructed Kanbun to reduce the number of fingers he used when doing finger tip pushups from five to three fingers, then two, to only his thumbs, and eventually with just his index fingers. He also had Kanbun go from palms to knuckles to finger tips when doing his hand-stand push-ups. One day, Hsu spread rice grains on two boards, one made of pine and the other hard wood. He instructed Kanbun to practice picking up the grains of rice one at a time with a pecking motion, like a hawk eating its prey.

Hsu explained, "Your fingers are already strong and the tips are tough enough to dent the hardwood, which I want you to do. For the other board, you should pick up a single grain with a quick flick without actually touching the surface. Doing both will toughen and strengthen your finger tips while developing a light touch for pin-point accuracy. Someday, you will be able to catch a fish with your bare hands when it surfaces in a pond or stream, snatch a frog mid-jump at the water's edge, or grasp a fly between your thumb and forefinger as it buzzes by your face. Some say that you should be able to pluck the eyes out of a fish as it swims in a stream or catch a frog by its belly or snatch the wings from a fly with two fingers mid-air while its body drops into your other hand, but I find that kind of talk fanciful."

"There is a story, however, that illustrates this training," he continued. "There was an elderly *wushu* specialist in Fujian named Song Li who had developed this pecking technique to a high degree. One day, he was sitting by himself in a tea house. A tough young man who had been training for some years in *wushu* approached him and sat in the chair on the opposite side of the table. The young man challenged him to a duel, but the specialist ignored him and continued to sip his tea. The young tough became frustrated and escalated his challenge to a threat. Still, Song Li ignored him and pretended as if he were alone. The young man lashed out with a strike toward Song Li's head, but he simply pecked at the blow horizontally striking the forearm of his attacker and blocking it away. The young tough swung with his other arm, and the result was the same. Unnerved and angry, the young man got up and left the tea house. The next day, the young man returned and Song Li was sitting in the same chair. The young man's forearms had swollen to be almost twice their normal thickness and he was obviously in pain. The *wushu* specialist gave him two medicines, one to drink and the other to apply to his forearms. The young man then begged Song Li to become his teacher, which he agreed to do."

Another time, Hsu led Kanbun outside the courtyard behind Jou's great house where several wooden posts were planted in the ground. At first, he had Kanbun stand on two of the posts with his feet spread wide apart and knees bent as if he were sitting on a horse. Next, Hsu placed two medium-sized flat stones on Kanbun's knees to increase the strain on his legs. Kanbun stood still and silent holding his weight and the stones. Hsu explained that Kanbun could develop strength and stability in his legs with stillness as well as motion and advised him to add this exercise to his routine.

The next day, after Kanbun had returned from his midday wanderings with Old Wu to Jou's estate, he caught the distinct scent of incense. When he entered the courtyard, he discovered there were two bundles of burning incense about 30 centimeters apart set on the edge of a table and a pendulum positioned behind them. Hsu told Kanbun to stand on the opposite side of the table and watch the pendulum when he set it in motion. After it had swung a few times, Hsu reached out and stopped the swinging pendulum. Next, he instructed Kanbun to come around to his side of the table, kneel on the ground, and place his head between the two bundles of burning incense. He said that he would re-start the pendulum and Kanbun should again follow its motion, but only with his eyes. If Kanbun turned his head, his cheeks would get burned by the incense. Hsu explained that it was important training to be able use the eyes without moving the body. There were also muscles that guided the motion of the eyes that needed to be developed, and there were times when he would need to use only his eyes and keep the rest of his body still for strategy and defense. Hsu instructed Kanbun with multiple varieties of training techniques pointed toward conditioning his sturdy body, sharpening his young mind, and energizing and focusing his will to improve.

The weeks passed into months as the seasons changed and Kanbun settled into his life in Nanyoi. The cycle of the seasons and the rhythm of agricultural life were especially prominent as the tenant farmers fertilized the land before the start of spring with manure from livestock and night soil collected from outhouses over the winter, plowed the fields with mules and oxen in early spring, sowed the crops in rows before the rainy season began, opened rivulets for the excess water to flow into the brooks, streams, and rivers, pulled away the weeds and grasses that choked the plants or robbed moisture and nutrients from the soil in the hot summer, gathered the produce during the harvest, took the goods to market for their share in the bounty, and stored enough that would hold them over once again until the season changed. For the several cold months of winter, when the soil, sun, and sky were inhospitable to growing much of worth, the farmers repaired their homes and equipment in preparation for the coming year. Interspersed in the annual, laborious, and demanding cycle of preparation, planting, growth, harvest, and semi-hibernation were festivals and ceremonies that celebrated significant events in the agricultural calendar, religious traditions, and tales of heroic deeds in the face of invading armies or the fearsome forces of nature. Kanbun was reminded of the colorful seasonal festivals in Motobu and Izumi and he felt more than a little homesick for the excitement of anticipation for the big days, the festive clothing, the rhythm and sway of drums, the tunes played on stringed instruments and flutes, the warmth of mixing with his neighbors and friends, and the opportunity to dance or perform *bo kobujutsu* with his friends and neighbors.

Kanbun continued to collect seeds and cuttings, plant them in a small garden he had dug, and watch and care for them as they grew. Old Wu explained the purposes of the plants, when best to harvest, and how to extract their essence, combine them with other materials, and store them for later use. Kanbun read through the books that Jou had lent to him and expanded his notebook of Chinese words and phrases, medicinal recipes, *wushu* descriptions, and observations from life in the rural area outside of Fujou. His understanding and conversational abilities in Chinese improved and Kanbun began imperceptibly to take on some of the features and characteristics of those around him. His replaced his worn out clothing from Ryukyu with Chinese garb, he tied his hair back as it grew longer, and his manner came to resemble other inhabitants of Nanyoi and Fujou. Jou continued to take Kanbun to Fujou from time to time so that he could sell on street corners and in front of temples the herbs he grew and the medicines he concocted under the instruction of Old Wu.

On one trip into Fujou, Jou invited Kanbun to join him at a teahouse to meet some of his acquaintances. Among them was a young man who despite his youth exuded a quiet confidence. He was educated and sophisticated, and the kind of person that others paused to listen to when he spoke. He was Wu Hsienkuei, a merchant who like Jou was classically trained and a landowner, but whose tenants grew tea bushes from which they harvested the deep green leaves in the spring and early summer before hanging them to dry in storehouses or grinding them into powder. Wu's clothing was finely woven and cut and he wore it well. He dealt in the trading markets in and around Fujou, Fujian, and even made regular shipping visits to Naha in Ryukyu. He spoke Japanese, some of the Ryukyu dialect familiar to Kanbun, and was a student of the white crane style of southern Chinese *wushu*. Jou introduced Kanbun to Wu and explained that they were comrades in *wushu* and that Kanbun could speak openly with such a trusted friend. For Kanbun, there was something immediately sympathetic and comfortable in meeting this acquaintance of Jou. He had the air of a kindred spirit.

Wu began by speaking in Japanese, "Shandi, where do you come from and what is your name in Japanese."

"My name is Uechi Kanbun and most everyone here, except Master Jou, calls me Shandi Wanwen, which still sounds a little funny to me, but I am getting used to it. Master Jou calls me 'Sanra,' he replied. Kanbun wrote the characters for his name with his finger tip on the table top, and Wu nodded.

"I am amazed because your Japanese is remarkable and you sound completely natural. I have missed speaking Japanese and am so glad to have this opportunity to converse with you. My home is a hill town called Izumi on the Motobu Peninsula in the Kunigami County in the northern districts of Ryukyu. My parents, grandparents, and younger brother live there and do farming and some fishing in the harbors of Motobu and Nago," he explained.

"I see," replied Wu, "which ship did you board to travel to Fukushu? I know many of the shippers, merchants, and traders at the port of Naha, but I have only passed by Nago or Motobu."

"I don't remember the name of the captain but the ship was the Heavenly Dragon. The captain spoke Japanese with a Chinese accent and had a first mate named Chen," replied Kanbun.

"Ah, I know who you are talking about," said Wu. "He transports cargo, and for an additional fee he takes on Ryukyu stowaways who are fugitives from the Japanese draft and the local authorities in Naha who enforce it. It is a risky business, but it is part of the exchange between Fukkensho and Ryukyu."

Kanbun had imagined that his parents had to pay a sum for his safe passage to Fukushu, but this was the first time anyone

175

had suggested that it might be costly. He knew that his parents had little cash and the only way they could afford his passage to Fukkensho was to trade some of their possessions or borrow from a money lender, which they never mentioned to him. In any case, it was certain they were doing with less at home because of his escape to Fujou. Kanbun imagined his dear and gentle mother selling her formal kimono that she saved for special occasions, such as his future wedding. He was saddened to have caused his family such a burden, and this was compounded by the homesickness he felt when speaking in Japanese with Wu. He pictured his family at home sitting on rice straw tatami mats around the low table at meal times, slurping on noodles and miso soup and digging with their chopsticks into simmered vegetables, fish, and rice. He could almost smell the briny fragrance of the miso soup and longed to see his family.

"At one time, Jou and I practiced crane style together. And, I have heard of *toodi* but have never seen it performed," said Wu. "I wonder if it resembles the *wushu* some of us practice here in Fukkensho. Would you mind showing me someday?" he asked.

"It would be an honor Master Wu," replied Kanbun breaking from his reminisces. "I only learned a little in Izumi, but Master Hsu and Master Jou are teaching me so much more. In Ryukyu, I also learned *kobujutsu* privately from my grandfather and in the village festivals, which for me was training with the *bo*. The *toodi* you mention is what we call the Chinese method of martial arts, which we learned from the Imperial Envoys from China who over the centuries have visited Ryukyu and attended official ceremonies at Shuri Castle," he explained.

"There is no need to be so formal here in Fukushu," replied Wu, "please feel free to call me Wu. And, I am sure 'Master Jou' would be equally uncomfortable with such a lofty title. Jou has told me that he has helped you as a student and a friend for about two years and that you show some promise. Let's practice together one day, but in a private setting."

Wu and Kanbun returned to speaking in Chinese and they chatted with Jou for a while before they were joined by several others in the tea house. The conversation flowed from the current typhoon season and its effects on the crops and markets to the local and national politics to a discussion of who in the Fujou area was the most skillful at differing types of *wushu*. Kanbun listened while Jou and Wu joined the others in talking about the weather and politics, but he noted that neither made comments in the conversation about *wushu* or the merits of one form over another. Those that did speak of the hard and soft styles, of the various systems based on the dog, snake, monkey, bear, cock, swallow, hawk, praying mantis, crane, tiger, leopard, dragon, and more, apparently had been studying from refugee monks from the Southern Shaolin Temple. These students risked persecution by the Ching Court in Peking for advocating against the government. There was such a mix of styles, flows of influences, and varying beliefs that it was difficult to determine who or what was genuine and effective. It was clear, however, that there were secrets that ranged from political intrigue to clandestine societies to criminal gangs to the practice of *wushu* and most everything else in between. Whatever this group of acquaintances expressed openly, there was much more occurring out of sight and in private conversations. Kanbun listened and tried to absorb as much as he could.

After the conversation had continued for a while, Jou and Wu prepared to leave; Jou for Nanyoi and Wu for the port of

Fujou. Wu turned to Kanbun and said knowingly in Japanese, "I'll look forward to seeing you again when we will have the opportunity to speak more."

"Thank you," replied Kanbun. "By the way, could you write your name so it will be easier for me to remember?"

Wu borrowed a brush from the owner of the tea house, wrote the Chinese characters on a piece of rice paper, showed it to Kanbun, and added, "As you can see, you read the characters in Japanese as 'Go Kenki,' which is what they call me in Naha."

***

On the way back to Nanyoi, Kanbun asked Jou about the *wushu* discussion in the tea house and the tiger style he was teaching.

"Well, Sanra, what did you think of the conversation," asked Jou in return.

"It was interesting and I learned a lot, but I am not sure they are very accomplished at *wushu*," replied Kanbun.

"That's right, they engage in important commerce in Fujou, but they are also a bunch of *wushu* amateurs who talk more than they train. Wu and I humor them with conversation, but we rarely touch the heart of the matter with them. There are many unscrupulous priests and teachers of *wushu* who charge a lot of money, either all at once or over a long period of time, for useless training and information, and those big talkers are their products." said Jou.

Kanbun continued, "So far, other than the dragon breathing I do with Master Hsu, there are no apparent animal movements in our practice. The training is great and I feel I have developed and improved in so many ways, but where are the animal-like motions that the others mentioned," asked Kanbun.

"What Master Hsu teaches, but only to very few and to the extent that I understand, is a system that utilizes the spirited breathing of the dragon, as you noted, but also the motions and techniques of the tiger and the crane," explained Jou. "I think I may have mentioned this about two years ago when you began training with my students. The dragon has fire in his eyes and breath and maneuvers well. The tiger has stealth and power and yet is light footed. The crane surprises because it is so graceful while being effective. My good friend Wu may have mentioned that for a while we practiced the white crane style together, which we did, but it is different from the tiger system I teach. I worked on it and other systems as well. Wu is the one who really focused on and excelled at white crane, so you should ask him about it if you want to know more."

Not many days later, Kanbun asked Hsu about what he heard in Fujou and his conversation with Jou.

"What you are learning is an amalgamation of the older hard and soft styles of southern China" said Hsu. "The soft styles rely on gently flowing movements, avoid direct confrontation, and summon energy from their inner spirit or *chi*. The best proponents of the hard systems are indeed very tough and hard to overcome. They can block and strike and take and give with great power. Some believe the correct way is to select one or the other, but I see no reason why you can't do both. It is my contribution to the theoretical and practical currents in *wushu* training and development. I am not the first or only practitioner of this *pangainoon*, which is an expression in this region with literal as well as figurative meanings, and I am fully engaged with it.

179

There are three main forms in *pangainoon*. You are working on the first, which is *sanchin*. The next is *sanseiryu*, but there is an intermediate form called *seisan* before that and together they contain elements of the dragon, tiger, and crane systems. You are now about ready to begin learning *seisan*, or 'thirteen' as the characters are read. It is taken from *sanseiryu* and *suparinpei*, the third of the main forms in *pangainoon*. It is yet another step in your progression, so you will see the tiger and crane movements of *pangainoon* in them."

"The animals you asked about are for mimicry," said Hsu. "They represent only a tool or a means to infuse you with grace, spirit, strength, speed, cunning, and especially unconscious motion. It is significant that insects, animals, birds, reptiles, and even fish can do so much more with their physical endowments than men. How many times have you seen a cat crouch and spring to a height much greater than its own, an ant carry food larger than its own body, or a bird catch an insect in flight? They are able to bring to bear their full capabilities precisely because they set aside consciousness and simply act. This resembles the practice of *Chan* or *Zen* as you call it in Japanese. Through the practice of *wushu*, we aspire to concentrate all the energy in our bodies in a focused movement, and then all of that into a single point for defending or attacking. We have the same or perhaps greater physical potential as other creatures, but our thoughts, judgments, and fears are barriers to achieving it. Have you ever mistakenly put your hand on a hot iron or dropped a grindstone on your foot? It is remarkable how we are able to react with speed, strength, and decisiveness precisely when there is no thought or pre-meditation. Our instincts are lightning fast, but conscious man is remarkably slow. With *wushu* we want to learn to act and react like the beasts, but live in balance and harmony as humans."

Kanbun took this in thoughtfully, while Hsu continued, "*Sanchin* is the basis for *pangainoon*. It is a triangle upon which stability, strength, confidence, spirit, and everything else we do is built. The characters themselves can be written as 'three conflicts' or 'three progressions.' They are the conflicts between the dimensions of man, earth, and the universe or the progressions of birth, life, and death or youth, middle age, and maturity. They may also represent the realms of the physical, mental, and spiritual development, of the soft, hard, and middling activities, of the lower, middle and upper body, and of much more. Three is the smallest, most fundamental, and most stable of the complex numbers. One and two, positive and negative, male and female, darkness and light are easily recognizable and observable in the everyday world, and there is a certain symmetry, balance, and elegance to the dualistic universe as described by the sage Lao Tzu. However, with the number three, we begin to understand that there is more, that the world is complex and diverse, and that our imaginations can go on until infinity. Lao Tzu may have believed, as do I, that the way of life is multifold and that which we do not see is greater than what is readily visible."

Sanchin," he went on, "like the number three, is the base, the beginning, and the launching point for comprehension, development, and potential achievement that reaches out beyond the horizon. The stepping sequence of *sanchin* when mapped out on the ground prescribes an ellipse with a triangle overlaid at the end. *Sanseiryu*, which in the Fujou dialect means "thirty-six' and as the number implies, is a substantial and complex development from the modest and subtle *sanchin* form. In *sanseiryu*, dragon,

181

tiger, and crane combine forces for protection, counterattack, and escape when necessary. With this form, we stretch the lines and directions of our movement, thinking, and consciousness. *Suparinpei* means "one hundred eight' and symbolizes yet another expansion from *sanchin* to extend three times beyond the reach of *sanseiryu*. It forms a circle to draw in all you have learned and prescribes a return to *sanchin* to embark on a new cycle. Of course, these numbers—three, thirty-six, one hundred eight, and even eight itself, which implies many-- are important in the practice, understanding, and development of Buddhism. You may have noticed this in some of the books in Jou's library. The practice of *wushu* is most closely related to the *Chan* school of Buddhism as most of what we do has some reference to its principles. Some priests and hermit practitioners of *Chan* Buddhism describe achieving a high level of consciousness through breathing techniques, chants, and mental exercises, which they do in a seated position. That is a passive form of meditation. *Wushu* applies similar principles to directed and spontaneous actions while imitating the movements of animals. This is an active meditation. The means may be different, but they are related and the objectives are the same. In any case, the philosophical and spiritual dimensions of *wushu* are a level apart from the physical and mental training we have done so far. The philosophical and spiritual aspects fulfill the third side of the triangle. Developing one side is inconsequential, two is an improvement, but three sides of the triangle are essential for comprehension, development, and awareness. Indeed, developing only one or two sides of the *wushu* triangle without counterbalance is incomplete."

"There is also sequencing that is significant to the learning path," he resumed. "We begin with the physical, which is the most obvious and actually the easiest, though, as you are learning, developing the body requires dedication, consistency, and the will to improve. After some time, the mental aspects rise in importance, which are a matter of guidance and exploration. This relates to our observations of how animals breathe, move, and act. They do so unconsciously with great skill and effect, but they can hardly be considered enlightened creatures. We want to mimic animals so that we attain their level of natural and reflexive existence, but we want to complement those instinctive skills with human qualities. And finally, there is the philosophical and spiritual domain, which is the most difficult level to achieve. You can think of it as the point at the end of the side of a triangle. However, it is even more complex than that, perhaps the point at the end of an infinite line. It is more than merely progressing from one stage to another in a straight line or predetermined path. At times we work more on one level than the other so that they are rarely found in equal measure or achievement. Sometimes we advance quickly in one aspect while one or two of the other sides of the triangle lag behind. Sometimes we may feel we are making steady progress in two sides of the triangle, while fulfillment in the third is somehow out of reach. I have to confess that I have read, studied, and tried to understand the philosophical and especially spiritual elements of *wushu*, but they remain mostly a mystery to me. I have never seen or met anyone who struck me as an enlightened soul. However, through *wushu*, if we can attain stable development in each of the three constituent parts at a high level, perhaps we will have reached a strong, advanced, and even enlightened stage. I suspect that *sanchin* means developing, integrating, and reconciling the 'three conflicts' or 'three progressions,' but I don't really know. It is something I look forward to learning more about over time."

He continued, "I have had this conversation with wise priests and other spiritual leaders, but they have been unable to explain what this means and how to attain a higher spiritual level. They have suggested that with the repetition of chanting and meditation, regulated breathing, and physical and mental discipline, one can or will reach a spiritually awakened and enlightened state of being. However, I am still wondering how this comes about. Is it a result of the repetitive practice? I don't think so. We know from *wushu* practice that merely repeating the same activity for many years may or may not lead to accumulated development, and there is no guarantee of mental or spiritual advancement. There are many in religious practice and *wushu* training who spend a lifetime in the same activities but never become enlightened. Will the practitioner, after many years of devoted effort, one day spontaneously awaken to a spiritual world? It is unlikely and certainly not automatic. We might also ask the question why some and not others achieve a higher spiritual level? Is it the role of an agent such as a teacher, mentor, or spiritual guide that opens the doorway to enlightenment? This may help, but I am doubtful that this by itself is the answer. Many teach and many more study, but only a few become enlightened. Is it something that only certain special individuals are born with or develop in their lifetimes? If so, it is a waste of time for the vast majority of us who will seek but never find. Why cannot those who claim to have reached a heightened level describe how they achieved spiritual awakening? Is it because in truth they have not? Is it imaginary? Is it merely a way of producing leaders and followers, but in fact resulting in limited or no spiritual advancement at all? I have more questions than answers about philosophical and spiritual progress. I am still seeking the way."

That evening, Kanbun lay on his straw matting in his room and began to think about what he had learned and practiced as a child, the understanding he gleaned from the books Jou had lent to him, and what he heard from Hsu that day. He recalled the traditional beliefs in the indigenous folk religion of Ryukyu that relied on women selected as priestesses to serve as mediators between good and evil spirits. Some people in Ryukyu followed the pantheistic Shintoism that had spread down from the north from mainland Japan. Others adhered more closely to the cyclical practices and beliefs of Buddhism. However, none was exclusive to the other and most people had some affinity to all. Though there were not many concrete or tangible points of intersection among them, somewhere at base they were compatible and complementary. It was intuitive for him that they all shared at least some common traits with each other, and that they would reinforce his practice of *wushu*. He also thought about the relationship Hsu had described between *wushu* and *Chan*, which he knew in Japanese as Zen Buddhism. This led him to consider ways of thinking that had not yet occurred to him or that others had devised and developed. It was challenging, even exhausting, trying to understand all that he had heard and was learning, not to mention contemplating the great expanse of what he had not seen or heard and did not know.

The next morning after his training session with Hsu, Kanbun did not mention to Jou the discussion they had the day before. However, Kanbun wondered and asked, "Why have you chosen me to train with Jiang and Lee and why take the chance of introducing me to Master Hsu and *pangainoon*?"

They sat down for a cup of tea, and Jou began by explaining, "There are at least several reasons. The first is very practical. I am only a little older than you and still have much to learn and develop. My students teach you, but you are also a partner for my own training. Jiang and Lee guide the group in the evenings, but I need someone from whom I can learn, to keep me sharp, and to push my own practice and thinking. As you become more proficient, I will also improve. Unfortunately, the students who attend the evening classes lack solid potential, are unlikely to amount to much, and probably cannot keep a secret. However, it is because I maintain a group for general practice, learning, and development that I am able to select a few who can become accomplished by training with me privately. I have trained Jiang and Lee in the same way, and I continue to work with them, but there are limits to how far they will go. You, on the other hand, strike me as the kind of man who can achieve a great deal, which is the second reason I have chosen you. You came to Fujou with a firm grounding in--- what did my good friend Wu Hsienkuei say it was, ah yes, *kobujutsu* and *toodi*. Before you arrived you had the physical elements and basic ingredients on which to build. And, there was more. You have a knack for solving problems that is simple and straightforward. I like that. Another reason is that I am curious. I have never travelled outside Fujian, and you are from another country. What better way is there to observe, learn, and grow than to have the stimulation of a friend who has had different experiences and thinks in other ways?"

Jou paused, and then went on, "As you probably understood from the conversation at the tea house yesterday, or even before from your own observations, my Chinese compatriots and I operate at multiple levels and move between layers of trust and friendship. There are many secrets and it is often difficult to discern people's true intentions. Among the talkers yesterday, there may have been a spy for the city or provincial administration seeking to identify anti-government forces or resistance groups and what their strength may be. There may also have been someone who ostensibly was an amateur, but who in fact was quite accomplished, trains under, and works for a significant *wushu* figure in Fujian. He may have been casting about to discover a weakness in another school, perhaps to exact revenge or to destroy a competitor. These kinds of dynamics occur across society and in most human relations here in China."

"Let me give you another example, something more personal," Jou added. "Young men come from the farms and villages to learn *wushu* from me. They do not know, and probably don't suspect, that there is more beneath the surface. I don't tell them that I train Jiang and Lee separately and at a different level. However, I don't tell Jiang and Lee about your morning sessions with Master Hsu, though they may suspect something. It is our secret."

He took a sip of tea and continued, "I have my own secrets, too. There is the external world of my house and servants, my school, my farmlands, my crops, and my trade. My inner world exists in my calligraphy, paintings, and books. Here in China, they are known as the 'Three Perfections.' I show all of these 'Three Perfections' to very few. For your purposes, *sanchin, seisan, sanseiryu* can be thought of the three perfections in *pangainoon*. And beyond that there are my own thoughts, impressions, motivations, and aspirations inside of me. Those, I reveal to no one.

A few weeks later, Kanbun received another lesson in how there were more secrets in *wushu* that he could only learn over time.

One morning, Hsu said, "Let's start on *seisan*. It is an intermediate step before the second of the 'three progressions' I mentioned, and you will begin learning it and its significance today."

Hsu walked Kanbun through the sequence of *seisan*, showing him where it was based on *sanchin* and where it expanded and developed in new directions. He took time to explain the multiple applications of each of the moves and what training it would take to employ them. At times he asked Kanbun to use his imagination or his own sense of *wushu* to explain how the movements related to *sanchin*, where they diverged, and how they might be utilized. They also discussed the ways in which the form was based on the movements of the dragon, tiger, and crane as well as the spirit from those animals that gave life and significance to them. It was a form that, while based on *sanchin* and opened with the same pattern, flowed with greater variety of movement in the arms and legs, starts, stops, and turns, attacking forwards and retreating backwards, and extending stances to new foot positions, all the while maintaining a low center of balance and stability along with measured breathing and greater exertion. It was refreshing for Kanbun to be able to add something new to his training routine, and the form of *seisan* hinted at what might he find in *sanseiryu*.

Hsu did not stop, however, with teaching Kanbun this new form. In the succeeding months that seemed to pass by quickly, he also introduced more and advanced training techniques. He also began developing Kanbun's skills in responding, parrying, and counterattacking. First, he had Kanbun sit in a kneeling position and performed only the sequence and motions of *sanchin* and *seisan* from the waist up. Next, they sat facing each other also in a kneeling position, and Hsu reviewed the multiple applications of *seisan* attacking with varying strikes from different angles while Kanbun utilized the dragon, tiger, and crane motions to block and counter. Also in a kneeling position, and then eventually standing as well, they worked on the important element of grappling when there was little room for striking, defending, or maneuver. Hsu moved on to free form combinations of attacks and counter moves so that Kanbun developed spontaneous defenses and learned to be on guard at any moment from unexpected directions. He also had Kanbun repeat the exercise that he had showed him of placing his head between two bundles of burning incense, but this time in a kneeling position. Hsu then continued the free form attacks so that Kanbun would develop his peripheral vision to see the strikes as they began. Hsu explained that it would be important to develop visual abilities to detect an attack but not become so focused on it as to miss the next one from a different angle.

To supplement, Hsu built on the training exercises Kanbun had learned earlier and extended their objectives. One day, Hsu took Kanbun to an area where there was a bamboo fence that had been set up to shield an area of the grounds behind Jou's great house. There were wooden posts inserted in the ground with cross pieces between them and vertical staves of bamboo lashed closely together at the top and bottom so that only slits of light could be seen between them. Hsu told Kanbun to thrust his arms straight out and with the flat of his hands held vertically to try to separate the bamboo poles. Kanbun tried but was only able to separate them enough to get a glimpse of what was on the other side. Hsu explained that he should practice doing this daily until he could divide the vertical bamboo staves and step between them on his own to the other side. Next, he had Kanbun do the reverse by extending his arms and squeezing the vertical bamboo poles together to try and make two openings in the fence. He also taught Kanbun to separate the bamboo by thrusting with his open hands and round kicking with the tips of his toes.

In addition to standing on top of two posts in a horse stance with flat stones resting on his upper legs, Hsu had Kanbun shift from one post to another while performing *sanchin* and *seisan*, blocking attacks from Hsu and counterattacking, and eventually closing his eyes while moving from one post to the other. Another time, Hsu took Kanbun to another area of the training area where he had hung cloth bags from four bars he had lashed to several upright posts and filled with sand and pebbles that formed a circle. He had Kanbun stand in the center of the circle and thrust with his finger tips, strike with a single knuckle, and attack with other parts of his hands, feet, and body to develop not only his striking surfaces but stability and strength in multiple directions. He also had Kanbun walk around the rim of a large, waist high ceramic pot, perform *sanchin* and *seisan*, and block and counter strike while maintaining his balance and keeping the jar in an upright position.

On still a different day, Hsu had Kanbun, with only his fingertips and toes touching the stone floor, arch his hips so they were higher in the air than the rest of his body. Hsu showed Kanbun how to dip forward with his chin, arch his back in the opposite direction with his hips low to the stone floor, and then reverse. Kanbun was strong and supple so he could do these rolling push ups. Next, Hsu had Kanbun repeat this movement continuing in a circular motion until he could do no more. They rested a minute. Hsu instructed Kanbun to do the same exercise but reversing the circles to lift his hips, roll his body forward on his arms, dip, return to the same position with his hips in the air, and then continue the circular motion. He also had Kanbun stand in wide and long stances, roll and rotate from side to side and front to back as he squatted and pushed with his legs. Then, Hsu pushed against Kanbun's shoulders, hands, and hips while he rotated to the sides and forward and backward. Hsu told Kanbun that these training methods would help him develop flowing, rolling, and dynamic energy or what he called "power in motion." He explained that this was the difference between strength and power. A strong man with large muscles could lift a heavy log, push a large stone, or break a thick post with his hand or foot, which were examples of strength limited to a single plane. However, a powerful man with well rounded and fluid force could sustain and direct his power in a way that far exceeded the strong man.

After nearly half a year of practice, Kanbun was able to separate the bamboo poles in the fence and step through to the other side. He showed Hsu that he could accomplish what he had been instructed to do. Hsu also extended his arms, separated the bamboo, though he seemed to do it with less exertion, and stepped through to the other side complementing Kanbun on his accomplishment. On the other side of the fence was a flat area that extended a short distance before rising sharply into the hillside behind the Jou's manor. There were several posts driven into the ground and a few medium-sized trees growing nearby. Hsu explained that the next stage of this particular training was for Kanbun to use his stance, strength, and concentration to pull a post from the ground. He demonstrated by bending his knees and dropping his hips, bending his elbows in front of him, grasping a post firmly with both hands, and extracting it smoothly from the ground. Kanbun tried, but was unable to budge the post. He tried again and failed. Hsu explained that failure itself would build strength and perseverance if he persisted until he succeeded with the proper application of energy and technique. He told Kanbun to consider this while trying to pull the post out of the ground. Hsu then led Kanbun to one of the young trees that flowered in the spring, though the fruit was bitter and unpleasant to eat. He instructed Kanbun to strike the tree with the tips of his fingers, the insides of his hands, and the flat top of his foot low to the ground. This was similar to the practice of striking the pillars and wooden slats Kanbun and the other students did in Jou's courtyard, but there was no thud when he hit the tree in the outdoor area. In fact, the tree did not budge and stood impervious to Kanbun's strikes. Hsu then demonstrated by bending one leg deeply and kicking the tree trunk low to the ground. The tree shook and a few leaves fell off the branches and fluttered to the earth. Hsu told Kanbun he should practice the strikes he had learned in *sanchin* and *seisan* until he was able to shake fruit and leaves from the tree. If he continued to do so until the leaves all fell and the tree died from his repeated strikes, then Kanbun would be ready to actually use these techniques.

By now, several seasons had passed and it was quite cold during the day and even more so at night in the midst of winter.

One evening, Jou mentioned to Kanbun that he wanted him to deliver a large grindstone for making flour to a relative who lived in a village closer to Fujou on the other side of a tributary of the Min River where they had first met. He instructed Kanbun to roll the grindstone along the ground and said Old Wu would show him the way. The next morning, the two men set out with Kanbun pushing and rolling the heavy wheel in front of him. They reached the Min River, but the old ferry boat captain who had been so grateful to Kanbun for retrieving his vessel amidst the flood several years earlier was no longer there. The new captain was young and impatient to get under way. Kanbun had brought no cash with him and was unable to pay the fare that the new captain required. Fortunately, Wu had brought some silver coins entrusted to him by Jou and proceeded to board the ferry, but again the captain stopped them. He objected that the grindstone was almost as large as and certainly heavier than a man and that Old Wu and Kanbun should pay the fare for three people to come on board. Kanbun thought a moment, as he was troubled by the difficulties with the ferry captain and the cost for an extra person, despite the fact there were only the two of them. Kanbun seldom handled cash, and then only small amounts when selling herbs and medicines. He lived and ate by the graces of Jou in Nanyoi and was by nature frugal and reluctant to pay the additional fare. Instead, he was reminded of the last time he was at this river bank and of the donkey he had enlisted to help him save the ferry. His thoughts also traveled back to Baro and his lessons in the bamboo grove with Grandfather. In a moment of inspiration, Kanbun leaned the grindstone against the river bank, stretched his back across the mill stone, reached around behind him to grasp the wheel, and rolled over clutching the heavy load supported by his lower back and hips. From there, he walked back to the ferry landing, boarded the boat, and told Old Wu to pay for two passengers. Kanbun held the grindstone in that position as the captain poled up the river. When they reached the far side of one of the river's tributaries, Old Wu told the captain to let them off. Kanbun descended from the ferry and set the grindstone down on the ground. Old Wu and Kanbun continued their journey, delivered the grindstone, and returned to Nanyoi. When they returned, Old Wu explained to Jou what Kanbun had done.

Jou laughed, slapped Kanbun on the shoulder, and said, "Ha, you are as economical as you are diligent, my friend."

Jou instructed Old Wu to prepare a better than usual dinner that evening for the two of them. He then invited Kanbun into the great house into one of the curtained rooms in the hallway he had seen the first night he visited Nanyoi. As Kanbun entered the room, he caught sight of a dim figure on the other side of the open space. There was something strangely familiar about it and he quickly realized it was a mirror and his own reflection. The only mirror he had seen before was a polished metal plate that his mother had used in Izumi when combing her hair and a similar one in the dining room of Jou's great house the first night he arrived in Nanyoi. This one was made of glass and taller and wider than a human being. He had never seen a glass plate so large, nor his own reflection so clearly.

Jou entered the room behind Kanbun and explained, "The mirror is a useful training tool in which we can see ourselves, imitate the movements of others, and improve our form. Run your finger over the glass. It is smooth and moist, isn't it? Try to imagine the surface of the mirror on another plane, for example under your feet."

Kanbun was puzzled by this last remark, but decided to leave his question about what Jou meant for later. He lingered in the room for a while looking at his reflection, standing in *sanchin*, practicing the movements of *seisan*, checking his posture, and watching his form.

The next morning, Jou told Kanbun they would depart Nanyoi for a visit to Gushan, or "Drum Mountain," behind the nearly thousand year old Gushing Spring Temple. On the way, they crossed the Min River, and Kanbun told him about his good friend Matsuda Tokusaburo and his failures and disappointments with training under Makabei at Gushing Spring Temple. Jou nodded in reply and explained that the temple was considered one of the great scenic areas in Fujian and the mountain behind it had four distinct peaks. Throughout Fujou's history, learned men and others well-known throughout China had visited the site and written poems or inscriptions that had been carved into the rocks along the 2,000 stone steps leading up the mountain. During the Tang Dynasty, a great Japanese Buddhist patriarch, Kunghai, arrived in Fujou and visited Drum Mountain. He was also a scholar, poet, artist, and founder of a sect of Japanese Buddhism.

"Perhaps you have heard of him?" asked Jou.

"Yes," replied Kanbun, "We know him as Kukai, the founder of what is called the Shingon or the "True Word" school of Buddhism in Japan.

When they arrived at the temple, they paused to offer prayers at one of the many altars open to the public. Kanbun asked one of the temple assistants if a man named "Matsuda" in Japanese or "Shaotian" in Chinese was still a resident. The assistant replied that Shaotian was there, but he had gone to Fujou for the day. Kanbun wrote a short message of greeting and gave it to the assistant asking him to deliver it to Matsuda. Jou and Kanbun continued on their way to the stone steps leading up the mountain. It was a cold day and the air grew colder as they ascended the mountain. They were warmed from exerting themselves during the climb, but it felt much colder when they stopped to look at the view or read some of the inscriptions along the way. At one point higher up the mountain, they paused to rest and Kanbun had never felt so cold before. He began to shiver. Jou laughed and they started on their way again. They reached a level area near the top of the mountain, where there was a sub-temple. It was painted deep red with thick wooden pillars, stone statues of mythical lion dogs clasping globes in their paws, sets of candles on long sticks set on the ground, and incense burning in large bronze pots by the entrance. There was a stone platform in front of the temple and a separate set of wide stone steps leading up to it. They warmed their hands by the incense, and Kanbun brushed some of the smoke toward his face for good health. The ferocious looking lion dogs outside the temple reminded Kanbun of the smaller ceramic lion-dog *shishi* that the people of Ryukyu placed in pairs at garden gates or on roof peaks of their homes. He wondered if the idea for *shishi* was originally from Fujian and not native to Ryukyu as he had thought.

Jou led them around the temple to a narrow trail that traversed the side of the mountain and passed through bamboo groves and other hearty bushes. Kanbun noticed that it had grown to be even colder as the wind seemed to blow right through his clothing. After a while they arrived at a small pond that was completely frozen over. Kanbun had heard of ice but never actually seen it before, not to mention a frozen pond. He reached down to touch the ice, which was indeed cold and to his surprise his finger stuck to the surface. Jou invited Kanbun to walk out onto the ice covered pond. It was not only cold, but slippery, which was also a new sensation under Kanbun's feet. Jou reminded Kanbun of the moist, flat surface of the mirror in his home and explained that in *wushu* the practitioner must be able to adapt to unknown and unexpected circumstances. His next stage of strategy would be to think about and exploit the setting, environment, conditions, materials, numbers of people present, whether attackers, onlookers, or sympathetic, so that one or a few could defeat many. Sometimes greater strength, position, and numbers in an attack could be turned against itself.

With that, Jou gave Kanbun a slight push, and the younger man slid a short distance and slipped onto his backside with a dull bump.

Jou laughed and said, "Now we will practice some *wushu*."

Kanbun rose, and they began moving about on the ice and feeling their way gingerly while striking, kicking, shifting, turning, and eventually engaging each other in free form. Sometimes they slipped and fell forwards or backwards, laughing as they did so. Kanbun found that he could keep his balance better by bending his knees and dropping his hips low to the ice as they continued their jousting.

Jou commented, "I can see you have discovered a strategy for encountering an attacker when under awkward circumstances, but what else do you suppose would be helpful to prevent you from slipping when on an icy or slippery area?"

197

Kanbun thought a moment, but had no ready answer. Jou walked over to the edge of the pond, took off his cloth slippers, which surprised Kanbun because his feet were very cold. Jou spat on the souls of his slippers and rubbed them in the dirt next to the pond. Kanbun did the same, put his slippers back on, and found that he had much better traction on the slippery surface. They continued their *wushu* practice for a while, and then they sat on a log to rest by the side of the frozen pond.

Jou asked, "What do you suppose you would do at night if there were no lamps nearby or a moon or stars in the sky with which to see an opponent?"

Kanbun thought a while, but again had no answer.

Jou explained, "If you keep yourself very low to the ground, you can see the silhouette of your opponent against the sky even during a dark night. It may seem there is no light and you cannot see, but actually there is some sky light and your opponent will appear darker in outline against it. You, on the other hand, will be low to the ground, which is also dark and you will be much less visible to your opponent.

He went on, "If you encounter an opponent at nightfall or daybreak, what is the natural advantage you could have in facing him?"

Kanbun thought a moment and responded, "It would be best to have my back to the sun on the horizon so that it shone into the eyes of the enemy."

"That is good," added Jou, "and even better if you block the sunshine with your body making a shadow, and then shifting just at the right moment when defending or attacking so that the full and bright sunlight suddenly strikes his eyes. When walking the streets of Fujou, it is best to keep a wide berth at corners, intersections, doorways, alleyways, or windows obscured with curtains. There may be someone laying in wait just out of sight. If you are close to a wall or building, you have less time to react. Taking away the strengths of an opponent or preventing him, even if you don't know of his existence yet, from doing what he intends to do is part of strategy. If you make space for your opponent, he can penetrate. When there is a need to attack, you must seek or create openings in the spaces around your opponent. A good strategy will depend on how well and quickly you read the situation, environment, conditions, materials, numbers of people and possible weapons-- whether to defend or attack, whether you use the physical setting, whether your senses are fully aware, and whether your mind is open. In the early moments of an encounter, your opponent is weakest. You must think about this deeply. A man with superior strategy can defeat a more powerful man or many men. Advanced technique or skill or power are all fine, but it is strategy that will win the day. This is true man to man, with multiple opponents, or in war."

He continued, "When we get back to Nanyoi, I will show you another book. It is called *Pingfa* by Suntzu, the master strategist from ancient times. You probably also noticed in the historical tale of the *Three Kingdoms* that I gave you Kong Ming was the great strategist of his day at the end of the Han Dynasty nearly two thousand years ago. You may recall the scene in which he sat calmly playing the zither in plain view of the enemy atop the main gate of a fortress that was clearly undermanned and unprotected. The enemy knew of Kong Ming's reputation and feared it was a trap. However, this was Kong Ming's strategy for avoiding defeat when there was no other way to defend against the impending attack. He did nothing more than read the enemy's perceptions correctly and devised his strategy accordingly. You should study not only what the great strategists did, but how they thought and how they employed superior strategy to overcome their opponents."

"If you know your enemy, you can defeat him. If you can keep your enemy from knowing you, you can defeat him. If your enemy knows you incorrectly, you can manipulate that perception to your advantage. The most dangerous enemy is the one you know nothing about, no matter how weak or strong he is. Walk calmly, whether there is a mountain before you or a tiger behind you," added Jou quoting from a well known proverb.

"And, when there is ice under your feet," added Kanbun, to which they both laughed.

Jou and Kanbun sat together a while longer and began their descent from Drum Mountain. They stopped in Fujou, had several cups of tea, and ate bowls of hot noodles at a shop not far from Gushing Spring Temple. Kanbun was glad to be indoors, protected from the wind, and warming his body with hot liquids. The windows of the shop were dusty, but they could see the shape of Drum Mountain from where they sat. Unexpectedly, Jou walked over to the windows, opened them wide letting the chill air from outside flow in, and returned to his seat.

The shop keeper stepped out from the kitchen in the back and said, "This must be terribly uncomfortable for you and our other honored guests."

"It is fine," replied Jou.

"But sir," the noodle soup will become lukewarm and no one will enjoy it," pled the shop keeper.

"Mm," grunted Jou, and the protesting shop keeper closed the windows.

When they returned to Jou's mansion in Nanyoi, as promised, he lent Kanbun a copy of the *Pingfa*. He also showed him some more of his brush work. There was a vertical set of four characters that Jou had drawn on the wall inside his studio that read "invisible," "inaudible," "intangible," and "unknowable."

Jou then asked Kanbun, "What do you think this means?"

"Well," replied Kanbun with an impish smile, there is the parable of the three monkeys who neither see, nor hear, nor speak evil, and I am probably the fourth monkey who knows nothing, so this is not really new to me."

Jou laughed, but he urged Kanbun to think a bit more deeply.

Kanbun thought for a while and replied, "This is what we seek in *wushu*."

"Pretty good," replied Jou, "that is close."

He also showed Kanbun a brush painting of a marshy pond mostly in black ink. It had a pair of yellow ducks with open bills facing to the left. However, the title of the painting was "Three Ducks."

Jou asked, "Why do you think this work is called "Three Ducks" when only two are visible?"

Kanbun shrugged and responded, "I am afraid I don't know much about painting or art."

Jou explained, "The two ducks on the water are anticipating a third one that is neither visible, audible, tangible, nor knowable in the picture, but its presence is felt."

Next, Jou hung a scroll beside them with the characters for "see," "hear," "perceive," and "comprehend."

Jou elaborated, "You must see the invisible, hear the inaudible, perceive the intangible, and comprehend the unknowable. Open your mind and senses so that you are aware as you do your training, as you eat, sleep, and wake, and as you walk along the road. *Wushu* should always be with you and you should be with it. You have senses so you can see, hear, taste, smell, and touch. Learn to develop these senses by themselves and together to reach a level above and beyond the information and sensations they provide individually. That is the difference between the five senses and perception. It is like seeing around a corner, sensing what is there when there is limited vision or light to guide you, hearing the fluttering of a bird outside while sitting in a crowded tea house, or catching the faint but familiar odor of dust in the afternoon air. A sword may be a clear threat in the hands of an opponent, but you must also hear the movement of his feet, see his positioning without looking, and be prepared for a potential kick. Do you remember the poem about Drum Mountain that I gave you?"

Kanbun understood instinctively a good part of what Jou had explained to him that day. At times, he had experienced glimpses of the thoughts that Jou had described, but he had never quite expressed them in that way. The view of the mountain may be obscured by the physical presence of mist around the peak or dust accumulated on a shop window. The dust was on the window, not on his vision or his perception. His senses and his awareness could be distracted, obstructed, or hindered, but that did not necessarily obscure his perception if his mind were open and aware. He had a distinct impression of what Jou was explaining, but he also had a sense there was more tantalizingly just out of reach. It was somewhere in his consciousness and needed only to be uncovered. He intuited that there was a spiritual dust that could veil the perception of what lived in his heart and mind, and he had to clear his mind to see through it.

Kanbun realized that Jou's movements, such as when he held a writing brush in his hand, were graceful and powerful, like that of a tiger. Step by step Kanbun would have to polish his skills to raise his mental abilities to that stage of development.

Sensing Kanbun's thoughts and impressions, Jou said, "Our training is like the trail up Drum Mountain. It is more than merely a step by step process or like climbing a ladder, but achieving successive stages, sometimes going sideways, perhaps retracing steps a few times or slipping on ice, but then going on to the next level of realization. If you merely aim to accomplish a particular level of competence by reaching for the goals you had when you began training in *wushu*, you will only achieve mediocrity. You must take the lessons you learn from your first struggles to improve, apply the knowledge you have gained from that process, and then seek and make a goal of the next level of ability, comprehension, and consciousness. If possible, and depending upon your stage of development, the energy you have, the relative importance of the task at hand, and the circumstances in which you live, the objective is to perceive and then achieve the next stage. One phase leads to another, rather than becoming the end in itself. You began with *sanchin* under Master Hsu, will go on to *sanseiryu*, and then complete the circle with *suparinpei* before starting over again. Here, take my copy of Suntzu's book on strategy. Read it carefully, study it closely, and apply it broadly."

With this, Kanbun felt he had made a significant step in his training. He realized that while learning from Hsu and Jou he must also think on his own, apply himself to new challenges rather than merely imitate what his teachers taught him, and develop his character and his *wushu*. He read the ancient work by Suntzu and he was reminded of the remarkable training, skills, strategies, and thoughts of Miyamoto Musashi in the *Book of Five Rings* that Grandfather had taught him about when he was a child in Izumi. He read both works in a new and more understanding light. What had been abstract or indistinct when introduced by Grandfather had become more accessible with Jou and Hsu. On top of that, he could sense that the advanced training and accumulated wisdom that had been passed down over an enormous stretch of time was now within his grasp.

Some months later on a visit to the tea house in Fujou, they met again with Wu Hsienkuei and had a conversation this time just among the three of them. Wu explained that he had heard of a contest set up between a man and a donkey. After paying five pieces of silver, a man could try to block the kick of the donkey to make his reputation as a first class *wushu* artist and win ten pieces of silver in return.

Remembering the day they met at the dock by the flooded Min River, Jou smiled at Kanbun and said, "Let's go see these donkeys."

After they finished their tea, Wu paid the bill and led Jou and Kanbun some distance to the edge of the city. They crossed several undeveloped fields until they came to a thick forest, which they entered through a narrow trail. Some distance later they arrived at a wide clearing where there was a small crowd of men and a farm hand with his donkey, which was chewing on a pile of hay and nosing his head in a bucket of water. The donkey was tethered to a post in the middle of the clearing and there was a leather strap tied over his back, across his ribs, and under his groin. Several men lay on the ground nearby. One was holding his ribs rolling on the ground and groaning. Another was holding a bandage to his forearm, which was clearly broken. Still another lay on the ground with a severe welt across his face, unconscious, and his companions trying to revive him with splashes of water. Wu, Jou, and Kanbun surveyed the scene while the donkey chewed on the dry straw.

The farm hand raised his voice and called out, "Is there anyone else who would like to test his strength? It is getting late and I will be leaving soon. I can even lower the price on the challenge if you dare."

After a few moments, a slight man beyond middle age stepped forward. It was Master Hsu, and the three men who had just arrived hear him say, "Will you accept two pieces of silver?"

"I suppose if you are willing to part with your money, and maybe your teeth," replied the farmer, "I can suffer you that much. Give me your two pieces for a chance at five. Come over here and stand behind the donkey. Remember, he is a tough beast and three men have already lost their good silver and their health today."

The farmer walked over to the donkey and slipped one hand under the leather strap over its back.

"I will see when you are ready, but I won't tell you when I will pull on the strap to make my donkey kick," he said.

Hsu, who by now had the attention of everyone in the gathering, took his position with his left foot slightly in front of the other and his hands clenched in front of his hips. The farmer gave a sharp and sudden twist to the leather strap. The donkey reacted instantly, kicking backwards viciously with both feet twice in succession. The slight though wiry Hsu adjusted as quickly, sliding back into a deeper stance, swinging his right arm around in a tight circle, scooping under the legs of the donkey, and then did the same from his left side on the second kick. With the second kick, Hsu, who moved more quickly and powerfully than anyone in the clearing would have imagined, threw the legs of the donkey to the left so that the animal tumbled over onto its side mewling and shrieking in surprise. The animal righted itself onto its feet, took a few unsure steps, and appeared to be stunned.

Everyone watching in the clearing was also stunned with what they just saw but did not move. Hsu walked over to where the donkey was standing, rubbed its belly gently with his right while leaning with his left hand on its back to loosen the leather strap and to calm the animal. Abruptly, he collected his reward and then left the clearing while everyone watched him disappear into the forest. When the onlookers turned their gaze back to the donkey, it had collapsed on the ground and lay dead. The farm hand gave a shout of dismay and ran over to the donkey, but it was too late. Again, everyone in the clearing was stunned. They edged closer to the dead donkey and the farmer who kneeled on the ground grieving next to his lost source of income. Wu, Jou, and Kanbun noticed there was blood oozing from the nostrils, mouth, and ears of the donkey. On the way back to Fujou, Wu, Jou, and Kanbun walked for a while in silence contemplating what they had just seen. What struck had Kanbun most, even more than the agility, speed, and power with which Hsu had dispatched the kicks of the donkey, was the fierce, animal-like, intensity in his eyes. Jou was the first to break their thoughts.

"I once met a great *wushu* practitioner named Feng Laohu who was visiting from northern China," said Jou. "He was much

206

older than me at the time and wore unusual clothing. His face was sort of square, his skin was fairer than what we normally see here in southern China, and his accent was quite different. He had the best *wushu* I had seen up until that point, though his style was unorthodox and hard to understand simply by watching. Other *wushu* practitioners in Fujou made fun of his style and openly doubted whether he was skilled or could be effective. One of them well known for his powerful legs challenged Feng to a match. The challenger let loose with a wild howl and a ferocious attack, and Feng responded by flicking his own leg at the man's kick. It seemed as if the attacker had pulled a muscle or hurt himself and sat on the ground holding both hands up in submission to Feng. Many of the local *wushu* students were offended that this outsider had defeated one of their own in such an easy and simple fashion. A succession of challenges from tougher and even better known locals followed with some attacking individually and others in groups. Each fell to Feng, but it was odd that he defeated some outright while others seemed to hurt themselves or the result was unclear like the strong kicker who was the first to challenge him. Finally, one of the best in the area pitted himself against Feng and appeared to defeat him with a flurry of strikes and kicks that left Feng crumpled on the ground. The locals gloated over the victory by one of their best. However, the next day the apparent winner fell ill and died soon afterwards. I went to see Feng Laohu and asked him if he knew his challenger would die. He replied that he did. I asked why he didn't defeat him outright and clearly. His reply was that there would be no end to the challenges if he did so. He went on to explain that in truth he didn't know his strength, its limits, and whether he could always win against ever stronger opponents.

What's more, he preferred not to find out because that would be the end of him. He said it was better to win unconvincingly or by losing, rather than provoke ever more attacks."

They stopped at a tea house on the edge of the city and spoke together in low voices.

Wu began, "I think Master Hsu just demonstrated for us the Iron Palm."

"I think you are right," replied Jou, "I have known Master Hsu for years, but never knew of his Iron Palm."

"What is the Iron Palm," asked Kanbun.

"It is a secret sort of *wushu* that is neither well known nor well understood," responded Jou. I have heard about it, but never saw it before and am not sure that I can explain. As you saw, it is a way of transmitting power from the body without much physical exertion. He killed that donkey just by making contact with its body, by laying a hand on it haunches and rubbing its belly. It is truly a mysterious system. He was clearly able to focus his full energy onto the surface of his hands and then deliver his force into the body of the donkey. However, it is unclear whether his high level of development was physical, mental, spiritual, all three in combination, or something different and greater altogether."

"It is a power I don't understand either," added Wu.

They all set meditatively for a while.

"What do you understand about power," asked Kanbun inquisitively to both men.

Jou thought for a while and replied, "There are multiple ways to power, but there are three basic kinds that I know about and work on. The first is the most natural and has to do with space. We all have the instinct for self-preservation. When you face an opponent, you are primarily concerned with defending yourself, and then try to find an opening for counterattack. A strategic part of defense is to stand without openings or weaknesses for your opponent to attack. In other words, you occupy a certain amount of space and you are safe as long as you do not open it to others. This can range anywhere from direct defenses with your arms, legs, and body to simply escaping by not being there when attacked to anywhere in between. You have done some of this already and there is much more to learn. The second is circular power, which you have probably trained with Master Hsu to develop in a variety of ways. It is strength in motion, at angles, and in arching sorts of ways. It is superior to mere strength that is pointed, inflexible, and unchangeable. The third kind of power is when you lock your body, mind, and spirit in tandem to focus your energy on a small area or a single point. Normally, we have backward and forward motion, fixed stances and moving postures, positive and negative energy, but you can only apply this power when all of your being is concentrated into single-mindedness. This is what I am working on in my own training these days. It may resemble the Iron Palm of Master Hsu in the clearing today, but he is far advanced in his training. You saw how skillfully he blocked the donkey's kicks and how effortlessly he applied his Iron Palm to destroying the animal. I understand that power, such as what we saw today, can be used in medicinal and healing practices as well. Like most other occurrences in nature, it can be used for positive or negative purposes. This power flows through the body like the electricity in a telegraph line, the steam in the great metal ships the Westerners sail on from Europe, and the water in the Min River. If you learn to access it appropriately, it can be used for great good."

Then Wu added, "I understand that there is more as well. Most *wushu* practitioners have a limited understanding of power, which you can see almost anywhere among those who talk more than they accomplish. Other more developed practitioners specialize in ways to power that are hard to see or understand, which apparently Master Hsu showed us today. And then, there is power that is outside our knowledge and experience altogether. There are those who have access to inner power and show us very little or nothing at all. They have learned something that is rarely taught, passed on only secretly within a tight circle or clandestine group, and is unavailable to everyone else. Who knows how this power is generated or applied? It humbles me to think how much I have yet to learn and I am not even sure I will ever have the opportunity."

The three men talked until after nightfall when Wu departed for his home in another section of Fujou and Jou and Kanbun headed toward Nanyoi. The two men from Nanyoi walked in silence thinking about the events and conversations of the day. Kanbun was inspired and yet puzzled. He had seen remarkable power that day and had followed closely the conversation with Wu and Jou. As much as he was making steady and significant progress under Master Hsu, there was much that was out of his reach. He would have to work with even more determination and hope that Master Hsu would lead the way.

One day, Wu visited Jou's manor in Nanyoi and the three of them sat together drinking tea and discussing *wushu* in the stone courtyard. Kanbun's language ability and skills in *wushu* had developed sufficiently that he felt comfortable conversing with the two men towards whom he also felt and expressed admiration and respect. Wu asked Kanbun to show him some *kobujutsu* and *toodi* from his homeland. Kanbun brought out a bamboo *bo* and went through the same routine he had practiced as a youth in the school yard in Izumi. Though Kanbun was a little rusty on the sequence because he had not practiced in years, he felt stronger, more supple, and confident in his movements. Next, he showed Jou and Wu some of the movements that Grandfather had taught him. These were more like combinations of formalized sequences, and Kanbun explained that he learned some simple movements of *toodi* that were meant to supplement his training with the bamboo staff. Wu then demonstrated his White Crane form. His stances were light and arm movements flowing, but his face showed fierce concentration and his breathing was forceful. His performance was elegant, powerful, and esoteric at the same time. He explained that he had learned it from a priest of the Southern Shaolin Temple in Fujian who had studied there before the Ching Court disbanded it. Next, Jou stood and performed something from the tiger system. It was powerful yet flowing, punctuated with bursts of condensed movement yet expansive in its range.

With the conversation and demonstrations of *kobujutsu*, *toodi*, and *wushu*, Kanbun was beginning to feel nostalgic about Ryukyu. Kanbun had not even written home or to Kazue about his life in Fujou for fear that his letters might be intercepted by the Japanese authorities and there might be repercussions for their families. Hoping to hear more, he asked Wu about his trading visits to Naha.

Wu replied, "Well, Sanra, trade is still strong between Fujian and Ryukyu and all up and down the coast of China and into Southeast Asia. Ryukyu itself still seems quite unsettled. There is nothing left of the old Royal Court in Shuri Castle and most

211

people of Ryukyu are unsure how long the Japanese will sustain their hold over the islands, though their grip seems only to be increasing with time. Some of your countrymen have adapted and in public call their homeland 'Okinawa' as designated by Japan, while continuing to use 'Ryukyu' in private. Others are holding back their endorsement of the Japanese administration, organizing resistance groups, or waiting to see what develops."

"A couple of years ago," he went on, "The Boxer Rebellion organized by the Righteous and Harmonious Fists of nationalists here in China was put down in Peking after about a three year insurrection. The Boxers had been trained by current and former priests of the Shaolin system, among others. They were angry with the weaknesses of the Ching Court in the face of foreign concessions, the spread of Christianity, the opium trade that has been disastrous for China, and the Unequal Treaties with the West in Nanjing. Ultimately, the foreigners themselves banded together, brought in reinforcements, and defeated the rebels. It was quite embarrassing for the Ching Court that it required the might of foreign powers to put down a rebellion in their own capital. The news has been reaching Naha regularly and in Ryukyu many fear the power of the Japanese. At the moment, Japan is much stronger than the Ching government and your countrymen worry that the government in Tokyo might expand trade with the Western foreigners and their 'Black Ships' with fearsome cannons in Naha and Shuri. The Japanese are also nervous about the possibility of a local uprising in Ryukyu similar to the Boxers. They are particularly strict and vigilant about even modest resistance. Among the ordinary people and those with whom I do business in Ryukyu, honestly speaking, there is more concern and uncertainty than confidence about the situation."

Sensing Kanbun's homesickness, Wu asked, "Would you like to accompany me on my next trading journey to Naha? You look a lot like a local man from Nanyoi these days, and we can disguise you as one of my trading partners from Fujou. It will be risky nonetheless, but you will be able to see your homeland for yourself."

"Yes," added Jou, "It would be good for Sanra to see his homeland, consider his own situation, and make plans for the next few years."

Kanbun was overjoyed with Wu's invitation and Jou's support. His face brightened and he replied, "Yes, that would be wonderful. Thank you so much. I will work for you on the journey in any way I can, even if it means only doing the job of the lowest crew member. But, may I make one request?"

"What would that be," asked Wu.

"I have a close friend who is staying at the Gushing Spring Temple. He and I escaped the Japanese military draft in a small group, crossed over to Fujou on the same ship, and initially studied *wushu* together at the temple. His name is Matsuda, or 'Shaotian' in Chinese, and it would be splendid if he could go too."

"Why not," suggested Jou, "Two might even be a better way to conceal an identity than one. "Besides," he added with a laugh, "these two ruffians can help provide protection against potential pirates and bandits."

With that, it was decided that Kanbun would contact Matsuda and invite him to join Wu and his crew on a secret return visit to Ryukyu. The next morning Kanbun wrote a letter in Japanese to Tokusaburo at the Gushing Spring Temple. He explained that he had been training in *wushu* for the past several

213

years and that a mentor in Fujou had introduced him to an honest and trustworthy man who could bring them safely on a short visit to Ryukyu. Three days later a very brief reply arrived from Tokusaburo arrived.

"I am ready," it said.

Kanbun consulted with Jou about what he should do to prepare. Jou took Kanbun to a barber in Fujou who shaved the front half of his head and braided his now long hair in the back into a tight queue so he had the look of a Mandarin. Jou also lent him a piece of jade to hang around his neck, rings for his fingers, and a brightly embroidered robe to wear that would stand in contrast to the single colored jacket and pantaloons most men wore in Ryukyu. Together, they went to the Gushing Spring Temple and requested that Matsuda come out to join them. A short time later, Tokusaburo appeared. His head was shaved clean, he had on the plain clothing of a young trainee at the temple, and he was carrying a small bundle of clothing that was held together by a thin cloth *furoshiki* tied around it. At first, Tokusaburo walked right past them. Kanbun called out to his friend in the local dialect of Motobu. Tokusaburo turned around and peered to the left, right, and behind him looking for the body connected to the voice that was sure to be from his friend Kanbun. When he realized that Kanbun had changed his appearance and had come with his friend, Tokusaburo fell down laughing and holding his belly on the ground.

"Ha-ha," he choked, "you had me fooled. But wait until our friends from home see you. They will think you..." And, he laughed some more.

"You are a pretty sight yourself," chortled Kanbun. "You look like a half Japanese, half Chinese itinerant monk who has been banished from his temple."

At last, Tokusaburo got up still chuckling and introduced himself properly to Jou in Chinese, "How do you do, sir. It is an honor to meet you. I am Matsuda Tokusaburo, but here they call me 'Shaotian' and I live in this temple. I was born in Motobu, like Shandi Wanwen, and came here together with him, but I would have never guessed that he had become a native."

He continued to laugh and explained, "We both wanted to escape serving the Japanese military and to learn Chinese *wushu*. It seems we have both been able to follow our paths, but what a different one Shandi Wanwen has taken. He looks like he has been studying Chinese theater in addition to *wushu*."

Jou then introduced himself and explained, "Sanra here tells me that you are a good and trusted friend and that you might want to join him on a visit to Ryukyu. I am happy to introduce my close compatriot Wu Hsienkuei who can take you both on the journey.

"Thank you, sir. I am indebted and will do whatever you ask," replied Tokusaburo.

"Ha," responded Jou half seriously, "I already told Sanra that here in China it might be dangerous to offer to 'do anything' before it is requested. I guess those priests in the Gushing Spring Temple haven't taught you all there is to know about China. But, your Chinese is quite good, so maybe the priests are of some use after all."

"It is a great honor to meet Shandi's respected friend, replied Tokusaburo, and you reminded me of what we used to call him."

215

"Ah, yes, he told me about his nickname and it has become kind of an inside joke in Nanyoi," Jou answered. When he has a chance, Sanra can tell you about it. Actually, now that I think about it, you will both need an alias while back in Ryukyu. Would Sanra also work well in place of Shandi Wanwen in Ryukyu?"

"Yes it would," replied Kanbun and Tokusaburo.

"I think I will use a regular Ryukyu name, like Higa or Oshiro, because I look like an acolyte from a Buddhist Temple, which are much the same in our homeland. I can pretend to be an advisor to Master Wu and 'Sanra' when we are in Ryukyu," reasoned Tokusaburo.

The three then turned and departed for Fujou, chatting on the way to a tea warehouse owned by Wu Hsienkuei. After arriving, they sat in the waiting room at the front of the building, sipping tea and continuing their conversation. Before long, Wu returned and greeted them warmly. After introductions, he said to Tokusaburo, "Shaotian, you are welcome to accompany us on the journey to Naha."

"Thank you very much," replied Tokusaburo seriously. "It has been some years since we visited our homeland, and I miss it very much. If there is time and it is safe enough, I hope to contact my family in Motobu while there. I thank you from my heart for your kind offer and generous hospitality."

"You are welcome," Wu replied, "but it is not all hospitality. I may ask for your labor or assistance during the journey and perhaps in Naha. You should also know that the situation has tightened for refugees from Ryukyu like you. Recently, the Japanese quickly and soundly defeated the Russian navy at sea near Lushun in northeast China by the Korean Peninsula. It was a surprisingly easy victory for the Japanese and a hard loss for the

Russian Imperial Navy. The Japanese have only recently modernized, while the proud Russians have been powerful for centuries but now seem on the decline like the Ching Dynasty in Beijing whom the Japanese also defeated about a decade ago. As a result, the Japanese have gained a great deal of confidence and have been extending their influence across East and Southeast Asia. You can feel this in Naha, which is only a small but relatively significant port for them. The Japanese authorities are checking the ships that enter and leave the harbor, and they are also arresting young men who try to escape their military draft."

"We understand the dangers and we are prepared to work on the ship or in the harbor," responded Tokusaburo and Kanbun.

"Good, we can leave tomorrow. Tonight, Sanra, you and Shaotian can stay with me," he added.

Jou nodded and departed for Nanyoi. Kanbun and Tokusaburo thanked Wu again and followed him out of the warehouse area to his home nearby. It was the home of a successful merchant with servants, fine furnishings, and a size that was far greater than ordinary. Tokusaburo, who had not been to such a refined household, was amazed with the quality of care, skilled craftsmanship of the design, fine materials used for the main structure and elegant interior, and the number of servants and assistants, especially having lived until that time in the austere atmosphere of a monk in training at the Gushing Spring Temple in Fujou. They ate and drank well that evening, and it was Tokusaburo who once again was most amazed by Wu's hospitality after the modest meals of rice, soup, stir fried vegetables, and no meat or fish at the temple. They chatted in Japanese, which Wu preferred to do before departing for Naha. Since they were speaking Japanese, the two younger men called their host "Go-san." This was less honorific than "Master Wu" that the merchant had suggested Kanbun refrain from using earlier, but was still a polite way to address a respected and trusted friend.

The next morning, the three men walked into Fujou. Quite unexpectedly, they bumped into Shingaki Tomohiro, who had accompanied Kanbun and Tokusaburo from Naha, on the street as he was pulling a cart piled high with compressed tea. He had more difficulty adapting to life in Fujian, was working as a laborer in the fields of tea bushes, and made his home alone in a shed. He had no close friends in Fujou and he looked forlorn. Tomohiro threw himself into a kneeling position on the ground and begged Wu to let him accompany his countrymen to Ryukyu. He explained that he had no plan to return to Fujou and would face whatever the consequences in Naha.

Wu thought a while and said, "It will be hard work, uncomfortable, and dangerous. You can come with us, but I will treat you as a laborer while Kanbun and Tokusaburo will be my associates. Would that be agreeable to you?"

Tomohiro stayed kneeling on the ground, put his forehead to the dirt, and thanked Wu sincerely. "My family will be deeply grateful, and you, your family, and your friends will always be honored guests if you visit our home in Ryukyu," he replied.

Tomohiro made no preparations and departed with them on the spot. They walked to the docks and got on a boat that paddled them to the harbor at the mouth of Min River, where they disembarked only to board a larger vessel that would carry them to Naha. Kanbun, Tokusaburo, and Tomohiro waited on the ship while Go took care of business at the warehouses behind the wharf. At last, he appeared and gave the signal to the captain to be underway. On the journey to Naha, it turned out there was little need for Kanbun and Tokusaburo to assist the crew, as Go Kenki had made adequate arrangements in advance, but Tomohiro stayed below the deck ill with seasickness. Kanbun and Tokusaburo spent time together catching up on what they had been doing over the past number of years and talking about their impending return visit to Ryukyu.

Kanbun began, "after leaving Gushing Spring Temple, I happened to chance upon Master Jou Tzuhe. I was sitting by a dock along the Min River after a heavy rain storm. It had become difficult to cross and the ferry was in danger of being swept away. I assisted with the recovery of the boat by getting a donkey to help me pull it ashore, which aided the ferry master and Jou, who lives on the other side of the river, so they were kind to me. Jou invited me to his home and I lodged for a few days, when I discovered he is a teacher of *wushu*. I was very lucky and he agreed to let me stay at his home and learn his tiger *wushu*. He also introduced me to another great man, Master Hsu, who has taught me so much but about whom I know so little. It seems that Master Jou also supports him, but I don't know any of the details. I don't know if Master Hsu is married, has other students, who his teacher was, or even his first name now that I think of it. He is a remarkable man in different sorts of ways. He is teaching me a combination of southern Chinese soft and hard systems, something he calls *pangainoon*, but it is so much more than a system. It is a way of thinking and being."

At this point, Kanbun paused in thought, and Tokusaburo picked up the conversation, "yes I hear about *pangainoon* from the priests in temple. It seems to be relatively widely applied to a range of styles that were taught in the Southern Shaolin Temple.

Some people mention the hard and soft systems of *wushu*, and occasionally they talk of the combination of the two."

"I have been living there, growing herbs and medicinal plants, selling them in Fukushu, and training in *wushu* two or three times a day," went on Kanbun. "I really have been lucky to meet Jou Tzuhe and have the chance to study under Master Hsu."

"My temple life has been pretty good, too," replied Tokusaburo. "There are a lot of young people who come and go at the temple. I understand it is quite famous and indeed it is a busy place that welcomes regular worshippers from Fukushu, pilgrims from other provinces, priests and acolytes from other temples, and wandering souls like you and me. We hear all kinds of stories and rumors, and it is hard to know what to believe. Those who are like me stay for a while, help maintain the grounds and temple buildings, tend to the gardens, and assist the acolytes who are serious about Buddhism and want to become priests. They give us a place to stay, some food, language instruction, and training in their *wushu*. Some people brag about the strengths of one kind of *wushu* in comparison to others, while others talk about all the instability in Peking and how it affects Fukushu. People who practice *wushu* here are very spirited, but there is so much variety, different kinds of training, and a mixture of styles that it is hard to know who does what and who is really good. Some people will pick up parts of one, two, or three systems, inject their own ideas, and make something different out of it altogether. It is not always clear how much depth there is to it, and I am often confused. It is not surprising that you say you are learning from Jou and Hsu at the same time. There seems to be a flow of influences and ideas that come together, break apart, and go in a new direction, unlike the straight line of master to student we are accustomed to in Ryukyu. Also, a lot of ordinary people seem insecure, and the merchants and traders are concerned they might lose control of their businesses and land to marauding warlords, boxer groups, political revolutionaries, foreign powers, or even the erratic and unpredictable Ching Court. Of course, there are secrets upon secrets and it makes my head spin sometimes trying to sort them out or to understand what is true and real. Last year, Makabei disappeared and the *wushu* training sessions at the temple have become disorganized. Instead, the temple priests have been tutoring a few of us."

"What do you mean Makabei disappeared?" asked Kanbun.

"Makabei was always ill-tempered and mean to others, especially newer students," replied Tokusaburo. "He was a little easier to deal with after you got to know him better. But, he was a very tough and strict teacher, and we all improved because of him. One day, he took a trip to Chanjou, which is another city south of here that is also a trading port where a number of people from Ryukyu live, but he never came back. Some people say he got sick and died unexpectedly, and others think he challenged another *wushu* expert who killed him. There is a rumor that the *wushu* expert broke one of Makabei's arms, then the next, and finally killed him with single blow to the side of his head. If that's the case, it would take an exceptionally strong and skilled practitioner to defeat someone as formidable as Makabei."

The two young men continued to talk for a while about their experiences and lives since arriving in Fukushu until Go Kenki joined them for a cup of tea after dinner.

"I am so excited about being able to return home and get in touch with my family," said Tokusaburo in Japanese. "Thank you very much, Go-san, for making these kind arrangements."

"You will probably find that the atmosphere in Naha is different since you departed some years ago," replied Go.

"Yes, but so little has changed in Motobu for decades or centuries that I can imagine my home village just as I left it. I miss the dragon boat races in Nago Bay in spring and the *chanpuru* my mother used to mix together with goya, carrots, mushrooms, tofu, pork, and soy sauce" said Tokusaburo wistfully.

"If I think about it about," added Kanbun, "Ryukyu and our people are kind of like *chanpuru*—a mix of flavors, textures, colors, and shapes from China, Japan, Southeast Asia, and our own islands. I hope to be able to contact my family and visit Motobu for a day or two if there is time. Do you think that will be possible?"

"We are making good time and should arrive in Naha on schedule or a little early. The winds are with us," said Go. "If the Japanese port officials are not too bothersome and we can conclude business reasonably quickly, there should be a few extra days for a side trip."

Kanbun thought about his own family and how much he missed his modest but comfortable home in Izumi. Would it be safe to see his family? For years he had not sent a letter for fear of being discovered, nor had they made any attempt to contact him as far as he knew. Grandfather would be happy and proud to see how much skill Kanbun had developed from his training in *wushu*. He hoped to be able show him some of what he learned from Jou and especially Hsu and how it built on but went far beyond the *kobujutsu* and *toodi* Grandfather had taught him. He pictured Kazue by the beach in Motobu, in the vegetable garden next to her home in Izumi, and in the village gatherings at the school. The gentle sway of her figure, the beguiling smile on her face, and the delicate perfume of her clothes were all near and real to him.

Go continued with his thoughts, "Ever since the Sino-Japanese War about a decade ago, the attacks from Chinese and Southeast Asian pirate ships have increased, while the Japanese authorities have become stricter and more attentive in Naha. The risks are great, but the demand for tea, lumber, ceramics, and silks are still strong and the profits are good, so it is worth the trouble and danger."

"I had no idea that the trade between Ryukyu could be so uncertain or hazardous," said Kanbun.

"We are from Motobu and know very little about commerce and trade," added Tokusaburo.

"Of course, there has been a very active maritime trade between the islands in East, Southeast, and even South Asia and the markets on the continent for many centuries," explained Go. "The commerce we carry on amongst ourselves has been beneficial, but the British promoted the opium trade, which has been a disaster for the Chinese people, society, and government. It began when the English started trading with India about three hundred years ago. Eventually, they took complete control of that country by military force, made it a colony of the British Empire, and presided over its trade and society. At the same time, they were also buying large amounts of tea, silk, and porcelain from China, which meant they would have to use their stockpiles of silver for exchange. In time, they contrived to export opium from India and trade it instead of silver for the products they wanted from China. The British created a huge market that made them prosperous and powerful, even though in China it has long been forbidden to import opium and those that smoke it face severe penalties if caught. The English continue to sell their opium to smugglers and pirates who transport and then distribute it in the illegal trade with unlawful groups on the mainland. Canton, which is south of here, and Fujian have been the main centers of this illicit activity and it makes it dangerous for legitimate traders like me to operate and succeed."

"Opium provides short term solace from toil and pain for hardworking Chinese laborers who suffer under harsh and difficult conditions," Go went on. However, the tragedy is that eventually they become addicted and indolent, stop working, and engage in crime to support their cravings. The British have no misgivings about selling the opium and causing wide social destruction, even though it is illegal in China and they have little use for it themselves. Twice, China went to war with England over the illegal trade in opium, but we lost each time. After the second of these wars about forty years ago, China had to settle by giving up trading rights at some of its ports, lowering its import tariffs, relinquishing the island of Hong Kong in Canton to the British, and yielding other concessions in a series of Unequal Treaties. This was a shameful outcome for the proud Manchus, the rulers of the Ching Court in Peking. These unfortunate circumstances also opened the door for other foreign powers, such as the United States, France, Germany, Russia, and Japan to be aggressive and seize trading rights in China. Subsequently, China has been experiencing an anti-foreign backlash, most notably among secret societies such as the Boxers, the White Lotus, and the Black Dragon Society. This is unfortunate because the world is changing and modernizing. Foreigners have built great steel railroads and steamships, burning coal rather than relying on the wind to power them, and they have developed many other technologies that help them get ahead and prosper, which we could learn about and use. Regrettably, in China we fight among ourselves, arguing over whether to welcome the future optimistically or retrench and restore the grand culture and glories of the ancient past. The Ching Court in Peking is too corrupt and unstable to be able to stand up to outside powers, or even internal, pressure to lead the country in new directions. I worry about the future of China."

"I am sympathetic to Ryukyu," Go added. "Your country, while beholden to the Ching Court, came under the jurisdiction of Satsuma in southern Japan, which usurped the rights and livelihoods of the native people. This left the King of Ryukyu and his administration in a delicate position to balance good relations with both China and Japan, who came into conflict with each other. When the 'Black Ships' from America stopped in Naha and demanded from Shuri Castle the right to use Ryukyu as a naval base before going on to force the Japanese to open up to trade with the West, it was another case of an outside power pressuring an undeveloped country for its own benefit. The Americans had no idea or interest in how delicate the relations with neighboring powers were for the Kingdom of Ryukyu to concede landing and storage rights to a foreign naval power that was planning to use that base to strengthen its foothold in China and gain concessions from Japan. And then during the last decade, the worst scenario for Ryukyu occurred. Japan went to war with China, and Ryukyu was again caught in the middle. In the end, Japan won the conflict and asserted complete jurisdiction over your kingdom, controlled your trade, and even changed the name of it to 'Okinawa' and making it one of the provinces of Japan."

Kanbun and Tokusaburo were amazed and impressed with the breadth and depth of his understanding and how current his knowledge was about China, Ryukyu, and the region. He explained the status of their Ryukyu Kingdom in relation to China, Japan, Asia, and the West in ways they had not considered before or realized.

"My family and I, as well as the people I know in Motobu, feel a closer kinship with China than Japan" said Kanbun. A lot of our customs, the kinds of food we eat, our rural way of life, and our beliefs are similar to those in China. Even though officially we speak Japanese, I noticed our Ryukyu dialect sounds closer to some of the Chinese spoken in Fujian."

The three men sat on the deck of the ship feeling the warm breeze and gazing at the view out over the East China Sea, which was lighted by a crescent moon and an ocean of stars in the sky. On the return journey, the shipped steered clear of Formosa, or what some now called "Taiwan." In addition to Ryukyu, which the Japanese now called "Okinawa," they had taken Formosa from China as spoils from their war ten years earlier and had changed the name to "Taiwan." The previous name of "Formosa" or the "Beautiful Island" had been established by Portuguese explorers centuries earlier. Unfortunately, during the current era of confusion amidst war and conflict, the north coast of Formosa had become a hornet's nest of smugglers, contraband, and illegal activities, even though Japan was working to establish its own orderly administration on the newly acquired island.

After a few more days at sea, the outer islands of the Ryukyu chain came into view. Kanbun and Tokusaburo heaved a sigh of relief and looked on expectantly as they realized they missed their homeland more than they thought. It seemed like many long years for both of them since they had departed Naha to take up new lives in Fukushu as renegades from the Japanese government and its laws on military conscription. Next in view was the main island of their homeland, and then the port of Naha. They felt like jumping overboard and swimming for shore, except that a good breeze was blowing from the west carrying them as fast as the ship would move. At last, they reached the docks, which were even busier with laborers, sailors, and traders than they remembered. They noticed the officious looking Japanese military police in the harbor patrol who officiated over the shipping activities in their stiff wool uniforms and tight caps. Kanbun, Tokusaburo, and Tomohiro suppressed their enthusiasm as the presence of the Japanese authorities reminded them that they were subject to Japanese law, justice, and penalties for having escaped Ryukyu several years earlier.

Kanbun assumed his role as a companion to Go Kenki, while Tokusaburo took on the character of a native guide. Tomohiro stayed with the deck hands wearing only britches and he smeared black sesame oil on his hands, chest, and face. Kanbun and Tokusaburo disembarked from the ship, assisted Go with accounting for their cargo, and moved on to a tea shop where the Chinese merchant conducted his trade. There was something familiar about the shop, and Kanbun and Tokusaburo realized it was the same place where the kind proprietor had given them fresh tea and friendly advice to the four youths from Motobu who were planning to escape to China at least a decade earlier. While Go was discussing his trade with the shopkeeper, several Japanese police appeared with pistols on their hips. They demanded to know who the visitors were and where they were from. Go explained that he was a tea merchant from Fukushu who regularly visited Naha for trade. He pointed to "Sanra," whom he introduced as a business partner in China who was hoping to engage in trade with Okinawa. Go told the police that Sanra spoke no Japanese. Kanbun clasped his hands together in front of him and bowed to the police without saying anything. Next, he introduced Tokusaburo as "Higa" who, as he explained was born and raised in Fukushu, though his family was originally from Okinawa. Higa bowed respectfully and told the police in Chinese accented Japanese that he had accompanied Go and Sanra to assist them with business contacts and negotiations in Naha. In very polite language yet firm and confident tones, Go repeated that they were visiting Naha for trade and urged the police to let them go about their business.

The police consulted separately among themselves briefly and brusquely announced that they would escort the men to their ship. Go and Tokusaburo were about to protest, but realized there was little they could do but comply. If they resisted, the Japanese police were likely to become suspicious and cause a disturbance in the shop of Go's trading partner and make things especially difficult when they returned to the docks. They asked the police in their most gracious and respectful language for a few minutes to conclude their business as they were making only a brief stop in Naha and would accompany the police forthwith to their ship. The police ordered them to finish their negotiations promptly as they would not wait.

The three traders from China and the local tea wholesaler switched to Chinese and sat down to discuss the situation. They spoke quickly. Go explained to the shopkeeper, with whom he had a long done business and trusted deeply, that Tokusaburo and Kanbun were indeed renegades from the Japanese draft. Kanbun thanked the shop owner for his kindness years earlier, even though he had not recognized the young men. The shopkeeper was surprised because Kanbun looked so much the part of a Chinese merchant. He mentioned that he had often come across young men from Ryukyu who were looking for ways to avoid forced induction into Japanese military service. Some were caught and imprisoned; for others, their families suffered persecution from the authorities. Some were able to escape, but few had returned to Ryukyu after going overseas. The shopkeeper offered to help them by trying to find out what would happen to the ship, the cargo, and crew. This might take hours or even days, and he suggested it might not be safe for Kanbun and Tokusaburo to stay in Naha in the meantime. Go agreed and offered to arrange return passage to Fujou as quickly as possible for Kanbun and to Motobu for Tokusaburo.

The police escorted Go, Kanbun, and Tokusaburo to the ship. The officials ordered them to cease unloading the cargo and for the full crew to line up in front of the ship. They asked the crew several questions, which except for Tomohiro who looked nervous, they could not answer. Dissatisfied, the harbor police ordered the shipment, of which about half was now sitting on the docks, to be returned to the ship and quarantined for the time being. They also pulled three of the sailors, including Tomohiro, out of the line and ordered them to the police station. They looked perplexed, uncomfortable, and fearful as Tokusaburo translated and explained to them what they were to do. Reluctantly, they fell in with the guards leading them away from the harbor and toward the police station.

That afternoon on board the ship they had sailed from Fujou, Kanbun drafted a note to his family. He explained that he had managed a short visit to Naha but it was too dangerous for him to stay or to travel to Izumi. He wrote that he missed them very much and hoped everyone was well, even his donkey Baro. He went on to explain that an acquaintance from Motobu, Shingaki Tomohiro, who had travelled both ways to China with him had been arrested by the Japanese authorities and did not know what would happen to him. He asked them to try to find Tomohiro's family, tell them that he was in jail in Naha, and to see if they might be able to arrange some help for him. Kanbun hid the letter in a crack in the boards under the deck. He went to sleep that night thinking about how to have the letter delivered to Izumi without being discovered by the port authorities.

The next morning, Go said that he heard from the tea shop owner that the Japanese police had taken turns keeping Tomohiro and the others awake at night and forced them to run with their hands and feet tied together with rope while denying them food and water. The police threatened to torture them unless the three men admitted more than they were saying. The three sailors held out saying the police were mistaken and they were merely visitors from Fukkensho. Finally, after non-stop punishment and new threats to crush their fingers in the metal door of the jail door, Tomohiro relented for the sake of the two Chinese crewmen and confessed to being a renegade from the Japanese draft. The police released the Chinese crew members, but threw Tomohiro in a small cell crowded with other criminals and prisoners.

Go explained that he had been to Naha a number of times, was known there in commercial circles, and generally had good relations with the port officials, but Kanbun might now fall under suspicion. He had arranged for Kanbun to change ships and it would be best for him to depart for Fujou the next morning when it would be ready to sail. Before sunset, Kanbun descended from the ship he was now holed up in and approached a workman on the dock. He gave the letter addressed to his parents and a small coin to the laborer saying that he should destroy the note rather than have it discovered. He could also deny that he knew the identity of the author of the letter, where he was from, or what was doing in Naha, which was all true. Kanbun re-boarded the ship not knowing if the letter would reach Izumi. He stayed awake and alert all night.

On the ocean journey back to Fujou, Kanbun had time to reflect on his situation in regards to Ryukyu and China. He felt nostalgic, even homesick, about Izumi. It was wonderful to have been able to come as far as Naha, but frustrating and ironic that he could not travel home to see his family and friends. Did this mean that he would have to live permanently in China? Would there ever be a time when he could return home without risk to his freedom? Would he see his family or Kazue again? He was certain of his Ryukyu identity, though his poignant thoughts and feelings also roused a sense of kinship with China that was deeper than merely braiding his hair, changing his clothes, and wearing rings on his fingers.

It saddened and troubled Kanbun that he had been responsible for causing difficulties for Wu, whom he respected and owed a great deal in gratitude. He had been a party to Tomohiro joining the journey home, for whom it had ended so badly. He was also worried because he did not know what would happen to his good friend Tokusaburo. He regretted not planning more carefully or thinking about how they could have protected themselves better.

These experiences led him to a new realization on the limits to individual power. Kanbun, Tokusaburo, and Go were all sufficiently trained in *wushu* and skillful enough to protect themselves against most ordinary men. However, as he thought about the dynamics of power, such as the power of the police in Naha to arrest and imprison Tomohiro, the power of the Japanese to overwhelm Ryukyu, the power of the American "Black Ships" and their cannons to open the seemingly unbeatable Japan to trade, the power of the British to engage in illegal commerce in China, and the failed power of the White Lotus Society and the Boxers to resist the foreign government and its intrusions, he realized that the successful application of power also required strategy, organization, and planning. He was reminded of Jou's explanation of the difference between strength and power, how it should move and flow. Makabei had been one of the strongest people Kanbun had ever met, but even he succumbed to someone with superior skills or strategy. Physical strength might be helpful or even life saving in unusual circumstances, but power required mobilizing multiple capabilities and focusing them toward a specific outcome. He began to see this was true for him as an individual in his own *wushu* practice, for groups hoping to improve their societies, and for nations when confronting each other in war. He began to see glimpses of applying the lessons he learned from Grandfather in

232

Izumi and pushing and pulling with his pet Baro, from Jou in landing lightly on the logs floating in the water ditch, from the books on strategy by Suntzu and Miyamoto, from developing strength that was circular as well as linear in his daily practice, from the way in which he instinctively escaped the three toughs who accosted him in Fujou, and from the extraordinarily concentrated power of Master Hsu who had blocked the kicks of the donkey and dispensed with the animal using his hard to reckon "Iron Palm." It all rushed through his mind. Parts were clear and unambiguous, while others required more thought.

Kanbun also realized that the sophisticated Jou, his friend Wu, and their colleagues were concerned about power. They were worried that the unstable situation in Peking was spreading all the way to the provinces like Fujian. If secret anti-government groups like the Boxers or bandit warlords, or even foreign intruders, were to organize and try to confiscate their homes, lands, and businesses in Fujou, there would be limits to what Jou and Wu could do to stop them. Kanbun now understood better why Jou was secretly training a group of *wushu* practitioners at his home. Like the stout wall surrounding his great house, his students were another layer of protection. It was by no means a foolproof or impenetrable defense, but Jou's cohort of youthful followers trained in *wushu* might forestall an attack if it were to come. Kanbun was reminded that he came from an extremely modest background and that he had next to nothing in the way of possessions. Even if he felt disappointed and lonely in his current circumstances, he had little to lose. Jou and his circle of acquaintances in Fujou, on the other hand, had much to lose, and it weighed heavily upon them. Realistically, as Kanbun thought about it, he had few choices. Continuing with Jou Tzuhe, Master

Hsu, and his livelihood in Nanyoi was the best, perhaps only, option open to him. Jou was open-minded, generous, and helpful. Hsu was a dedicated and high level *wushu* instructor. Kanbun had much to be grateful for.

Fortunately, Kanbun's actual journey to Fujou was as uneventful as his first one, though fraught with questions and concerns. This time he had so much more to think about, the world was far more dangerous than he had even imagined those years earlier, and he had so much more to reflect upon. After returning to the great house in Nanyoi, which by now had become familiar and comfortable like another home to him, Kanbun explained to Jou the difficulties he, Tokusaburo, and Wu had encountered in Naha. He reiterated his gratitude to Jou, apologized for being troublesome in Naha to his friend Wu, and made a renewed commitment to following his guidance in pursuing the path of *wushu*. Inwardly, Kanbun resolved to make the most of his time in Fujou, however long that would be, and to re-dedicate himself to training in *wushu* and to the development of himself as a man.

In the weeks and months that followed, it seemed to Kanbun that Master Hsu led him to another level in his *wushu* practice. He added a training session in midday. He taught Kanbun the next principal pre-arranged form, which was *sanseiryu* in his hard-soft *pangainoon* system. It was more expansive than the intermediate *seisan*, and its range was spread out over greater space. Physically and strategically, it contained new information, techniques, situations, movements, and dynamics. In order to supplement his instruction in *sanseiryu*, Hsu began working with Kanbun on specific techniques as well. They practiced together, dissecting and analyzing every move in *sanseiryu*. Hsu taught

Kanbun how to use the single knuckle punch introduced in *seisan* and which he had strengthened by pounding the padded beam in Jou's courtyard and thrusting through the bamboo fence in the area behind the manor. Hsu showed Kanbun that he could destroy an opponent's attack by striking the strike with a single knuckle punch.

"Strike the punch with your single knuckle," said Hsu, "and your attacker will falter. Block your opponent's kick by striking it with the four-knuckle fist and you will either break his leg or cause so much pain he will be unable to walk. If the kick is low, use your kick against it. Your feet and toes are conditioned enough to stop it before it hits you. Apply the finger flick and the tiger hand to deflect an attack and counter strike simultaneously. Do not give your opponent the space or opportunity to develop a second or follow on attack. This is the 'hard' element of *pangainoon*."

Hsu told Kanbun to meet him early the next morning while it was still dark. He had Kanbun sit in a kneeling position facing the east until the sun rose above the horizon.

Hsu instructed Kanbun, "Clear your mind by letting every thought escape from you. Think of your brain as a muscle that you are letting relax. It should become supple, untroubled, and free from care or thought."

Next, while Kanbun was in an upside down position with his feet against the courtyard wall and progressing through his routine of placing his hands flat against the stone floor, in fists, with wrists bent, and up on finger tips, Hsu instructed Kanbun to steady his breathing, count his breaths, and calm his mind. Kanbun, though exerting himself physically in these positions, steadied his breath, began to breath normally, and then even relaxed comfortably.

"This is the 'soft' of *pangainoon*," said Hsu.

One evening, Jou, Jiang, Lee, and Kanbun sat sipping tea after practice. The night was warm and there was a pleasant breeze blowing across the fields. It seemed an opportunity for Kanbun to learn perhaps something new from his seniors and mentor. Kanbun began with a question he had wanted to ask, but had refrained from doing so until the right moment.

"Master Jou, who was your teacher," he asked in earnest.

Jou at first looked a little puzzled, but then replied with a knowing smile, "Oh, you mean my teachers. I have worked hardest at the tiger style, but actually learned different kinds of *wushu* from at least several teachers. It is best to think broadly, deeply, and openly about multiple sources of information and training. One day, like Jiang and Lee, you will be able to go forward and develop your own way."

Kanbun's next question was, "is our training similar to what Feng Laohu used to develop himself so effectively?"

Jiang and Lee looked blank.

"Who?" asked Jou.

"You once told Wu Hsienkuei and me the story about Feng Laohu, the *wushu* master who was capable of defeating many, but eventually feigned losing to end the fighting," he reminded him.

Jou burst into laughter, "Ah, now I remember. I made up that story to illustrate a point. There is no need to take me so seriously."

Kanbun was embarrassed by this response, dropped his questioning, and sat silently with the three men.

Hsu continued his advanced training of Kanbun for some months, during which time he explained the significance of the in-between spaces in *sanseiryu*. He described the turns, pauses, shifts in direction, and seemingly unimportant parts as the glue or the chain that held the sequence and flow together. He taught Kanbun to focus not on the central action taking place, such as the block, strike, or kick, at which he was already skilled, but rather the transitions from one to the other or the places in-between.

"By watching what goes on away from the center of action, you can assess the skills and power of a *wushu* practitioner," said Hsu. Watching the in-between spaces is not just theory or an abstraction, but also has a practical application. Just before or after an attack, when commencing or recoiling, your opponent is at his weakest and it is the best timing for counterattack."

"The spaces between movements in *sanseiryu*," Hsu went on, "are also like your back and spine in relation to your upper and lower body. The upper body has the shoulders, arms, and hands, while the lower body has the hips, legs, and feet. Each has its function and strength, but it is the soft middle of the body that connects the upper and lower centers of power together. That is why we focus our central energy while doing forms by tucking under our hip muscles, firming up the belly in the front, lowering our body weight, and breathing forcefully like a dragon. The middle connects the extremities, and without it the upper and lower body are separated and weaker. This is true for the pauses and spaces in-between in *sanchin*, *seisan*, *sanseiryu*, and *suparinpei*. You must be firm yet flexible, tying together the whole body with movement. This is yet another meaning of the hard and soft of *pangainoon*."

He elaborated, "There are also sequences of actions that connect the truly important and significant events in your life. There were many things that you yourself did, but also others that occurred in your homeland, many of them seemingly inconsequential, before you departed Ryukyu and led you to Fujou. There was a separate series of events that led our friend Jou and you to the Min River bank where you met, and all of them when tied in a sequence and added together became the result of where you and I are today. The same is true with strategy. Alter one element in the chain that leads to an interaction or a conflict, and the outcome will be different."

Time seemed to fly by for Kanbun as he devoted himself to training in *wushu*, all the while learning still more about materials, recipes, and applications of herbs and medicines and studying strategy from the books in Jou's library and in discussions with Master Hsu. He continued to note new information and insights as well as his thoughts and impressions in his journal, though there was less need for his dictionary. He could feel that he was beginning to excel, and at some indistinct point along his path Kanbun began to devise and invent his own training methods.

One day, Kanbun twisted his left thumb in a particularly intense training session and could practice only with his right arm. At first, he was angry with himself and frustrated that the injury would require an unwanted distraction and delay in his training. He tucked his left hand into the sash at his waist and practiced *sanchin*, *seisan*, and *sanseiryu* using only his right arm. It felt quite different and asymmetrical. Even going through the full forms without using his left arm, his hand on that side began to throb. Next, in frustration, he sat in a kneeling position closed his eyes, and mentally walked through each of the three forms and other practices and training. This gave him an opportunity to review where he felt most confident and strong and where he needed work to improve individual moves, transitions, steps, stances, and more. He decided that when his left hand healed, he would sit in the kneeling position and practice the routines to strengthen his concentration, clarity of mind, individual movements, transitions, and upper body movements in general. Kanbun then began to think about the sequence of forms without any arm or upper body movements focusing only on his lower body. He stood and walked through the forms, again noting how it felt different to emphasize only his foot positioning, legs, transitions, and lower body strength. Next, he decided to deprive himself of another part of his being while practicing the forms. He closed his eyes and walked through the sequences. To his surprise, he learned that his balance was not as stable as he had thought and his steps and turns were not as consistent or squared as when his eyes were open and he was able to use them for visual reference. In fact, he ended up in a different spot and facing an angled direction rather than straight forward when he finished one of the routines and opened his eyes. He repeated the forms with his eyes closed, but this time using his hearing, the touch of his feet, and his other senses to achieve better bearings, awareness, and balance throughout the forms. He could feel the air on his skin, the heat from his body, gravity beneath his feet, the hair in his follicles, and the perspiration under his clothing, as well as smell the moist and verdant breezes that blew in from the fields, the odors that drifted from the corners of the courtyard, and dry wooden walls surrounding him. He could hear the rustle in the kitchen and smell the tastes that rose from the flour that Old Wu mixed with other ingredients frying in a saucepan. It was an increased level of consciousness and it reminded Kanbun of Jou's words regarding being able to see the invisible, hear the inaudible, perceive the intangible, and comprehend the unknowable. He understood how this special practice could help him reach beyond his everyday senses, observations, and experiences to develop greater awareness, comprehension, and perception.

While his left thumb was still healing, Kanbun practiced running, jumping, and landing on balance on the lip of the waist high ceramic pot in the courtyard. He went on to develop kicks, leaning from one side to the other, and doing hand stands on top of the great pot without tipping it over. Kanbun also practiced jumping ever more lightly onto the logs in the water pit. As he became confident and skillful at doing this, he began to jump from log to log, skipping back and forth, crossing his legs, changing his direction, leaping up high, and landing on balance.

Some weeks later on a spring day while on an expedition foraging for plants and materials to mix medicines that Old Wu had shown him how to make, he walked by a grove of poplar trees and sat down to enjoy the warm turn in the weather. He surveyed the landscape before him letting his mind wander over his life of study, practice, and training in Nanyoi and Fujou. He watched as caterpillars ate at the leaves and beetles scratched at the bark of the poplars. How could these diminutive and soft creatures tear open the trees? Out of curiosity, Kanbun reached up and grabbed a branch hanging near the ground where he was sitting. The branch stretched and broke after Kanbun gave it a pull. He stood up and tried his hand against a larger limb and found it breakable but more challenging. Next, he set his fingers against the bark on the remainder of the broken limb, dug in his nails, and peeled back the surface. It was different from the exercises he had done to strengthen his fingers, but it was good training, too. He grasped the trunk of the tree with his hands and burrowed his finger tips into the bark. He gripped and pulled and succeeded in tearing away a piece of bark. Not only had Kanbun progressed in his *wushu* more than he realized, but he was devising ways to develop his training further and perceive his world differently.

Toward the end of summer and in the midst of the typhoon season that year, a great storm struck the southeast of China including Canton and Fujian. It arrived with fearsome bursts of wind, rain, and damage to land and property. The inhabitants of Fujou and the surrounding areas stayed indoors to avoid injury. Kanbun sat in his room waiting out the storm and reading his books until he feel asleep. During the night, he was awoken by a crash, which was the sound of the wind ripping the heavy wooden door to his room away from its fasteners and blowing it out into the yard. Kanbun rose and went outdoors leaning against the wind and rain to fetch the door and return it to the opening in his room. The wet, slippery door twisted in his grasp and pushed against him as he lifted it and the wind blew fiercely. Kanbun dropped the door on the ground and returned to his room to pick up a length of rope. He tied one end of the rope around the middle of the door and the other around his waist. Next, he pulled against the weight of the door and the wind against his body, dragging the wooden boards on the ground across the yard, past his room, and toward the open space behind the great house. He strained, pulled, stumbled, and surged against the driving wind and rain and the heavy door that slid along behind him in the darkness. When he reached the incline on the other side of the clearing, he paused but then continued his effort until, covered with mud and soaking wet, he stood on top of the hill behind the great house. He stopped to catch his breath and to look at the storm gusting and blustering across the sky. He hoisted the door up in front of him, set his feet firmly on the ground, and lifted the sturdy wooden boards against the wind. He grunted, struggled, and raged against the storm as he held his position, neither losing the door, his posture, nor his composure. He had met the storm's challenge.

Before long, the wind lessened as the eye of the typhoon reached the outskirts of Fujou. Kanbun untied the rope from his waist and threw the door into the darkness. He heard it tumble and slide down the hill. He sat down on the grassy and muddy ground with the breeze cooling his thin wet summer clothing. Kanbun felt physically stretched but mentally at peace. There was little he could tangibly see, hear, smell, taste, or touch on top of the hill in the eye of the dark storm, and his thoughts turned inward. He recalled the triangular shape that Jou had described to him in which there were physical, mental, and spiritual planes to his training. Kanbun began to see that there was another dimension, that the triangle could become a pyramid. There was depth below and height above the triangle of dynamics and skills that he was learning and developing. He was not yet able to articulate this vision in clear thoughts or concrete words, but his sense and perception told him it was there and he would strive for it.

A few days later, Kanbun told Hsu about his experiments with new training and practice and holding the wooden door up against the storm. Hsu encouraged Kanbun explaining that he was reaching a new level in his development and that he should continue to observe, combine, experiment, invent, and expand his thinking about training in *wushu*.

Another time, while enjoying a midday meal with Jou, his benefactor began to talk about longer term planning for Kanbun. He mentioned that Jiang and Lee would be "graduating" and would leave his school soon to start their own training halls. They would be taking some of the students with them but return occasionally for consultation, training, and practice together with his students. Jou felt confident in their abilities and loyalties, and there was more than enough interest in *wushu* among other young people in the Fujou area so the two young teachers would have a reasonable chance of success.

"I suspect that one day other young men from Ryukyu will come looking beyond Fujou in places like Nanyoi for instruction in *wushu*," said Jou. "They can go to Jiang or Lee or eventually study from their students. I already have a student from Ryukyu in my school, which is enough," added Jou with a twinkle in his eyes. Turning more serious, he went on, "I want you to take their position as instructor for the younger students in the evening classes in the courtyard. Your skills in Chinese language, medicine, and *wushu* are sufficient to lead this group, and I want you to continue to train with Master Hsu in the morning. It is early yet for you to open a school. What's more, there are some in Fujou who equate Ryukyu with Japan, even calling it by its new Japanese name of Okinawa, and there is still much anti-Japanese sentiment left over from the Sino-Japanese War that was only a little more than ten years ago. Some have criticized me for teaching you, but I tell them to mind their own business and that you are really Chinese. However, there might be trouble if you were to start a school on your own. In any case, it appears you will be in Fujou and Nanyoi for a while. I suggest you get married, start a household, and settle down for a while," he added. "You do look rather Chinese now, and you can even become a Chinese husband," he said with a laugh.

Kanbun protested, "I don't know the tiger system well enough to teach it."

"Oh, that doesn't matter," replied Jou, "teach what you do know. What we do in my little courtyard behind the garden walls is merely what I know from multiple sources. 'Teach your students everything they know, but not everything you know' is a well-known proverb among Chinese teachers. Besides, it is unlikely that any of the students will have the dedication and energy, not to mention the time after working in the fields, to develop much skill anyway."

Kanbun had no immediate reply for Jou in regards to settling down. He had never given a thought to marriage and starting a family of his own in China and was startled by Jou's suggestion. His thoughts turned to Kazue and the warm feelings he kept for her. However, his life had changed so much since he had grown up in Izumi and it now seemed far away. He had matured and was much more aware of the ways of the world, its opportunities, and its dangers than when he was a country bumpkin from Motobu when he had arrived in Fujou about a decade earlier.

A few weeks later, Jou invited a farmer named Gao, who lived nearby and apparently had a large number of children, to his home and introduced Kanbun to him. A girl, presumably Gao's daughter, accompanied him, but no one addressed her, took notice of her, or even mentioned her name. The girl, who was attractive in her simple peasant clothing, seemed shy and nervous. Her long hair flowed over her shoulders in the back and she sat straight and attentively. Though she spoke not a word, there was something sympathetic, understanding, and appealing about the way she entered, listened patiently, and nodded politely. Jou explained to Gao that Kanbun, though lacking in formal education, was reliable, hardworking, and clever, and he had grown up in a farming village like Nanyoi. He looked just like other Chinese, except that he was originally from Ryukyu and had been staying with Jou for about ten years. He offered a small house nearby in which Kanbun and the girl could live and from which he could forage for ingredients for traditional medicines part of the time and assist Jou at his home when needed. The farmer spoke not at all to Kanbun, but agreed to Jou's proposal and the agreement was sealed with cups of wine.

Kanbun learned from Jou that the girl's name was Weiya, and soon afterward they were married. They settled into their home and over time began to get know each other. She cooked the meals he liked and asked no questions about how he spent his time with Jou. Kanbun continued to sell herbs, remedies, and medicines, and entrusted his new wife with the small savings he had accumulated until then, along with the modest income he received from his commerce in the local villages and on the streets of Fujou. One day, while cleaning, Weiya discovered Kanbun's Japanese to Chinese dictionary with the bookmark in it that Kazue had given him. She asked Kanbun if she could use the dictionary to learn some Japanese. Kanbun, though struck by the irony of her request and the origin of the dictionary, nonetheless let her look through the book and encouraged her by helping with pronunciations. Kanbun was surprised and delighted to be greeted at home pleasantly in the evening after instructing the students in Jou's courtyard with an "*Okaerinasai*," or "Welcome home," from his young and warm-hearted wife. Weiya often practiced using everyday words in Japanese and asked him to teach her the names of objects around their home. They became comfortable with each other's presence and enjoyed their meals together. The next spring she bore him a child, a girl, which pleased neither his father-in-law, nor his mother-in-law, nor their family, which seemed distant and cold to Kanbun. His wife's mother scolded Weiya that she had better bear a son the next time. Her brothers and sisters said nothing.

Kanbun continued to train daily under Hsu and in the evening he kept a strict yet fair atmosphere with his students in Jou's courtyard. His conversations with Hsu included thoughtful discussions about *wushu*, its origins, and his objectives. One day, Hsu asked Kanbun if his students were improving and whether he had any prospects for special training. Kanbun replied that it was still too early to say for certain. Hsu then explained to Kanbun more clearly his approach to training.

"I have little faith that they will develop into much, but you never know what the effect will be when you throw a stone into a pond," Hsu counseled with a nod. "The small waves spread and some day a student with promise will surprise you. Most students will only achieve a superficial understanding and think they have learned a great deal by observing a wide arch of activity. They never realize or see the depth to which the stone can sink into the pond. This is similar to the discussions we have had about the distinction between the surface and the depth, what can and cannot be seen, what is beyond immediate view, and what can be sensed by using your full consciousness."

"There is a difference between doing one thing a thousand times and accumulating the experience of one thousand repetitions," Hsu added. "It is like ascending Drum Mountain. The casual visitor will mount the two thousand steps and make his legs stronger. The thoughtful visitor will read the inscriptions, look at the small shrines, and take in the view while ascending so that he gains wisdom and experience on the way. It is similar to the distinction between a technician and an artist with a brush and ink: one does the same thing over and over again so that his brush work is technically perfect. The other develops talent with multiple repetitions. One form of practice is static, the other is organic. The first only repeats the motion, which is one dimensional; the second can apply variations of his skill to different situations, all of which describes the art of my good friend Jou."

"Keep your senses sharpened for those who see the surface but also know there is the possibility to touch the depth," he continued. I have helped train you, along with Jou, and you should seek your own depth, your own way of doing things, and explore new directions. Use your senses to discern the distinction between surface and depth, what is happening outside the view of the eyes by using your ears, nose, touch, and even taste."

After pausing, Hsu resumed. "Sanra, you have learned particularly well about Chinese medicines. Your *wushu* is good, but there is more to learn and I hope you will continue on the way working especially hard. For example, Jou has told me about seeing for the first time when you leapt over the wall to escape the three attackers in Fujou. That was good thinking, because you knew it was better to withdraw than to stand and fight when there was a good possibility you might lose. And, you realized quickly there was nothing to gain by fighting those three toughs, though it was also possible you might have won. Strategy is related to wisdom. And, there is a better strategy to learn from that encounter about ten years ago."

"Let me tell you a story," he continued. "Once there was a feud in Fujou, which is about as rare as the rice grains that grow on the green and brown stalks in the fields, between the Liang and the Hao clans. There were open clashes, concealed attacks, and losses on both sides, some of them fatal. No one outside the families knew the origin of their animosity, but after many years the Liang clan had somehow gotten the upper hand over the Hao. Both families were well known for their traditions in differing styles of *wushu* that had been handed down from one generation to the next. I was a young boy at the time and had heard about them from friends who lived in the city of Fujou. One day, I was sitting with my first instructor, Master Chen, who taught a soft style of *wushu* and was its foremost proponent in Fujian at the time. We sat in the same tea shop where Jou saw you across the street selling medicines. We drank tea and watched the activity on the street outside the shop. After a while, we saw a senior member of the Liang clan passing by on the opposite side of the street just where you had set up to sell your medicines. Suddenly, two other men who were probably from the Hao clan ran at him from opposite directions each holding a staff. It happened quickly, but the man from the Liang clan continued on casually until the attackers swung their poles to strike. He jumped straight up in the air so that the attackers missed completely, except that their poles struck each other with a loud whack. Both of the attackers fell down from the impact, while the Liang clan member continued to walk on comfortably down the street. I nearly fell off my chair laughing because the two attackers had completely missed their target and knocked each other down. I was also amazed that the man from the Liang clan had easily avoided being hurt and was completely undisturbed. I told my teacher that I wanted to learn *wushu* like that and be able to defend against attackers without having to engage them. I noticed my teacher was laughing, too."

"Master Chen said that the man from the Liang clan was skilled, but he was immature in the development of his strategy. I asked Master Chen what it was the Liang family member had done, and he told me it was known as esoteric *wushu*. Its proponents specialized in avoiding confrontation and escaping from harm, rather than defending and counterattacking or even responding to an attack. Their practice consisted of physical conditioning with a different strategy, and had none of the blocking and parrying utilized in tiger or in *pangainoon wushu*. We have forms that simulate actual conditions of defense against thrusts, kicks, or attacks from many directions and from multiple opponents. Their form is esoteric in that they try to be as intangible as a shadow, as ungraspable as the mist. We block, parry, and counterattack against imaginary opponents, while they pretend they are the invisible counterpart that we strike only in our imagination. Their philosophy is to take the imaginary and turn it into *wushu*," said Jou.

"Master Chen explained to me that most practitioners of esoteric *wushu* learned to escape an encounter, as the man across the street had, but with even more strategic sense he would see, know, or sense when an attack was imminent and avoid a clash before it developed. An expert strategist would not have been there at all; instead there would be nothingness. Though well trained and reasonably proficient, neither the Liang nor the Hao had developed sufficiently, which is why their feud had continued with much loss to both. It is a wiser strategy to intuit the intentions of an opponent, to have your enemy fight himself instead of you, and then not be there when his actual attack comes. This is not always possible in every situation, but something to remember in your thinking," he concluded.

***

The next year, after the spring rains had initially flooded the rice paddies, a drought descended during the hot summer and lingered into autumn. The parched rice stalks withered, unable to draw life and nourishment through their weakened roots that reached into the thick soil. Even wells were beginning to go dry. This caused a great deal of apprehension among the peasants and their landlords alike. There was already instability in the grain, vegetable, and fish markets as there were increased rumors of foreign encroachments, open insurrections, and countless clandestine activities across the land. The people of Fujou could see that everyday society, even at a distance from the capital of Beijing, was affected by weak and indecisive public leadership. There was a palpable sense that the old imperial regime would not be able to stand up to the inexorable march of modern and Western technology and ideas.

Kanbun and Weiya were relatively unaffected because he had stable support and employment under Jou as well as access to the wild herbs he sold, which grew well in most conditions. However, Gao and his large family struggled to sustain themselves. His rice fields were distant from the river, which was the source of the water for his crops, and the flow had slowed to a trickle with less rain. He and others like him often borrowed sums from their landlords or the rice brokers to hold them over at the end of the growing season until they could harvest the grains and cover the loans. This year, there were less funds available to sustain the farmers in that normally short period between the time green rice shoots bent over at their tops, brown and laden with grain. It was clear there would be much less produce at the end of the season and indeed some were in danger of losing their crops altogether.

One evening, when Kanbun was walking home from *wushu* practice to his simple cottage where Weiya and their young daughter would be waiting, he was deep in thought about his life in Nanyoi. There was only a crescent moon and few stars to light the sky and a cool breeze chilled the back of his neck and the shoulders of his light robe jacket where he had perspired earlier. He wondered what his family in Izumi might be doing and whether they saw the same crescent moon. Would they be enjoying the autumn harvest festival celebrating the bounty of the fields and the gifts from the sea in contrast to the difficult situation in Fujou? Along the narrow road ahead, there was an ever so slight rustle in the leaves of the bamboo stalks in front of a small family warehouse that might normally be filled with sacks of rice at this time of year. As Kanbun passed the front of the warehouse, suddenly a dark figure burst from behind the bamboo in a hostile leap with a knife extended towards him. Kanbun instantaneously swept his left arm in front of his body with his elbow low, lowered his body weight, drew his shoulders down, and exhaled firmly ready for another attack, but then instinctively struck in one swift motion at the mid-section of the attacker with the single-knuckle fist of his right hand. The attacker grunted and landed flat out, prone on the dry, hard, and rutted cart path.

Kanbun deftly and defensively took a step back in case the man rose to continue his attack, but there was no more movement. Kanbun carefully bent on one knee to survey the motionless attacker whose head was turned toward the right and was still holding tightly the knife in his outstretched right hand. Kanbun placed his fingers against the man's nostrils, but there was no breath. Kanbun knew the attack was over, though no more than a couple of seconds had elapsed.

Kanbun stood and wondered what to do. His mind was clear, but his next actions would take some thought. He lifted the limp body over his right shoulder and held the legs against his chest. Next, he hastily returned down the path to Jou's mansion where several lamps were still burning. Kanbun placed the still figure on the ground in the *wushu* practice courtyard and called in a low voice to Jou. His mentor appeared in the lit doorway in loose and comfortable evening clothes.

"Yes, Sanra, what is it?" he asked.

"Master Jou, I have a problem," he replied. The formality in his voice alerted Jou that there was indeed something serious to discuss.

"Tell me, you have my confidence," Jou went on.

In simple and direct terms, Kanbun replied, "there was an attack on my way home, and I brought the body back here."

Jou brought a lamp out into the courtyard to see for himself what Kanbun was talking about. He sent Kanbun to fetch Master Hsu, and when they returned he held the lamp over the dead man and then closer to the inert face. Hsu looked genuinely surprised and then queried Kanbun about what had happened. Kanbun gave a brief account of the details of the past half hour or so, though to Kanbun it seemed all to have happened in less than a few moments.

Hsu opened the front of the dead man's robe to examine his chest. He paused deep in thought and then turned to Kanbun.

"I don't know how you discovered the 'heart-stopping blow,' but that has killed this unfortunate attacker," Hsu said after a momentary pause. "I have been meaning to teach you this special skill, but waited because I wanted the timing to be right. Just a relative handful of the most accomplished and dedicated *wushu* men know it. Among others it only exists as a rumor or a superstition. However, unlike most other common rumors or false beliefs, in this case it happens to be true. It requires a remarkable combination of speed, power, and accuracy to strike a special location just below the heart. It is highly secret because it is dangerous and carries great responsibility with understanding it. It is one of those secret lessons in *wushu* and I was planning to teach you one day, but you have reached a high level of skill even before I realized you were ready. The other significant feature of the 'heart-stopping blow' is that it leaves no mark on the body, so it is nearly impossible to determine the cause of death or prove that such a technique exists. It seems that you have progressed in your training more than even you were aware. "

Hsu went on, "The attacker may have been a desperate thief—there are some who have turned to robbery in these difficult drought conditions—or it is possible that it was someone who was targeting you particularly."

Kanbun's eyes grew round and wide, "But why?"

"The attacker was your younger brother-in-law," Jou replied. I don't know his motivations, but he may have been jealous of your success and relative comfort. What's more you are foreign. Your in-laws regrettably have been slow to warm to you."

The three men stood in silence for some time contemplating the implications and possible repercussions for all of them. Jou had supported Kanbun and introduced him to Master Hsu; Hsu had taught Kanbun a powerful *wushu*; and, Kanbun had used it to slay an attacker who turned out not only to be local but related to him. They each were entangled and bore some measure of responsibility for this tragedy.

Eventually, Jou spoke in measured terms to Kanbun, "Take the body of this young man to the house of your father-in-law nearby. Explain that you came upon him on the way home and apparently he needs a doctor. Say no more than needed or asked of you. If you try to explain the circumstances as you did for us, they will not believe you and they may blame you anyway."

Kanbun nodded, hoisted the body again over his right shoulder, and left with his burden to the home of his in-laws. When he arrived, some of the family was there, and he explained just as Jou had suggested. His in-laws were shocked and called out angrily to one another. A younger brother was dispatched to fetch a doctor and there was general confusion in the house. No one stopped to thank Kanbun for bringing the son home, nor did they take particular notice of him. He left quietly and returned to his own cottage, where he explained to Weiya that her younger brother needed urgent medical help. She departed quickly carrying their baby daughter with her. Kanbun sat at a table sipping tea and thinking deeply.

In the following days, there was a funeral for the young man. Kanbun offered to explain what he knew to Weiya, but she replied that she would not ask and he should not put forward information if it would be unwelcome. Some weeks passed and rumors began spreading that the young son of the farmer may have been killed, rather than dying of natural causes. At first, some suggested it may have been an outsider attempting robbery, but then others began to ask why there had been no wound on the body. Only someone with remarkable skill could have done that. At first, a few village elders visited Jou to ask respectfully what he thought and if he knew of anyone capable of such a deed. Jou did not answer directly saying that he had been home that evening and could only guess at how something like that could have happened. The elders were largely satisfied with this response, but one or two continued to question how it could be. By the time Jou's words had filtered through to the wider circle of peasants in the area, the doubts had become more firm. Some wanted to know if Shandi were capable of this. After all, he was an unknown to them, a foreigner who could not be trusted, and he was not liked by his wife's family. Perhaps there had been a dispute between them. Kanbun's father-in-law did nothing to dispel this potential explanation and instead let the rumors spread. Jou's prediction about Weiya's family was correct. More people in the village and beyond began speaking ill of Kanbun.

During this time, Kanbun spent more time talking with Jou than training with Hsu. Jou explained that China had developed advanced martial skills and techniques long before the arrival of Chan Buddhism, what is called 'Zen' in Japanese, from India during the period of the Northern and Southern Dynasties of well over a thousand years ago. Chan Buddhism helped complete the third side of the triangle with philosophy, meditation, and awareness. However, what was not well known was that secret information related to modern *wushu* had also been transmitted along with Chan Buddhism. Legend had it that an Indian aristocrat had conducted thorough research on human anatomy and physiology by instructing his doctors and healers to perform experiments on the slaves among his holdings. They used different striking points from the hands, feet, elbows, and knees of their assistants, as well as various weapons to determine vulnerable points in the human body. The used hammers to discover how much pressure on different locations would produce a variety of results, affect nerve centers, and death spots that killed instantly or gradually. They also probed with sharp needles the internal organs of the slaves to learn about the location and relation of those organs to the nervous system, muscles, bodily functions, pain, and the senses. Over time, as this Indian knowledge spread and mixed with Chinese practices of acupuncture and moxibustion, Buddhist adherents and *wushu* practitioners became more deeply aware and understood energy centers in the body that could be altered and controlled with pressure, heat, or cold. Conversely, they also discovered massage and exercises for stimulation and energy, healing and repair, and breathing and circulation. In Jou's view, the 'heart-stopping blow' that Kanbun had accidentally discovered was probably a vestige of the mysterious information that had been transported from India to China many centuries earlier.

On other occasions, their tea merchant friend Wu joined their conversations, which inevitably also dealt with the contemporary period. In the modern world in the fading twilight of the Ching Dynasty, the feudal system was collapsing. The old order had become corrupted beyond repair. Many civil servants, petty bureaucrats, provincial governors, government ministers, and even the Eunuchs in the Imperial Court achieved their status through bribery and cronyism rather than the traditionally honored merit-based system of rewarding scholarship, insight, and courtesy. Jou knew the peasantry was being pushed dangerously close to revolution. If all the oil were squeezed from the sesame seed and not even the kernel left for replanting, the cycle of life would be choked. Eventually it would wither away and starve to death. There was a great deal of unrest across the country with insurrections sometimes led by charismatic but much misinformed leaders. Warlords had carved out provincial areas for supplies of food, resources, materials, and weaponry with their own armies so that they became the sole arbiters of local rule, each with a different character. It was unsafe for anyone, not to mention for foreigners, especially for those perceived to be from Japan, to travel around the country.

Around that time, the drought in Fujou had become so severe that some farms failed with great loss to those families who worked on them. The anti-foreigner sentiment had become stronger as China weakened in the face of superior development in foreign countries and many were willing to misplace blame for their misfortunes on what they neither knew nor understood well.

One day, Wu had received a packet of notices and letters from Ryukyu, one of which was addressed to Kanbun from his mother in Motobu. The letter was partially water damaged, but Kanbun was able to read enough to understand that his father was seriously ill. Weiya grew increasingly worried about the safety of Kanbun and their daughter because she had heard the rumors, too. She knew little of his *wushu* skills, but Kanbun understood that any man could be defeated, especially when challenged by large numbers of attackers, governmental authorities who had been manipulated to believe false charges, those with firearms, or even his in-laws because he would be unable to resist out of respect for his wife. He was reminded of the arrest years earlier of Tomohiro in Naha and his thoughts afterwards on the ship returning to Fujou. Jou, Wu, and Kanbun discussed these developments together and decided that though a return to Ryukyu would be risky, it would be safer for Kanbun to return home for a while. The letter from his family in Izumi only added urgency and weight to their decision.

Hsu had wanted to teach Kanbun *suparinpei*, the next principal form in *pangainoon*, but now there was no time. Instead, he demonstrated it for Kanbun and his pupil began to see how the movements, motion, animal spirit, breathing, glare in the eyes, and more all tied into Hsu's overarching descriptions of the history and essence of *pangainoon*. It was indeed another level of action, development, and existence. Also by now, Kanbun's journal of medicinal recipes, practice, training, strategy, impressions, insights, and wisdom had become a considerable collection of materials. He spent the next several days gathering his notes, documents, and essays together but still short of a systematic work of reference for himself and perhaps others in the future. He had no time to examine his writings, but organized them so that he could review and bind them together at a later date. He found the cotton *furoshiki* that Kazue had used to wrap around the dictionary she had given him. On it, he found a slender but long thread of hair. He picked it out in the faded light and realized it must have been one of Kazue's. He held it fondly while feeling a mixture of irony and pains of conscience that flooded his heart. A dozen years earlier he had fled danger and possible persecution in his homeland for the opportunity to learn *wushu* in the relative safety of Fuzhou. Now, he was reversing his

258

direction to escape potential harm in Fujou as a result of his *wushu* training.

He decided to take as few possessions as possible with him to avoid attention and suspicion by the local villagers. If they saw that he was preparing to leave, they might try to waylay him. If the situation settled down in his village, in Fujou, and perhaps across China over the next period of time, he could return to Nanyoi, his family, and his *wushu* practice and teaching. He was torn, but there was no better alternative.

On the last evening, Kanbun invited Master Hsu, Jou, and Wu to join him in the parting ritual from Motobu of drinking strong liquor from a ceramic pot while viewing the reflection of the moon in the liquid. They sat soberly together sipping silently with their thoughts. After a while, Jou handed Kanbun a letter and suggested he read it when he had time and a clear mind. Then, Kanbun took leave of his closest friends in China.

The next morning, Kanbun gave a restrained yet deeply felt farewell to his wife and daughter and set out for the port of Fujou dressed as a tea merchant. Ironically, the disguise that had served Kanbun so well when he had returned to Naha earlier and had helped him escape detection by the Japanese officials was now useful for traveling to Fujou locally among the Chinese. He wanted to stop at the Ryukyukan Juenenki for the night, give his regards to the gentle old man and lady from Ryukyu, and catch up on the latest news from the island kingdom. However, his disguise would either disqualify him from assistance at the Juenenki or give away his identity to others. Besides, he was not sure if the elderly gentleman and kind lady were still there or even alive. Instead, he kept to himself, avoided areas where he might be recognized, and stayed in an inexpensive inn where there was simple bedding on the floor and on bunks for eight or ten sojourners like him per room. He arose early the next morning, set out for the port, and arrived on foot at the mouth of the Min River. From there, he took a small boat to the port island where he could embark for Naha. It was a journey to a place completely familiar and yet where the circumstances were unknown.

Return to Motobu

Around the close of the first decade of the twentieth century, a number of disparate and regional warlords and revolutionary groups joined Dr. Sun Yat-sen who combined his forces with them and led them to overthrow the last Imperial Dynasty of China and establish a republican government. Shortly thereafter in Japan, Emperor Meiji, passed away and his mentally deficient son Taisho became the head of state in the fledgling democratic state. In Ryukyu, the Japanese administrators, under the designation of Okinawa Prefecture, for the first time authorized the right of the local citizens to vote for their representatives in the national assembly in Tokyo. It was indeed a time of churn and change, of lurching forward into the modern era for these historically feudal societies. Within the next two years, the countries of the West plunged into World War I, which upended their civilizational order that had been established centuries earlier. Japan, seeking to take its place among the modern and industrial nations of the world, joined the conflict. Amidst the disorder of the day, Tsarist Russia fell to a cabal of revolutionaries and the appeal of communism as a political ideology became integrated to varying degrees with governments across the globe. Whatever vestiges remained of the nineteenth century when Kanbun had departed Ryukyu, the world had now entered a new age.

On the sea journey to Ryukyu, Kanbun had time to think and reflect. He took out the letter from Jou and read.

Dear Sanra,

The timing and, even more so, the reasons for your departure are unfortunate. However, we must face life and our options with good sense and practicality. You were the first from a foreign land to join me and my *wushu* study group. However, I know of no other, Chinese or not, who trained so successfully under the tutelage of Master Hsu learning his *pangainoon*.

Unfortunately, there are those who cling to ancient ways and utterly reject the new without comprehending it. They are like an idle pond that has become stagnant and choked with weeds. They are overfilled with the drink of self-importance to admit fresh clean water. Nature takes its course. Spring rains fall, the mountain runoff rushes in torrents, and the ground water wells up from below so that the once still and tranquil pond overflows and becomes a flood. Upheaval, confusion, misfortune, and disaster rule the day. Eventually, the rush of the flowing mass recedes, but not before the traces of good left from the past and the mitigating influence of the old have been swept away. A new era begins. New ideas, habits, and practices are by nature fraught with danger because they are as yet untried. With wisdom, judgment, insight, and the aid of good fortune a fresh idea, modern technology, or a different approach may be wedded peaceably and profitably to traditional beliefs. It is prudent to embrace the new and the unusual, especially that which will improve the quality of life for others. We see this in our own day-to-day lives and in the world at large.

At the same time, hold steadily and reverently to the accumulated wisdom transmitted across the ages, particularly that which is good and useful. There are some who become blinded by the appeal of change without realizing the consequences or stopping to be grateful to those who provided for their livelihood or their very existence. They are like thirsty dogs in the desert chasing after mirages. They are so desirous of relief that they lose their sense of direction not knowing where they came from or how to sustain themselves. It is the rare individual who has the depth of character and foresight to select a worthy goal and to lead others to a better world.

You have made remarkable progress and become highly skilled in *wushu*, even more so than I would have guessed. However, we are all fallible and we all make mistakes. It is inevitable and unavoidable. What is more important, though, is what you do after you make a mistake: make amends, correct your path, learn and develop further as a human being and as a productive citizen. Most importantly, learn to avoid repeating your errors.

You are about to re-trace your path, but it will be different from the one that you took to arrive in Fujou. Whether the final road you take is to your homeland, a return to this country, or somewhere different still, the way will be an accumulation of your past and a set of new experiences you will encounter.

Know that you are always welcome in Nanyoi.

Jou Tzuhe

Upon arriving in Ryukyu, Kanbun kept his disguise as a Chinese tea merchant, slipped through the port and past the attentive Japanese in Naha, and headed north for the Motobu

Peninsula and his home in Izumi that he had missed so much. While traveling home, he sent no notice of his impending return for fear it may be intercepted by the Japanese authorities. It was still a real possibility that he could be apprehended and imprisoned, like Tomohiro, for avoiding the Japanese draft. As he was to learn soon, his good friend Matsuda Tokusaburo had spent a year in prison for draft evasion after returning some years earlier to Motobu.

While on route to Motobu, Kanbun cut off the long braided queue at the back of his head, changed his clothes to a robe jacket and pantaloons in simple designs familiar to Ryukyu, and put away his Chinese accessories. He arrived in Izumi only to discover that it was his grandfather and not his father who had been described as ill in the damaged letter he received in Nanyoi through Go Kenki. Indeed, Grandfather had just passed away the night before Kanbun arrived. The anticipated death of Grandfather and the unexpected arrival of Kanbun induced a mixture of grief and happiness, loss and recovery, for the Uechi family. Kanbun felt the weight of the loss of his grandfather most keenly. It was a shock, rather than an expectation, and he had looked forward keenly to discussing with him all the wonderful ways he had been able to build on their extended practice in the bamboo grove and to develop so much more as a man of *wushu*.

In the next few days, there were first and foremost preparations for the funeral of the family patriarch to attend to, and then some brief opportunities to re-acquaint himself with his relatives, neighbors, and friends who had grown in differing ways and changed over the past dozen years or more. He could not help but realize with a sense of irony he now noticed things that he had taken for granted growing up in Izumi. The ground felt differently, the vegetation was more green, and even the sun seemed stronger. People bowed frequently even during ordinary conversations, repeated greetings, thanks, apologies, and questions even in casual interactions, and often paused to gather thoughts, show respect, and express thoughtfulness with whom they were talking. The houses, fields, and even the people seemed smaller and bunched in closer together. There was little distance between any of them and they somehow seemed inter-connected, unlike Foujou where it was a mass of disjointed distant confusion. The food at home was delicious, as he had very much missed his mother's cooking, but it was also plain and salty compared to the great variety of flavors and spices and ways of preparing meals in Nanyoi. He had grown so used to wearing slippers indoors and out in Fujou, so that now he was conscious of removing his sandals when entering his home, whereas it had been as natural as opening the door when growing up. There was no midday siesta, so he had to keep himself awake by drinking stronger tea after lunch. It was remarkably familiar and everyone looked and acted much the same as he remembered, except they seemed to be even more like themselves.

The Uechi family and its close relatives gathered for reminisces and consultations. There was the family line to maintain, and Kanbun was the eldest son in successive generations of eldest sons. He was already into his thirties with no wife or immediate prospects to continue the Uechi line. What would be more natural than for his parents and elder relatives to choose a wife for Kanbun? This was the tradition throughout most of China, Japan, and Ryukyu, and the sooner it was carried out the better. Uechi elders and family members gathered to discuss a good match for the families and society in Izumi. It was most common for a go-between to arrange for the two sets of parents to meet formally, and then a decision was made. The individuals in question entered marriage with very few expectations, bore their duty, and learned to live together and depend on each other.

Kanbun's mother Tsuru sensed diffidence in Kanbun and wondered whether there was something causing him to hesitate or he was merely unsure so soon after his return from being far away for a long while. He had changed, and had more than just matured since he had departed as a youthful teenager. He seemed happy to be home in the bosom of his family but also wary in his interactions with others. He had developed a presence that exuded from his body, his voice, and especially his eyes. For his part, Kanbun wanted to speak with his parents about Weiya and his daughter in Nanyoi and discuss what would be the best path to follow. However, his relatives and the family guests often stayed late into the night eating and drinking heavily, and it was the responsibility of Kanbun's family to host and provide for them, even leaving some to sleep where they dropped off on the tatami mats around the low dining table in the modest family home. His relatives were happy and grateful that he had returned home safely, particularly at a crucial time for the Uechi family. However, for the most part their conversation was absorbed in village affairs. They talked about the planting season and debated whether their allegiances should remain with Ryukyu or they should take on the identity of the new era and Okinawa. There were very few questions and little time for Kanbun's thoughts, hopes, or experiences in China.

Within a matter of weeks, one of several neighborly women had found a probable match for Kanbun. She introduced

Kanbun's father and mother to the parents of Toyama Gozei, a shy and younger girl from a neighboring village. She was quiet but seemed easy to talk to. She had thick hair bunched around her round face but her posture was lean, firm, and pleasing. Her clothing was the simple top and bottom robes of the natives of Ryukyu, but she also had the aura of being clean, neat, and well prepared for the introduction to Kanbun. The two male heads of family spoke respectfully to each other while discussing their means of living. Kanbun and Gozei said nothing and barely raised their eyes to survey one another. The two women discussed the dishes they most liked to prepare, drank tea, and easily agreed. The marriage was decided upon, and the men toasted a good match and their family futures over a cup of *awamori*.

One morning a few weeks before the carefully selected wedding date that was aligned with the stars and good fortune, Kanbun passed near the home of the now retired Izumi Headman Kobayashi. Kanbun had wavered over whether he should visit and offer his greetings. Would Kazue still be nearby? How would she be, and more importantly how should he act after all these years? Would she be friendly or businesslike? Would there still be the same light that danced in her eyes and the charm that warmed her smile? Kanbun carried with him the now dog-eared dictionary Kazue had given him more than a dozen years earlier.

A girl and a younger boy played together in the Kobayashi family yard. There was a woman hanging *futon*, the padded cotton mats spread on tatami before retiring in the evenings, to dry in the spring air on long poles hung from the veranda. Kanbun recognized her bearing immediately as Kazue. Kanbun tucked the dictionary into the folds of his jacket. He approached and called to Kazue gently. She turned with the same beguiling and unmistakable smile but now as a full woman. She had changed somewhat, but undeniably she had become more attractive than the years before.

"Oh, welcome home," she called back warmly, "I had heard that you returned."

Kanbun bowed and hesitated, but then it was if he had never been away. He smiled widely and said, "I missed Izumi."

The two young children scampered about behind Kazue and asked, "Mother, who is this stranger?"

"Why, he is from Izumi," she replied, "now go and play."

They trotted off unconcerned.

Kazue suggested they take a walk along the edge of the clearing that made up the open area behind the thatched roof house. They came to a small path that looked out over the descending hillside and down to the ocean, and she led him along it.

"They are healthy and good looking children," Kanbun began.

"Yes, in the years after you left Izumi, my family and relatives were worried that I would become an old maid. I was able to put them off a number of times, but in the end they arranged for me to get married. Nobody knew when, or even if, you would come back."

She went on, "My older brother Gonta was drafted by the Japanese military despite my father's best efforts and their assurances he would be exempt. He became a naval officer, but then was killed about a half dozen years ago in the Russo-Japanese War."

268

She paused, and Kanbun said softly, "I am sorry to hear. It must have been a terrible loss for your family."

"Yes," she replied, "and it meant that when I married, my husband would take our family name, and together we would become responsible for caring for the family farmhouse. We have been looking after my parents and raising the next generation since then."

She paused a while, and then added with slightly moist eyes, "Kanbun, I am sorry."

Once again, similar to when he was a teenager, Kanbun found it difficult to summon the appropriate words for Kazue. Instead, he changed the subject.

"Kazue, do you remember the Japanese to Chinese dictionary you gave me? It helped me so many times in Fukkensho. I even added to it converting some of our Ryukyu language to the local Fukushu dialect and I brought it back with me to Izumi. Here, have a look," he added.

Kazue smiled warmly, but this time said nothing. Soon, they came to a small clearing with a few rounded "turtleback" tombs, the customary way of constructing a burial site in Ryukyu. Indeed, it was well into the fourth month, notable for the *Seimei* grave cleaning rituals, the time of year when families paid respect to those who had passed away. There were flower vases, incense holders with ash residue, and offerings of fruit and sake outside the tombs.

"This is the Kobayashi family tomb and my brother's ashes are inside with our ancestors," she said.

Kanbun picked up a wooden bucket to gather some water to wash the exterior of the stone monument. Kazue picked some wild flowers and took a piece of incense from her pocket to light and set in front of the tomb. They bowed solemnly, their shoulders almost touching, and said silent prayers. Kanbun recalled the friction he had felt with Gonta, but now was sorry for his death. If Gonta were still alive and had been able to carry on for the Village Headman, perhaps Kazue's situation would be different. But, he dismissed the thought and instead remembered fondly the delightful times he had with Kazue and the youthful affection he had felt for her. He could not help but also sense the irony that often comes with the passage of time and the accumulation of experience. The steady, happy, and simple life enjoyed by the villagers of Izumi had become forever altered with the intervening turns of history that affected Ryukyu, China, and Japan so deeply. It was the same for Kanbun and for Kazue.

After their prayers, Kanbun drew a brightly decorated lacquer charm from his sleeve and offered it to Kazue.

"It is a souvenir from my travels in China," he said, "and the least I can give in return for the dictionary."

Kazue hesitated a moment, but then accepted the gift and thanked him for remembering her and being so thoughtful. They returned to the Kobayashi family home without speaking.

Kanbun married the next month and the following year Gozei bore him a son, Kan'ei. In the years that came afterward, Kanbun and Gozei also had two daughters, first Kame, and then Tsuru who was named for Grandmother who passed away around that time. More than ten years after their marriage, a second son, Kansei, was added to the family. They led a quiet, unremarkable life as rural farmers. Kanbun did his best to avoid notice and stayed distant from the Japanese authorities who still might arrest him for escaping the draft. He attended to family matters, looked after his parents, managed the household, observed their agricultural traditions, and participated in village gatherings and activities. One of these activities was helping to organize and participate in village festivals. Though the youth in Izumi often demonstrated their *kobujutsu* skills with traditional farm implements of the *bo*, *sai*, *kama*, and *tonfa*, Kanbun and Tokusaburo let others guide these activities and refrained from displaying any of the abilities they had acquired in Fujou. They were sensitive to the eyes of Japanese authorities and the rumors that might spread of their skills with 'Chinese Hand.'

Kanbun had been away from Izumi and Ryukyu for more than a decade, and social and cultural changes had gone from perceptible to concrete for the island nation and its people. Standard Japanese, rather than the Ryukyu dialect, was now taught in the schools in rural areas so that a generation was growing up with a different set of sensibilities. Similarly, the Japanese enforced the use of "Okinawa" rather than "Ryukyu" on signs and in official documents so the usage of the former had become more widespread. There were other ways the Japanese authorities indigenized Okinawa during that time. For example, they removed many Chinese elements from the language and other continental features of the island society and substituted them with those that looked, sounded, and felt more familiar and comfortable to the central government on the Japanese mainland. They placed pictures of the Japanese emperor and the national flag in schools, municipal offices, and public buildings to remind the residents of "Okinawa" to whom they owed allegiance. In schools, students were required to bow to the photo of the Japanese emperor at the beginning and end of each day. Social organization and government structures were reconfigured to match the calendar, national holidays, laws, and regulations of mainland Japan.

During World War I, Japan had expansive interests in acquiring foreign strongholds in the region and seized territories to include parts of China, Russia, and the South Pacific. However, following the war, like much of the rest of the world, Japan suffered a severe economic downturn. In the role of a backwater to Japan and with virtually no natural resources, Okinawa was particularly hard it. There was little or no industry and there were minimal prospects for employment for most young men. Many migrated to the Japanese mainland where there was a need for able-bodied men to work for low wages in the industrial and commercial centers in the area centered on Osaka.

One year, around the time of the autumn festival honoring that year's meager harvest of sugar cane, rice, millet, flax, buckwheat, and vegetables, as well as preparation for the coming semi-dormant winter months, Kanbun learned that a trading ship from Fujou would be visiting near Motobu. Out of curiosity, he, his son Kan'ei, Tokusaburo, and a couple of others from Izumi went down to Nago Bay and waited for the vessel to arrive. Kanbun and Tokusaburo were surprised and excited when they saw that the small trading group was led by Go Kenki. Kanbun stepped forward and warmly welcomed his friend from Fujou.

Kanbun apologized, "my own home would be too modest for such a gentleman as Master Go to stay overnight, but I will arrange the best dinner possible for you and your compatriots."

"Kanbun, my good man, do you still need to call me 'Master Go' when we are as close as cousins," he replied. "My ship is comfortable enough for lodging, but we would be honored to share some of your local *chanpuru* and *awamori*!"

Kanbun and Tokusaburo introduced Go to their friends and neighbors. Next, he instructed Kan'ei to pick up some fresh fish at the Nago market and sent him running ahead to let Gozei know that she should prepare a special feast for a larger than usual number that evening. Together the two small groups of Chinese traders and local farmers climbed the hillside path to the village of Izumi. They walked to the far side of the village, where Tokusaburo showed Go some of his rows of tea bushes on the side of the hill that he along with his fellow villagers cultivated and harvested in spring. The size of the area for tea cultivation in Izumi was no where near the vast plantations that Go owned and managed in Fujou. However, he did understand well the cycle of the tea growing season and how best to develop the leaves of the bushes for harvesting, drying, and brewing the local varieties of tea. When they arrived at Kanbun's home, he introduced Go formally to his father Kantoku and explained how much he was indebted for his care and hospitality in Fujou. Kantoku kneeled on the veranda, bowed deeply and repeatedly touching his head to the boards, offered several kinds of thanks, and invited Go and his friends into their small home. The visitors removed their footwear and stepped up onto the veranda and then into the open interior. Gozei, assisted by her daughters Kame and Tsuru, placed around the low table small *bingata* cushions for them to sit on, set out tea and rice crackers that she had learned to make from her mother-in-law, and then left the men to converse.

Relatives of Tokusaburo and Tomohiro from Motobu also joined the Uechi family at their home, which crowded the small farmhouse, but made for a lively gathering. All of them were eager to show their gratitude with gifts of food and liquor to Go Kenki for his hospitality to their sons while in Fujou and for

273

arranging a journey for them back to Ryukyu. The men reminisced about their days together in Fujou, caught up on friends in common, and events in Fukken, China, and Ryukyu, but Kanbun did not mention Weiya or his daughter. Go took this clue from the conversation and did not touch upon the family or difficulties Kanbun had left in Nanyoi. Two of the men with Go were his students in the White Crane style of *wushu*, so there was much in common to talk about. They ate well, drank plenty, and talked late into the night. Kanbun and Tokusaburo invited Go and his men to stay a few days so they could see the autumn festival that would be celebrated in Motobu and attended by people and families from Izumi and the other villages in the area. Go accepted the warm invitation, presented Kanbun and his family gifts from Fujou, and departed down the path to the harbor at Nago where they would spend the night on board their ship. Before the group from Fujou departed his home, Kanbun gave them a large ceramic jar of *awamori* that they could draw from whenever they liked, whether moored in the harbor or at sail at sea.

The next day, Kanbun excused himself from the preparations in Izumi for the autumn festival and joined Go and his group for lunch in Nago. In the afternoon, they walked to Motobu and took seats with the gathering of villagers, elders, chieftains, housewives, and children who grew in number as twilight turned to darkness under a sky lit by a full moon. There was a bonfire in the central area of the festival and pots of fire and torches on poles for light near the edges of the clearing. Some of the men beat drums, plucked the stringed *shamisen*, played the flute, sang local harmonies, or simply clapped to the slow rhythm. Women and children dressed in brightly patterned evening kimono, and even some of the men danced in prescribed patterns in the central area along with the women. Others helped by bringing dishes of food, cakes, snacks, tea, sake, and *awamori* and offered them to those known and unknown alike. As the night wore on, some of the intoxicated dancers picked up bamboo poles and swung them about in mock battles of *kobujutsu*, while others feigned punching, kicking, and jumping about. At one point, a village leader invited Go Kenki to demonstrate some of his 'Chinese Hand,' to which he at first demurred, but then after repeated requests directed his students to show their forms. When they finished, some in the audience applauded politely and shouted for their teacher to demonstrate next. Unable to refuse further, Go Kenki reluctantly stood near the middle of the large circle by the bonfire, removed his upper clothing, and announced he would perform *seisan* from the White Crane system of southern China. His sequence of movements was a graceful, flowing, and spirited form, light on his feet and quick with his hands. There was more cheering and applause as the men shouted out their approval of both his *toodi* and his Japanese language ability. Next, Go announced that there was an expert of the *pangainoon* system of *wushu* from southern China in the crowd, someone well known in the village of Izumi. He invited Kanbun to join him in the circle. Kanbun was hesitant at first, but eventually came forward because he could not refuse his guest from China who had been so helpful and such a good friend in Fujou.

"Uechi Kanbun is the man of whom I speak," said Go, introducing Kanbun to the larger group. "In China, he is known as Shandi Wanwen. His skills are perhaps greater than he realizes," he went on knowing that Kanbun would understand the private reference to his encounter in Nanyoi.

Regaining his poise, Kanbun stood before the crowd and announced that he would also perform *seisan* as he knew it. He stood briefly, bowed solemnly to the group of village leaders, and straightened his back, pulled down his shoulders, and exhaled firmly pushing with his belly while bending his knees to lower his weight to the ground. He was like a tightened spring with his mind and body fused together. Next, he launched into a series of steps and arm motions that no one except Go Kenki had seen before. His eyes reflected the flames of the bonfire. His movements flowed powerfully and his breathing was measured yet fierce. The audience at the autumn festival, young and old alike, quieted and watched intently as he completed his *seisan* with a great leap back, then immediately forward. The whole performance lasted less than a minute, and the villagers held still for what seemed longer.

A young boy spoke loud enough for most in the crowd to hear, "Daddy, I am scared."

This broke the tension as the men chuckled, the women went back to filling cups with tea and sake, and the musicians returned to plucking their *shamisen*. There were no more calls for performances, the bustle and activity lessened, and the fires seemed to diminish. Soon, families and groups began bowing to each other, taking their leave, and heading back to their homes. Among the group were a contingent from the slightly offshore island of Iejima, and among them was a young man named Shinjo Seiryo who had watched intently, inspired by the demonstrations of Chinese *wushu*.

In the following weeks, several of those who had been at the autumn festival called upon Kanbun at his home in Izumi asking if he might teach his 'Chinese Hand' to them. However, Kanbun had other plans. He was now well into his forties and his prospects for income to support his family were modest at best. Okinawa lacked development and opportunity, so Kanbun had decided, like many of his compatriots, to migrate to the mainland the next year to secure better employment and a steady income. Tokusaburo left soon after the autumn festival and well before Kanbun for employment in Osaka. Kanbun made his preparations, left his family to manage the vegetable fields in Izumi, and boarded a ship with other men from Izumi, Motobu, Nago, and Iejima bound for the Kansai area of Japan. They disembarked in Osaka and made their way to the neighboring prefecture of Wakayama where there was a growing population of migrant Okinawans who had formed a fraternal organization called the Okinawa Citizens Association. There, Kanbun found the support and inroads to the local society much in the same way he had at his first stop in Fujou at the Ryukyukan Jueneki. Soon he found employment in a textile mill and secured a reliable place to live in company-provided housing so that he was able to send small sums home to his family in Izumi. Another Okinawan younger than Kanbun, Tomoyose Ryuyu, who had travelled from nearby Iemura in Motobu, befriended Kanbun as they worked together in the same mill. Somehow Ryuyu was able to glean from the way that Kanbun engaged in the physical labor they did together that Kanbun had some special skills and strengths. Ryuyu learned their birthdays were the same day but twenty years apart and looked up to Kanbun for friendship and guidance. He asked if Kanbun would explain to him the source of what seemed liked an unusual power. At first, Kanbun refused. However, Ryuyu persisted and convinced Kanbun that it would be beneficial for the Okinawan migrants who felt vulnerable in their transplanted community to develop some strength, gain confidence, and feel able to protect themselves if needed. Together, they carefully selected a few dedicated young men like Ryuyu, such as Uehara Saburo, Matayoshi Yoshitada, and Akamine Kaei, who originated from Okinawa and would be discrete about training together. They met in an open storage room at the textile mill and practiced in the evening after they had finished their duties. With his success at landing stable employment and establishing himself in the migrant community, Kanbun sent word for his son Kan'ei to join him in Wakayama. Within in a couple of years, word of Kanbun's *pangainoon* had become more widespread and other transplants from Okinawa applied to join the group. After a while, they gathered together their modest resources and helped Kanbun establish a formal school called Pangainoon-style Karate Training Hall. Included among them were Shinjo Seiryo and others from Iemura, Motobu, and Izumi. Kanbun was able to resign from the textile mill, rent space for himself and his son to live, open a miscellany shop, concentrate on karate training, and teach his students something about Chinese medicine as he had done in Nanyoi. His son Kan'ei worked and practiced by his side and eventually Shinjo Seiyu, the son of Seiryo, became old enough to join the training hall. With the formal operation of a training hall, Kanbun's students began to wonder where and how he had developed such high level skills. They asked Kanbun who had been his teacher.

Kanbun paused and responded, "My teacher was Hsu-*sabu* in Nanyoi outside of Fukushu-shi in Fukkensho, China." He had paused because there were so many more than a single teacher or person from whom he had learned and to whom he felt deeply indebted for his life there. Rather than confuse his students, he did not elaborate. This was also in part because the person from whom he had learned the most was indeed Master Hsu, though in truth he knew so little about him after training daily under his guidance all those years.

In the following decade, Japan began a period of expansionist policies in the Western Pacific. However, as much as it initially prospered and succeeded, gradually it began to overreach its ambitions. Resources became scarce and many Okinawans who at first had benefited from the growing demand for industrial labor in mainland Japan were now the first to lose employment when the economy turned. Gradually, they began returning to Okinawa and the comfort of their homes and the society that was familiar to them, even if not much more secure.

During World War II, large parts of Japan and most of Okinawa suffered great loss and had been turned to rubble by bombing from above and the ground war on the islands. The lives of families were disrupted as many became separated or they lost members. Kanbun's eldest son Kan'ei and others originally from the Motobu area had departed the Kansai area before the end of the war because it had been heavily bombed and there were no longer homes or employment available to them. Kan'ei returned to Okinawa, set up a new home in Nago, and began teaching what had become known as Uechi-style Karate. Kanbun's younger son Kansei, along with other young and able men from Okinawa, had been drafted into the Japanese military and dispatched to Manchuria. At the end of the war, he was captured by the Russian Army and imprisoned for two years in a Siberian labor camp before returning to Nago.

In the aftermath of World War II, it was once again a period of upheaval. Ironically, neither Japan nor China, which had fought each other bitterly without either side gaining complete victory over the other, could lay claim to Okinawa any longer. The United States had decisively defeated Japan and was leaving China much to its own devices. This distant and Western power now occupied and ruled over Japan and Okinawa. The people of Okinawa, or "Ryukyu" as many in the island nation still considered, had their own culture and identity. Historically, they were neither Chinese nor Japanese, and certainly not American, but they were also uncertain about their future.

Kanbun faced his future with this same uncertainty as the economy, government, and society around him were unstable and unsustaining. He decided to leave Wakayama, which he did accompanied by Shinjo Seiryo and Seiyu, two of his dedicated students. He turned his Uechi-style Karate Training Hall over to his trusted student and friend Tomoyose Ryuyu. However, before departing, they gathered outside the Training Hall to say their farewells. Kanbun brought out a nearly empty ceramic jar of homemade and murky liquor that he poured into small cups for each of them to drink while reflecting on their training and experiences together over the past two decades.

Upon returning to Okinawa, Kanbun continued to train in Iejima as he had done in the years earlier in Wakayama. Shinjo Seiryo and Seiyu, a few of his other students who had repatriated to Iejima, and a few beginners, including Tomoyose Ryuko, the son of Ryuyu in Wakayama joined him in practice. After one of the training sessions in which they sat discussing *wushu*, *kobujutsu*, *toodi*, and karate, Kanbun offered some advice that he expressed visually and physically. Kanbun seemed to be reaching not only back into his past in Fujou, but even much earlier to his days as a youth who practiced the *bo* and performed in festivals in Izumi. He selected a thick and sturdy bamboo pole from a rack on the outside of the building. He crouched and set his toes in the crack between the base of the sliding door and the tatami mats. Next, he invited his students to push the pole against him. First one, then two, and then all together, but they were unable to move Kanbun. Kanbun simply chuckled and said that his power came from *sanchin* and they should apply themselves fully to the practice of it.

The next year, Kanbun felt a growing discomfort in his midsection just below the ribs. It reminded him of the pain he had experienced when Makabei had broken his bamboo staff and defensive move against the strike with the lead filled *bo* at the Gushing Spring Temple training hall. He tried treating the pain with mixtures and prescriptions he was able to make from herbs he had gathered in Iejima, but he was unable to find the best ingredients for kidney ailments in the local climate, soil, and flora that were different from Nanyoi. By now, Kanbun had grown much older and was less active in the training hall. Mostly, he observed and encouraged his students with comments and suggestions. He had declined physically, but somehow he still felt the power flowing from his insides out to his eyes, the tips of his fingers, and down to his feet.

One unusually warm morning in autumn, Kanbun rose painfully from his infirmity. The pain sapped his body and dizziness flooded his head. From somewhere deep inside, he forced a rebuff of his illness. He seemed to be floating in Grandfather's sailboat with Hiro, bouncing and rocking on the waves that washed over the coral in the clear water beneath them. Next, he was in the East China Sea on the Heavenly Dragon that carried him to Fujou. He realized that once again he stood on the edge of history. But this time, with his heart throbbing and the weight of the humid air pressing against his lungs, he slipped back to his sick bed. Soon, there would be other great events that marked the flow of the world. There would be another generation and another to follow that. As he lay prone on his narrow cotton mat in the tatami covered room, he felt the pull of the earth against his back, the ground slip beneath his feet, and the power rush away from his finger tips. He drew in a breath, exhaled, and expired.

Epilogue

In an extraordinary display of loyalty and devotion, Shinjo Seiryo and his son Seiyu transported Kanbun's body in a boat they rowed from Iejima across the approximately two kilometer strait between the island and Motobu Peninsula. From there, they carried the figure wrapped in white cotton covered by canvas to the home of his sons Kan'ei and Kansei, then living in Nago, several miles away. Kanbun's family, students, and friends held a funeral memorial and entombed Kanbun's ashes in Nago.

In the next decade, Kan'ei moved to the Futenma section of the mid-island city of Ginowan, and with the assistance of Shinjo Seiyu and Tomoyose Ryuko built a home and karate school. Seiyu quit a good and secure job with the postal service in Motobu and relocated to Kadena near to Futenma to train under Kan'ei. Ryuko also moved to central Okinawa in order to be near Kan'ei and continue the tutelage he had begun under Kanbun. The Uechi family also relocated Kanbun's burial urn to a new family grave site in Futenma, a short walk from Kan'ei's home and training hall, where the ashes of Uechi Kanbun, his son Kan'ei, and grandson Kanmei now rest.

During the tumultuous era of Kanbun's life, he became one of three major figures that included Funakoshi Gichin and Miyagi Chojun to bring Okinawan karate to mainland Japan and thus extend its spread from China to the wider world in the aftermath of World War II. Among those three, Funakoshi was the oldest and had learned his karate in Okinawa. He became the earliest and strongest proponent of karate on mainland Japan with a system he called Shotokan. Kanbun spent 13 years in Fujian, a

283

center in China for the most advanced forms of wushu, and later taught only a small group of students in Japan. His karate is known as Uechi-ryu. Miyagi was the youngest, studied briefly in China, and combined what he learned there with what he had learned in Okinawa to formulate what he called Goju-ryu.

Made in the USA
Monee, IL
21 October 2021